D0576331

my beating teenage heart

also by c. k. kelly martin

I Know It's Over

One Lonely Degree

The Lighter Side of Life and Death

my beating teenage heart

c. k. kelly martin

random house new york

Visit us on the Web! www.randomhouse.com/teens

Educators and librarians, for a variety of teaching tools, visit us at www.randomhouse.com/teachers

Library of Congress Cataloging-in-Publication Data
Martin, C. K. Kelly.
My beating teenage heart / C. K. Kelly Martin. — 1st ed.
p. cm.
Summary: Two unexpected and heartbreaking deaths cause the lives of two very different
teenagers to become intertwined as one struggles to deal with his grief and stay in this world,
and the other finds herself inexplicably caught between this world and the next.
ISBN 978-0-375-86855-9 (trade) — ISBN 978-0-375-96855-6 (lib. bdg.) —
ISBN 978-0-375-89925-6 (ebook)
[1. Death—Fiction. 2. Grief—Fiction.] I. Title.
PZ7.M3567758My 2011
[Fic]—dc22
2010027985

Printed in the United States of America

10 9 8 7 6 5 4 3 2 1

First Edition

Random House Children's Books supports
the First Amendment and celebrates the right to read.

For anyone

who has ever wondered

if they could stand another day

Rage on

my beating teenage heart

one

The first moment is utter darkness. The absence of thought, the absence of everything. An absence that stretches infinitely backwards and threatens to smother your sanity—if there was a you, that is. But there's not. I am nothing and no one. I never was. I must not have been because otherwise, wouldn't I remember?

Don't look back. Don't let the darkness inside you.

If I'm talking to myself, there must be a me. That in itself is a revelation. I exist. The second before was starkly empty and now I'm swimming with celestial stars. They're as silent as stones but they shimmer, glimmer and shine. I think . . . I think I can hear them after all but not in a way I've heard anything before.

The sound isn't music and it's not whispers. I don't have words to describe it. If teardrops, blinding sunshine and limitless knowledge combined to make a noise, it would be the one the stars hum while I float amongst them. I don't know much, but this is something I'm certain I'm learning for the first time: the stars know things that we don't and they always have.

And then, just as my mind begins to expand with questions

—who am I?

—where is this?

—how am I . . .

I'm falling, plummeting through the glittering darkness at a speed that would normally make your stomach drop. Instinct kicks in and makes me throw out my hands to break my fall. Only, I don't have any—no hands and no stomach either.

The fear of falling exists in my consciousness and nowhere else. There's nothing I can do to stop my descent. Beneath me continents of light beam their brightness as I speed towards them.

Catch me, stars. Help me.

But they're not stars, as it turns out. They're the lights you see from a jumbo jet when you're coming in for a night landing. They make civilization appear minuscule and for some reason that makes me want to sob but I can't do that either. No hands, no stomach, no tears.

What happens when I hit bottom?

I'm so close now that I can spy individual cars, streetlamps, house lights left on.

Is someone, someplace, waiting for me, leaving the light on?

Where am I supposed to be?

A pointed suburban roof reaches up to meet me, and if I have no body, surely there are no bones to shatter, no damage to fear, but my consciousness flinches anyway. It quakes and tries to yank whoever or whatever I am away from the solid mass shooting up underneath me.

In the split second it takes to realize I've failed, I'm already through the ceiling. Inside, falling still. Falling . . . and then not.

I don't crash. I don't even touch down. All I can do is stare into the pair of blinking eyes below me. They're not even a foot away. They're the distance you hold yourself from someone when you're on your way to a kiss. I don't remember my own kisses but I remember the concept the same way I remember what a roof or a jumbo jet is. I remember romance, yearning, love and hate in a way that has nothing to do with me. Maybe I've never been in love—or maybe it's happened a hundred times but so very long ago that I've forgotten each of them. I can't decide which idea is sadder.

The eyes open and close as I stare at them. *His eyes.* The white boy's. They're not staring back at me, but looking clean through. If I had a body I'd estimate it was hovering just above his, toe to toe and head to head with him.

It's night and we're cloaked in darkness, the two of us. But he's the only one who's truly here. *Here.* Wherever that is.

I'd move if I could, give him the space he doesn't realize he's lacking. I feel awkward, embarrassed about all I can see from here—his pores, his nose hairs, a cracking bottom lip that could use lip balm—even though he doesn't appear to have a clue he's being spied upon. But there's nothing I can do about it. I'm like a camera, picking up images but not in control of angles or focal length.

So I watch the boy's eyelashes flutter and listen to him breathe. What his lungs expel sounds like a steak knife slashing into meat. Not like an asthmatic but like someone so steeped in despair it's a wonder he hasn't drowned in it. How long can someone live like this? It hurts to hear. My nonexistent hands clamp themselves over my nonexistent ears.

Outwardly, my focus barely shifts. I'm still floating over him, listening to breaths of bottomless anguish. *Wait* . . .

I must be asleep. My fall from the stars and the hurt I hear in this boy's breathing, they can't be real. This vision I'm watching is nothing but a wildly vivid dream. When I wake up tomorrow, with my stomach, my hands and all my memories intact, I'll shake my head at my panic. Then I'll grab a pen and jot the details down before they fade to nothing. I imagine how crazy every bit of this will seem when I read it back in the morning. Stars that make a noise of wisdom. The power to read emotions through someone's breath.

Insane. Even for a dream. Why not dream of something my eyes would want to linger on—the rapturous merging of two bodies or a purple sky hanging over a majestic blue-green waterfall? Why dream of this sad boy?

I examine him, attempt to cement the details in my mind so I can record them when I wake up, and as I'm watching I realize I can shift the camera here and there after all—not much, but a little. Yes, I can stare at him from the end of the bed if I prefer, or from a blue acoustic guitar leaning against the wall near his window. Maybe I can even . . . No, I can't escape the room, can't leave him behind. That's beyond my power. He's meant to be the star of this dream for reasons my unconscious isn't ready to share with me. I notice that when I turn away from him to study the room, my gaze jumps inadvertently back to him before long.

And when it does this is what I see: a white boy of about

sixteen or seventeen, curly brown hair framing his face. His eyes are light but in the dark I can't determine whether they're green, blue or even hazel. The boy's lying in bed in a gray T-shirt, his bare arms stretched over the covers. He's motionless. Stiller than still except for the blinking. The horrible breathing has stopped, or so it seems. When I listen more intently I realize I can still hear it if I choose. There are some things I can control within this dream, evidently, and this strange audio ability is one of them.

I watch the teenage boy close his eyes. A cell phone rings on the bedside table next to him. My eyes follow his as they dart to the phone and I wonder if the call is important in the scheme of this dream fiction. Perhaps the real action is finally getting started.

Who wants to stand by and be a helpless witness to the grip of misery? I hope, since I'm being forced to take in this vision, that the dream's preparing to morph into something more entertaining—maybe something more closely resembling an action movie or thriller. Do I like chase scenes and gunfire in movies? Shouldn't I be able to remember that, even in my sleep?

Once the phone falls silent, the boy reaches for it, looks to check who called and begins to set it down again. It erupts in his hand and I could swear this time it's louder, almost like a siren. If I have to guess I'd say I'm hearing the phone the same way he is—with added urgency. This time he switches his phone off before returning it to its space on the bedside table.

The boy's gaze flashes away from his cell and towards the alarm clock next to it: 12:23. He lies back in bed, his eyes glued to the ceiling where I both am, and am not. Long moments pass like this. 12:24. 12:25. 12:26. I begin to feel like I'm waiting for a change of scene that will never occur. At last a light tap at the door breaks the spell.

The boy's eyes snap shut as if on cue.

"Breckon?" a middle-aged man with a receding hairline whispers as he pops his head around the now-open door. The man's tie is askew and he smooths it down with one hand and then eases the door open wider, waiting for the boy—Breckon—to stir.

Breckon does no such thing, although I know he's awake. The man pads towards him, sighs silently and sits on the side of his bed. He does this carefully, so as not to awaken the boy I now know to be Breckon. I wonder if the man is his father and if he wishes Breckon would open his eyes and speak to him or whether he prefers this false silence.

The sound of Breckon's breath still hurts if I let it, but I don't. I use the special volume control that allows me to swing down the audio on that alone. His father, or whoever the man is, doesn't seem to hear anything unusual. At first he surveys the moonlit walls—a key-chain collection hanging from four curtain rods mounted one beneath the other on the far wall, a surreal Dalí print tacked up close to the door and nearer the bed posters of Pink Floyd's *The Wall* and a photographic image of a soccer ball sailing through a blue sky.

Dalí. I remember Salvador Dalí. Jumbo jets, kisses, Salvador Dalí and Pink Floyd too. *How I wish, how I wish you were here.* I hear the lyrics play inside my head and the memory of them makes some currently unknowable part of me ache.

Breckon's father curves his hands around the edge of the bed. He transfers his attention to the boy next to him, peering down at Breckon until his eyes well up with tears.

The movie inside my head isn't an action film but some kind of tragedy, and I've seen enough for one night. I begin to struggle with my brain. *Wake. Up. Open your eyes!* My subconscious brain is obviously stronger than my conscious one. It's not ready to depart yet. No matter how many mental shakes I give myself, my focus holds on Breckon and his teary-eyed father. *Please, please, please let me wake up.* I try it like a chant. *Please, please, please.* With profound longing.

But no matter how much I plead with myself, I can't regain consciousness. I'm trapped inside these four walls.

Slowly, Breckon's father rises and starts back towards the door, closing it gently behind him. That leaves me as Breckon's sole witness and, helpless, I continue to watch him pretend to sleep, his lips parted and his breathing shallow. I suppose at some point the pretense becomes the truth because it lasts until morning light. What should unfold in hours feels more like minutes, and when the sun rises and birds begin chirping outside Breckon's window, I'm no clearer about who I am but at least there's more to see.

Breckon rolls onto his side, curling into the fetal position. He lifts his head and then tugs the rest of his body out of bed with it. In the daylight his eyes are a smoky blue. They match the stripes on his sweatpants. Now that he's standing I can see that he's lean and medium-tall. There's a bump in his nose, which could mean it was broken at some point, but don't ask me how I know that when I couldn't tell you my own name.

Breckon's fingers dig into his head and scratch. I circle him, testing out my camera skills now that I have an active subject. I'm able to swirl 360 degrees around his body or sharp-focus on his bare feet or the back of his skull, if I like.

I can cling to the ceiling or dart over to the window at the speed of light, but the real trick—soaring *through* it and fleeing into the open air—is a magical feat that I can't muster. Meanwhile Breckon himself has opened his bedroom door and is shuffling into the hall. My being follows like we're attached by an electrical current. Staying in his bedroom is suddenly as impossible as leaving it was just moments ago.

In an instant a dog that is little more than tufts of fiery orange and white races towards Breckon with a high-pitched yelp. It launches its front paws up to rest them on Breckon's left leg. The dog stares at him beseechingly.

"Moose," Breckon scolds. It's the first thing I've heard him say, and his voice is deeper than I would've guessed. Breckon bends to push the dog roughly away from him. First his father and now the dog. Is there anyone this boy does want to interact with?

I home in on his breathing, only for a moment, but that's long enough for the ache to register. Things aren't any better for him this morning than they were last night.

Moose whimpers as he's shoved aside. He lets Breckon pass, his eyes trailing him, when a forty-something-year-old woman appears in the hallway in pale linen pants and a cardigan. Her long brown hair's back in a ponytail, and her eyes are near enough to the same color as Breckon's. It would be difficult to decide which of them looks more tired.

"Morning," the woman says. She leans in towards Breckon to wrap her arms around him and he lets her.

"Morning," he mutters back.

"I was just about to go down for breakfast," the woman tells him as she straightens and steps back, one of her hands still touching his arm. "Is there anything you'd like?"

Breckon rubs his dry lips wearily together and shrugs.

"How about some eggs?" she suggests.

"Sure." He scratches at his T-shirt. "Thanks."

As they head downstairs together, Moose following, I've begun to doubt my initial assumption that the woman is Breckon's mother, but she's clearly someone he knows well. Someone who wants to make him eggs because at least that means she's doing *something* for him. Or am I reading too much into their exchange? Perhaps she doesn't have an inkling about the pain he's feeling.

Down in the kitchen, Breckon collapses into a wooden chair and watches the woman pull eggs out of the refrigerator and retrieve a frying pan from the shelf beneath the stove. He clears his throat and sets one of his bare feet on the chair across from him. "So did Sunita get home okay?" he asks. "Did you talk to her?"

"I did." The woman pivots to face Breckon. She smiles for him, but the wrinkles in her forehead proclaim something other than joy. "About an hour ago. She complained that the man in the seat next to her was sneezing nonstop during the flight last night, but other than that she seemed fine."

Breckon nods in response, a yawn creeping into his mouth and making him open his jaws.

"Do you want some toast too?" she ventures. "Juice?"

Breckon shrugs like he doesn't care but the suggestion of juice jolts through me. *I remember.* And this is different than with jumbo jets or Dalí. I remember something specific about *me.* I like orange juice. Apple too but orange more. I'm not even thirsty, but the mere mention of it sends me into an orange craving that would rival an alcoholic's yearning for vodka or whiskey. Nothing in the world seems more appealing than a tall glass of freshly squeezed orange juice at this exact moment.

Wake up, I urge. *Don't you want to get out of bed and pour yourself some real-life orange juice?*

While I'm busy having a personal revelation (I love orange juice!), a second woman has entered the kitchen. In many ways she resembles the first. In fact, if the first woman didn't have her hair tied back, I might mistake them for the same person.

"Dawn," the first woman announces, reaching out to stroke the second's arm. "I'm about to fry Breckon up some eggs. Can I put a couple on for you too?"

Dawn cradles her chin like this is a difficult, almost unanswerable question. One of her blouse sleeves is unbuttoned at the wrist but she either hasn't noticed or doesn't care.

"Go on, sit down," the first woman adds, leaping over her original question. "I won't be a second with the eggs."

Dawn bobs her head and trudges towards the table, where she stops and studies the apricot-hued wall behind it. What appears to be a recent school picture of Breckon hangs next to an empty hook and then a family portrait. I study the photos along with her, confirming that Dawn and the man who sat on

Breckon's bed last night are his parents. I haven't worked out who the woman making breakfast is yet, and there's a girl in the family portrait—young with white-blond hair cut as short as a boy's—who has yet to make an appearance.

"Oh," the woman at the stove remarks, her mouth drooping around the word as she notices where Dawn's stare has landed. "I have to drop by the funeral home and pick up the photos. I'll do that later today."

Oh. I feel the sting of the implications behind that syllable too and I hope I'm wrong. The girl in the family portrait is much too young to die. In the photo she can't be older than six. But the woman's reference to a funeral home could mean anything—an older relative's passing. It's only a dream anyway, I remind myself. Nobody's died, not really.

Breckon's mother sits across from him at the table. They nod at each other but remain quiet. The sole sounds in the kitchen are of a wall clock the shape of a sunflower ticking and the woman at the stove scraping a spatula against the bottom of the frying pan.

"Lily?" Breckon says, breaking the silence.

The woman with the ponytail turns to look at him. "Hmm?" she says, tilting her head.

"I'm going to hit the shower," he tells her, already on his feet. "I'll have the eggs when I'm finished, okay?"

"Sure, honey." Lily's face is gilded with sympathy. "Whatever you want. I'll keep them warm for you."

Breckon glances down at his mother. Her eyes are blue too, but brighter than his, and she points to her feet, where Moose is sitting on the tile floor, dazedly watching the three of them.

Dawn's mouth flaps open as she struggles to formulate her thoughts. "He's been so—"

"I know," Breckon cuts in. He turns abruptly away and makes for the stairs, taking them two at a time like he can't escape the kitchen quickly enough.

"Breckon," his father calls from the top of the stairway. Breckon's shoulders curl towards his chest as he looks up at his father. "I heard your cell ringing in your room just a second ago," his dad continues, hands dipping into the deep pockets of his navy-blue robe. His face radiates the same unhappiness that everyone's inside this house does. *And still no sign of the little blond girl,* I note. *But can't people change their dreams if they want to?*

If I concentrate hard enough, imagine the face from the family portrait and wish her into being with all my might, will she materialize in front of us, white-blond hair still mussed from being flattened against her pillow? Can I create a miracle in my sleep?

They call that lucid dreaming, I think, but either I'm doing it wrong or it's a phony concept in the first place, because nothing happens when I envision the little girl in the hallway with us. Absolutely nothing.

"I'll . . ." Breckon's fingers dive into his curls. "I'll check messages when I get out of the shower." He squints as he continues his climb, maybe remembering the same thing I am—didn't he switch his phone off last night?

Breckon passes his father on the stairs and lurches through the second-floor hall and into the bathroom, where I watch him tear off his T-shirt and sweatpants. He leaves them in a heap on the floor and reaches, naked, for the shower tap. Inside he stands under the stream of water, bowing his head and letting droplets run down his face. He closes his eyes and hooks his fingers into his armpits. His shoulders begin to shake. His face crumples. He cries quietly into his own chest as the tremble takes hold. Breckon's face is red with agony. He quakes and sobs under the sound of running water, and the sound of that undercover weeping is worse than his tormented breathing, though I can still hear that too.

If I've ever seen anyone cry like this, I can't remember it, but I'm certain that even in my waking life, I won't forget, and with the pain of that thought, finally, finally my brain changes gears and starts to release its hold on my dream world and let me go. Not through the roof and stars the way I came, but with a simple fade to gray and then black, Breckon dropping away from me as I fall into pure, blessed silence.

two

Something has gone horribly wrong. Panic sets in as I thrash around in the darkness. Just try to thrash without a body and see where that gets you. Frustration and fear with no form. Indistinct half-thoughts tumbling in a void. Grasping, without hands, for certainties that don't exist.

Nothing. And that goes on forever.

Nowhere. Except for the spot you wanted to leave behind. That place still exists: the boy, Breckon, sobbing in the shower. I can hear him in the distance, as though he's standing at the opposite end of a long tunnel, when I tune my ears in to the sound. Apparently I've switched off visuals the same way I turned down the audio on his breathing earlier. It happens that I'm capable of blocking his world out entirely with no trouble.

The problem is, when I switch off that noise and matching pictures, there isn't anything else to replace it. Just some weird essence of me in the blackness.

This is no regular dream. I would've woken up by now. *Try*

again, I tell myself. *Maybe you haven't really tried with everything you've got.* So I thrash harder. I rail against the darkness, fighting for my consciousness like my life depends on it. Maybe it does. Maybe I'm in a coma in a hospital somewhere. That would explain my amnesia. Brain damage. Some kind of head injury or a high fever.

Scream, I advise myself.

Let the nurses and doctors know you're still in here.

Advising myself is well and good but in practice the screaming proves exactly like the thrashing. While I don't have the use of my body, I suppose it can't be any different. All I can do is *try* in the exact same way.

What if I don't ever wake up? What will become of me?

Don't think like that, I command. *You can't lose hope.* That might make things worse still.

I don't even know what I have to lose; I don't know who I am. A few very select personal details have bobbed up inside me and made themselves known while the real world goes on without me. Hoping for more, I concentrate on those details by keeping the lifelike vision of Breckon and his mourning family at bay. Alone, turned inward to delve for information about myself, my dream world temporarily ceases to exist. This is what I imagine being blind and deaf is like.

Silence isn't golden, it's like being the last person on earth, but it helps me think. To review, this is what I now remember to be true:

1. I like orange juice.

2. I'm female (a fact I only realized when I watched Breckon

take off his sweatpants and climb into the shower, but that somehow didn't come as a complete surprise).

3. There's a good chance I haven't seen a guy naked before (I gratuitously lingered on certain parts of his anatomy while simultaneously feeling self-conscious about that, even in my invisible state).

Breckon's dog is a Pomeranian. (I didn't recall the breed name when I first saw him but now I remember it along with others—cocker spaniels, beagles, Great Danes, bloodhounds, chow chows.) I continue listing them in my head for so long that it leads me to the next detail, which is:

4. I'm a dog person, not a cat person.

5. I don't like snakes or big creepy crawly things, though the smaller ones don't bother me.

6. I like songs you can dance to (but I can't conjure any specific examples).

7. I don't like sad songs except when they're breakup songs (not one of which currently resides in the near-blank slate that is my mind).

8. My favorite color is aqua.

9. I'm right-handed (I think). I imagine reaching out to open a door, and in my imagination my right is the first to extend itself.

But what else? Who are the people closest to me—my friends and family? When they call my name what is it they say? When they look at me who do they see?

On those matters my brain sputters, stalls and refuses to budge. I'm like a novel with all personal references methodically cut out, leaving only inconsequential words like *"the," "that," "from"* and *"said."*

I have no plotline, hardly enough information about myself to form the most basic character. When I wake up will I even be able to feed and dress myself? And if not, who will be around to help me?

The only people who exist in my memory are ones I don't know. Salvador Dalí, the members of Pink Floyd (and I don't know their names either). Who else? *Think.* Musical groups. Painters. Which ones can you remember? Leonardo da Vinci! Mona Lisa smiles her enigmatic grin in my mind. Vincent van Gogh. He lopped his own ear off. Michelangelo painted the ceiling of the Sistine Chapel.

The Beatles sang "I Want to Hold Your Hand." Marvin Gaye: "I Heard It Through the Grapevine." Tina Turner: "River Deep, Mountain High." But these are old songs, aren't they? Somehow I sense that, although I can't recall what year it is out in the real world. So what's the last song I heard? And what's my very favorite song?

I have no idea. I make a mental note of what I know about the world and try to measure it against my personality and history.

The world is round, not flat. The earth revolves around the sun. Those are facts they teach you in school, but I don't know precisely who taught me them. Something even simpler then—do I like the sun?

10. I do. I like the sun and

11. snow too.

What do I *do* in the snow? Do I skate? Do I ski?

Memories of lacing skates and slipping boots into skis flit effortlessly through my head. No people. Just skates and skis.

12. I can do them both but I'm not sure how well.

13. Swim too.

14. And stand on my head.

So what do you like besides orange juice? What do you eat?

15. Ice cream, but then doesn't everyone? So what flavor? Orange, of course! But also chocolate, butter pecan, bubble gum, black cherry, cookies and cream and Ben & Jerry's pumpkin cheesecake.

So it sounds like I'm fond of ice cream. There are an infinite number of flavors swimming in my head and none of them seem unappealing. Images of various scoops—strawberry, coconut, mint chocolate chip, raspberry ripple—flash through my unconscious. My hand, holding dripping cones. *My hand.*

The image of it is still in my memory. My hand is darker than Breckon's, more of an olive tone. My God, if I can see that, there must be more. My body, my age, my name.

There's a part of me that remains *me* even without that knowledge, I've discovered. And that part is racing through the darkness without moving, searching for the countless parts of myself I've mislaid. Reaching . . . Remembering . . .

Yes.

I've got it. No doubt Breckon's still crying in the distance, if I bother to listen, but that barely matters. I'm reveling in my true identity, dancing in the dark.

I'm me and no one else. I love orange juice and ice cream and someone from the real world will find me and bring me back any moment now.

I'll open my eyes, dance in the sunlight, cry out my name at the top of my lungs and make people I don't know stop and stare. Their eyes on me will make me laugh and shout until I'm all out of voice. *I'm me! I'm me and no one else!*

I'm almost sixteen years old and my name is Ashlyn.

three

breckon

When I get out of the shower I feel shaky, like I could fall down and throw up at the same time. I sit on the floor next to my T-shirt and tilt my head down towards my knees. I don't want to pass out. The last thing my parents need right now is to have to take me to the hospital. It doesn't matter how much medication they're on, that would push them over the edge completely. My aunt Lily would be the one who'd have to bring me. If there was something really wrong with me, her girlfriend, Sunita, would fly back from Ottawa to keep Lily from falling apart.

But I know there's nothing wrong with me that anyone can do anything about. I slide myself along the tiles and lean over the toilet. I let myself cry too much; I can't do that. When I lose my grip it's too hard to get it back. Stupid.

I envy Skylar for being dead. I'd trade with her anytime.

Shit, here it comes. I throw the lid up and heave liquid into the bowl. I haven't had breakfast yet and I can't remember if I ate anything last night. It looks like there's nothing but spit for me to lose.

Okay, I need to get it together. I've already been in here too long. Lily will be downstairs watching my eggs get cold and worrying about me—about all of us.

I haul myself up, stomach still churning, and stare at my reflection in the mirror. I look red and shriveled. If I was bald I bet people would think I had cancer.

Breathe, asshole. Get your shit together. You can't go anywhere looking like this.

I run the tap and splash cold water on my face. There's just my toothbrush left in the toothbrush holder now. Someone has already packed Skylar's away. It's a shock to notice it missing, the same way seeing her school picture missing from the kitchen wall came as a shock to my mom. There's a new shock every sixty seconds. She's gone. BAM. You'll never in your life see her again. BAM. They just keep coming.

I know she's gone and everywhere she isn't still comes as a shock.

I grab my toothbrush and brush so hard that my gums begin to bleed. I spit the blood into the sink. It leaves a weird, metallic taste in my mouth but I don't care.

I dripped on my sweatpants and T-shirt after climbing out of the shower. They're pretty wet but I throw them on because I forgot to bring in a change of clothes. Once I'm back in the wet stuff I make a beeline for my bedroom to check phone messages that I don't care about either.

My cell's lying facedown on the carpet where it's turned

itself on. If Skylar were here she'd probably say a ghost did it. Two months ago I made the mistake of letting her watch a documentary with me about a haunted house in Connecticut and she's been obsessed with ghosts ever since. Scared too sometimes but she wouldn't admit it. Well, not to me.

I only know because I caught shit from my mom for letting her watch the thing. A couple days after we'd seen it, my mother said Skylar was having trouble sleeping because of it and didn't I realize she was only seven years old?

It would sound like I was making excuses if I said that sometimes with Skylar you can forget, but I've seen it happen with other people too. She can hold entire conversations with adults (or people my age) about their day and you don't have to dumb things down for her. Other times she'll break herself up with her own homemade jokes and sing in a loud, on-purpose off-key voice that will make you want to clap a hand over her mouth.

Another thing you can almost forget about Skylar sometimes is that she's a girl. She scowls at Bratz dolls and anything pink and hasn't let my mom put her in a dress in almost three years. She keeps her hair short because she says she hates when it whips around in the wind and that long hair makes her head feel heavy. Her favorite toys are the race-car track she left laid out in the family room for all of March and a bunch of action-figure explorer and wilderness sets that come with stuff like tiny weapons, boats, little tents and canned food for the ranger figures to cook over a campfire.

About a month ago Moose swallowed the miniature pair of binoculars that came with one of the sets, and Skylar's so hung up on all that explorer gear that for the next twenty-four hours she kept checking out his shit to see if she could find them. She never did. They could still be parked in his intestines. With any luck the binoculars will go septic and kill him in his sleep. Then the dumb dog could stop wandering around the house looking for Skylar like we've hidden her away behind a fake bookshelf or something.

I pick my cell up from the carpet and it would be warm and fuzzy for me to say that it was Skylar's ghost that threw it there but anyone who would think that is just deluding himself. I didn't answer my phone once yesterday so there are a bunch of messages. Some of the people I go to school with have texted their condolences. The girls send lots of "xoxoxoxo" and "((hugs))." The guys mostly just say "sorry."

Lots of them were at the funeral yesterday too but I made sure that I hardly spoke to anyone. I heard some of the girls from my school crying when the church started playing "Bright Eyes." My grandparents picked the song because my parents and I couldn't come up with one. I couldn't remember the name of a single song when the minister asked me for suggestions, but it would've been better if they hadn't played one at all. Some other people were crying during "Bright Eyes" too but the girls from school wailed the loudest. I wanted to tell everyone to shut up. Most of those girls never even met my sister.

Aside from the texts there are a few voice-mail messages from closer friends asking me to let them know if there's anything they can do. One of them is from my best friend Ty. In his message he sounds like someone stomped all the air out of him. He says call whatever time I want, even if it's four a.m.

Jules has called multiple times. In the first message she says she loves me and that she's been thinking about me, the others just say, "It's me again." I throw on a pair of pants that I haven't worn since all this happened, a clean T-shirt and a checked long-sleeve shirt over it. When Jules sees me wearing it she likes to say that I'd look like Kansas farm boy Clark Kent in it if I had straight hair. Superman's the only superhero either of us likes, so it's a compliment.

I pick at the stitching on my sleeve and think about returning Jules's call but in the end I switch the phone off again and go downstairs. Lily heats up my eggs for me and toasts two pieces of whole wheat bread. Then Mom, Dad, Lily and I sit ourselves in front of the TV until my grandparents (Dad's parents) and Mom's mother (her father came down with bronchitis and coughed during the entire ceremony yesterday) show up. The grandmothers itemize the meals other people have brought over, squishing their own contributions into the fridge along with them. Then they wash the few dirty dishes in the sink (one of my grandmothers complaining how hot the water is) and clean things that don't really need cleaning.

Dad and his father stand around in the backyard so my grandfather can smoke a cigarette, and Mom, Lily and I stare at an old disaster movie on TV. Eventually we eat reheated chicken stew and when my grandmothers get me alone one of them asks if there's anything of Skylar's she should take away or tidy up but I don't know what to say.

She sniffles, pats my hand and says, "Don't mention it to your mother. I don't want her to have to give anything a thought today."

I nod numbly, excusing myself to find my grandfather and ask if he's ready for another smoke. We head off to the front yard this time, and he hesitates before shaking the package in front of me and asking if I'd like one. I don't care what I do so I take one. Jules smoked vanilla herbal cigarettes for a couple months last fall. They were supposed to taste like marshmallow mixed with vanilla but instead their flavor was more like moldy leaves that you rake up off the lawn in October and after a while I couldn't even bring myself to kiss her if she'd just finished a cigarette, which is like the equivalent of Superman losing his lust for Lois Lane.

My grandfather's brand tastes more like a cigarette is supposed to but mostly I just hold it between my fingers and keep him company until Lily walks out the front door and says she's going to the funeral home to pick up the photographs. If she was going somewhere else I'd offer to keep her company but I don't want to see that place again.

When my grandfather and I go back into the house Moose jumps on me like he did this morning and I snap at him again, without meaning to. "He just needs some TLC," my grandfather says, scooping Moose up in his arms like he feels sorry for him. "Don't you, boy?"

Moose stares at him in the same annoyingly blank way he's been staring at everyone in the past few days. "He's driving me crazy," I tell my grandfather, my voice nearly breaking.

My grandfather scratches under Moose's chin and dips his head like he understands.

"You want a dog?" I ask, trying to make a joke out of it. "You can have him dirt cheap."

My grandfather bounces Moose up and down in his arms like he's a baby that he can make laugh. "You hear that?" my grandfather asks him. "He's trying to unload you for a quick buck. You better try harder to earn your keep."

Moose barks, wanting to be let down. "Ah, go on then." My grandfather lowers him to the carpet and Moose trots off down the hall looking as unmoose-like as ever. "Your sister sure had a sense of humor," my grandfather mutters, rubbing at his left eye. "Imagine calling a little bit of a thing like that Moose."

Skylar wanted a big dog—an Akita or German shepherd—but my mom said she wouldn't have a horse in the house, so this is what we ended up with. Skylar gave him a big-dog name to compensate but Moose doesn't realize he has a big-dog name and acts like a little dog or even a cat. Sometimes, when he's really content, he makes a purring noise and if you take him for too long a walk he flat out refuses to take another step and you have to carry him home in your arms. Lucky for Moose, Skylar ended up loving him despite all of his deficiencies.

At the end of the day, when my grandparents have gone home, all of Skylar's photographs are hanging back where they should be, and I think I can finally be alone, Moose scratches insistently at my bedroom door. I ignore the noise for a while, thinking he'll get bored and wander off, but then the sound of his claws on the door starts to wear on me so I let him in. He zips into the middle of the room and just stands there with his head cocked, wanting something I can't give him.

She's not here, idiot dog. She's not anywhere you can find her.

I point silently towards my open door and hope he'll get

the message and leave. I don't want to yell at him anymore today.

Instead Moose hops straight up onto my bed and sits down, eyes still watching me. I don't care how much he gawks. I'm not letting him sleep at the end of my bed like he used to sleep on Skylar's. "Down," I command. I don't shout but I'm not using my happy voice either. I snap my fingers and repeat myself.

On a normal day I don't have anything against the dog, but we're done with normal days around here. I can't keep an airtight lid on myself and feel sorry for him too. There's not enough of me left over for that. If Moose is depending on me to get him through this I guess he just won't make it.

Moose obeys my command, leaps down from my bed and scurries out of the room. I shut the door behind him, reach for my cell and speed-dial Jules before I can lose momentum. Usually she's the easiest person in the world for me to talk to but I don't have the energy for anyone right now.

Jules answers on the first ring and I hear her mother calling "Julianna" in the background—like she's always doing to let Jules know her cell is ringing in another room—as Jules picks up.

"Hi," Jules says to me and then shouts to her mother, "I've got it, Mom."

"I picked up your messages earlier," I tell her, "but I couldn't talk. My grandparents were around for most of the day." I sit on the bed and notice the clump of orange fur Moose left behind on my bedspread.

"I figured there'd be people over. I just wanted to make sure you were doing . . ." Jules pauses and tries to start over. ". . . that you were—"

I cut her off. "Thanks. I know."

Jules is quiet and waits for me to continue. When I don't, she says, "Do you want me to come over?"

I don't want anything, really, so it's impossible to say. "Maybe I'll just try to get some sleep." I knock Moose's flyaway fur to the ground.

"That's a good idea," Jules says in a soothing voice.

"I don't think I slept at all last night." I close my eyes and yawn. I didn't feel tired until this second and now I'm down to the bone exhausted.

"Sleep," she tells me, the word itself sounding like a lullaby. "*Sleep.* I'll come over after school tomorrow."

My stomach twinges as my eyes pop open. "But I bet I'll just lie here, that I probably won't be able to drift off, no matter how tired I am." The minute my head hits the pillow I'll either lie there as numb as a dead thing like I did for hours last night or lose it the way I did in the shower.

"You know, your parents probably have pills that would help," Jules says into my ear. "Didn't you say you thought they were both taking something?"

They're like zombies, so yeah, they're sure as fuck on something but . . . "I don't want to ask them," I admit, my voice strained.

"I can bring you something," Jules promises without a moment's hesitation.

I can't imagine what she has access to—Jules doesn't even really like smoking weed—but I say okay and to call me when she's outside because I don't think my parents are ready for visitors that aren't family, not even my girlfriend.

My mom didn't like Jules much when we first started going out last year after the tenth-grade trip to New York. I told her that Jules was big into theater and really independent-minded—one of the least superficial people I'd ever met—but when they met I watched Jules's nose ring, dyed black hair and the battered burgundy combat boots that she wore all last year overpower the good things I'd said about her. As far as my mother was concerned Jules's personal style indicated that she—and by extension *I*—was on the way to becoming a drug addict or homeless person. Not that my mom said anything like that, but she'd get this slightly pained squint when she'd look in Jules's direction and she didn't say much to her until about the fifth time Jules came over.

Skylar had found this frog at the park down the street and smuggled it home in her hoodie pocket. When my mom found out she told Skylar she had to bring it straight back and Skylar got so sad and quiet (but she didn't cry, Skylar hardly ever cried) that my mom told her she could have an hour to say goodbye to it.

Enter Jules and me, interrupting Skylar's bonding time with the frog, which probably only would've made saying goodbye harder anyway. Jules started to make up a story about how the frog's family would be waiting for him back at the pond and I helped pile on the details. It probably sounds stupid now and it's not like Skylar believed a word we said, but it seemed funny at the time and when we took Skylar out later to return the frog to nature she didn't seem so sad anymore.

My mom thanked Jules and me and I could tell that she'd changed her mind about Jules because she didn't have the squint in her eye anymore when she looked at her. I never asked Jules if she noticed any of that but it's ancient history because now both my parents like her a lot. This is the first time I've ever suggested that she meet me at the side door so I can sneak her in. Maybe my parents wouldn't mind her being around, but I don't want to take any chances.

So fifteen minutes after we hang up Jules calls back and says she's standing outside. I hear the family room TV on as I head downstairs to meet her. Someone's still up, but if we're lucky we won't run into them.

I unlock the side door for Jules and raise a finger to my lips to let her know we have to be quiet. In place of her nose ring she has the clear retainer thing in, the same way she did at the funeral yesterday, her hair's tied back in a messy ponytail and she's wearing the chunky black Mary Janes, which are her favorite shoes these days.

She nods at me and grabs for my hand, squeezing hard. I lead her upstairs. Our steps don't creak much and we make it upstairs without a soul intercepting us. Inside my room I turn the radio on low to cover the sound of our voices and Jules sits on my bed and holds out her palm to reveal five white caplets. "You only need one," she whispers. "I brought extras in case you need some for the next few days."

I can't imagine how things could be any better after the

next five days but I tell her thanks, pluck a caplet from her hand, slip out to the bathroom and gulp water to chase it down. Then I go back to my room, sit on the bed next to Jules and mutter, "How long do they take to work?"

"It didn't say on the bottle," she says apologetically. "But I guess most things take about thirty minutes to kick in." Jules motions to my bedside table. "I stuck the rest of them in there."

I open the drawer and look at the other four tablets laying across the sheet music for the Beatles tune "I've Just Seen a Face." The song always reminds me of Jules and I was teaching it to myself just before Skylar died but now I never want to play it, or hear it, again. With all that's happened, I can't believe the music's still there and that I haven't torn it up and burned the pieces to ashes.

I shut the drawer and ask, "Where did you get the pills?"

"My parents' medicine cabinet. Sometimes my dad has trouble sleeping." Jules runs a hand loosely along her dark ponytail and adds, "His job stresses him out."

She's never mentioned that her dad takes sleeping pills before but I nod. I still can't make up my mind whether I really want her here or not.

Jules rubs my back and pulls me nearer to her on the bed. "Do you want me to stay?" she asks. Jules's parents don't hit her with a curfew when they know the two of us are just hanging out at my house and not a party somewhere but she's never spent the night.

"I told my mom I was coming over and that I thought maybe I should stay if you wanted me to," she adds, her voice soft and supportive. The sound pushes me a step closer to crumbling.

The air in here's too heavy. My lungs fight to breathe.

"Why don't you get in?" Jules suggests, taking charge. "I'll get the light." She slips off her Mary Janes before ambling towards the light switch and flicking it off. Then she stands in front of my key-chain collection, examining them in the dark. "I'll go before your parents wake up in the morning," she whispers, reaching for one of the key chains in the second row. My eyes haven't adjusted to the dark yet but I think it's the toy penguin that Ty found on the steps of the Royal Ontario Museum back when we were in seventh grade.

Ever since I started collecting key chains at ten years old, everyone I know has felt compelled to pick them up for me when they go away on vacation or stumble across bizarre novelty ones. You wouldn't believe all the weird things they make into key chains. I have emergency condom key chains in three different colors given to me by three different people; a pregnant woman key chain that's clear so you can see the baby inside her; a fish-shaped one that works as a TV remote, bottle opener and flashlight; and a solar-powered LED key chain that flashes "Barack" every two minutes. I take off my pants and shirt and slip under the covers in my boxers and T-shirt, continuing to itemize my collection in my head to see if that levels me out any.

Jules strips off her skintight black jeans and gets in next to me. I leave the radio on and turn onto my side, Jules spooning protectively up against me. "You're chilly tonight," she murmurs as she lays her hand against my abdomen.

I feel her bare legs, cold, against the back of my calves. Jules is always freezing but she's right, tonight I'm cold too.

Most of the time that I'm not on the verge of losing it, I'm working backwards in my head, trying to redo things with Skylar and make them turn out differently. It's like my brain still believes I have another chance, for a millisecond, before it completes the equation and realizes it's all over. BAM.

If I'd known how precarious life was I would've kept track of the details and never allowed this to happen. I didn't realize how everything could change in an instant. I don't know how I could spend almost seventeen years on the planet without learning such a fundamental fact about life.

I squeeze my eyes shut just as they begin to drain. Jules feels my chest collapse and hugs me harder. "I'm sorry," she says to my back. "I'm so, so sorry, Breckon." She says it over and over again, for I don't know how long, until I'm sure the damn pill she brought over must be about as potent as children's aspirin and that I'll never sleep through the night again. And then, in a terminally slow fade, the cold and pain disappear and there's just dark.

four

ashlyn

Levitating in the center of what I can only describe as my mind's eye, it's as though someone left a single tiny lamp on in an attempt to illuminate infinite darkness. But the light isn't nearly powerful enough to stretch far enough. It can't and even if it could there's not much to see. *Oranges. Vague memories of snow and ice. The knowledge that my name is Ashlyn. Ashlyn Baptiste to be precise.*

Grateful as I am for my lightning-bolt moment, I wanted more. A landslide of information, the story of my life flashing through my head with the speed of a super computer upload. Instead, so far I'm not any wiser about myself than I was yesterday morning. I'm that same cutout novel I described before, name and age pasted on the cover but so full of holes it's unreadable.

The funny thing is that even with the majority of my backstory missing, I'm feeling more like myself, as though my thought patterns are homing in on my Ashlyn nature, digging down to the core and dragging up a more distilled Ashlyn, even if they don't know what that means yet, to the surface of my being.

I don't know what *any* of it means yet. I can't digest why my mind would offer up this gloomy grieving vision of Breckon and his world. If it's to keep my brain occupied until I regain consciousness, wouldn't it make more sense to drop me into some kind of brain-teaser reality, a puzzle that I have to solve? Watching this boy is really only accomplishing one thing. It's making me *feel,* and what I feel is sad.

Could it be that the empathy I feel for him is meant to make me fight harder to return to my own loved ones? But I don't know how to fight any harder than I am right now.

Surely every second of this darkness and despair must be making my cells ache with the desire to wake up again. I want to live, but not like this. I swear to God, or whoever else could be listening, that if I wake up I'll do the right thing for the rest of my life, no matter how difficult that is. And I won't be afraid of anything or anyone. I'll be brave and true and make a difference somehow. I'll help and heal people like Breckon and his family. I'll do whatever it is you want, if only I'm allowed to wake up.

Please, please, please. Give me my life back.

This is what I do now. I make promises to the darkness.

In front of me, Breckon and his girlfriend are beginning to stir. That makes a day and a half that I've been watching him now, following him around like he's the star of a 24/7 reality TV show. Yes, I've learned I can stop watching, turn down the audio and video and retreat into the darkness, but it's so lonely on my own that I don't like to shut him out for very long. At least Breckon has the pills to make him rest. My mind never stops. I have two choices—I can watch his every move or wrestle with my memory in complete solitude, but either way there's no such thing as sleep.

Maybe that's because technically I'm already unconscious.

I'll go stark raving mental in here with only my own thoughts or images from someone else's train wreck of a life to keep me company. How will I stand it?

Breckon's girlfriend is leaning over him in bed. She watches him adjust his head on the pillow and swing his arm over his eyes—an unconscious reflex reaction to block the sun's rays—but it appears that she doesn't want to wake him. She lies back next to him until the alarm clock reads 8:42, at which point she throws her legs over the side of the bed and reaches for her jeans.

When she turns to face him again, jeans on, Breckon peers up at her with sleepy eyes. I zoom in on them in an extreme close-up and am glad to spy the telltale crusty residue underneath his lashes that proves he's been asleep and not faking.

I marvel at the cleverness of my brain to create such an intricate plotline. Breckon. His parents and extended family, complete with a cigarette-smoking grandfather, grieving Pomeranian and deceased little sister.

If my mind has the energy for that why can't it bring me back?

So many questions and no means to locate the answers.

"Hey," Breckon's girlfriend says quietly as she works her hair free from its ponytail, brushes it with her fingers and then reknots it in place. "I didn't want to wake you but I'm late for school.

"I don't have to go," she adds, bending her leg to rest one of her knees on the bed.

"No, you should go." Breckon clears his throat, looking groggy. "Besides, my parents probably wouldn't be cool with you hanging out here all day."

I wonder if they might be, if they thought it would help him.

His girlfriend pauses in place, her Mary Janes still on the floor next to the bed. "Well . . . what are you going to do today? You should do something." She sits down on the bed and curls her arm around his waist. "I mean, maybe being busy will—"

Breckon scrunches up his forehead, his eyebrows leaping together. "Being busy won't do shit. Nothing changes the facts."

Breckon's girlfriend winces at the bitterness in his face and tone and I know her suggestion wasn't meant to be callous, just the opposite, but that she can't think how to get that across without risking saying something else he'll take the wrong way.

"What?" Breckon challenges, squaring his jaw.

"Nothing." She moves her hand away from his waist to caress his face. "I just want to be here for you."

Breckon blinks heavily. "I know. But I'm not even here now. You know that, don't you?"

Breckon's girlfriend nods and reaches for his hand. Their fingers automatically entwine. She bends towards their interlocked hands and presses her mouth to his skin, changing his demeanor entirely.

"Thanks for bringing me the pills last night and everything," he tells her. "But it's okay. You can go to school, Jules."

Jules, so that's her name. It's possible Breckon mentioned it before when I wasn't really listening. Now that I know she's a Jules instead of an Emily or Megan, I can't picture her being anything else.

Jules studies Breckon, trying to determine whether it's really okay to leave him.

"I'll talk to you later," Breckon continues, hauling himself out of bed and into yesterday's wrinkled pants and shirt.

"You sure?" Jules asks.

He nods and messes with his hair. "I might even go back to bed for a while."

Jules pulls back the straps on her Mary Janes and jams her feet into her shoes. One of her fingers brushes against her bottom lip. "I'm glad the pills worked." A stiff smile stretches onto her face. "I'll check messages at lunch. You call me if you need anything else, okay?"

Breckon bobs his head in agreement and reaches for the doorknob. He and Jules stand in the open doorway, both their faces dropping in surprise. Out in the hall Breckon's father stops and registers their twin presence. His mouth slumps too but only for the briefest of moments before he rectifies that by saying, "Julianna, hello."

"Hi, Mr. Cody." Jules pronounces his name cautiously, as though in anticipation of being forced to admit a mistake.

The only names I've picked up so far are first names, and I perk up at the nugget of information and tuck it into my memory.

"I'm just walking Jules out," Breckon explains, avoiding his father's eyes.

"Ah," Mr. Cody replies, as though this makes perfect sense. I congratulate myself for guessing Breckon's parents would be more understanding than he gave them credit for and watch Mr. Cody turn and continue his way along the hall. Breckon and Jules hang in Breckon's doorway until his father has disappeared back inside his own room. Then they proceed quietly along the hall and down to the side door where Breckon thanks her again.

"Stop thanking me already," Jules says, grabbing the end of his shirt.

Breckon's pupils are tiny. He looks every ounce as tired as before he went to bed last night, and he wraps his arms around her and holds her to him. "Do you want me to get you a cereal bar or something?" he asks as he pulls away. "You can eat it on the way to school—what do you have first period anyway?"

"Bio." Jules frowns at the thought. "And it's okay, I'll swing by Second Cup and get some coffee on the way."

"Bio," Breckon repeats. "Right. Now I get why you'd want to hang around here instead. You don't want to deal with Gallardo's early-morning rantfest."

"Yeah, so you should really think about letting me stay." Jules fingers Breckon's shirt again. "Save me from a fate worse—" Her lips pause on the unspoken words, her face creasing in regret.

"Worse than death," Breckon finishes. His shoulders jerk up into a detached shrug. "Saying it doesn't make things worse than they are."

Jules sighs soundlessly and steps towards the door. "Okay, I'm going. Call me later?"

Breckon nods in confirmation, and once she's gone he heads directly back upstairs, steps out of his clothes, digs another sleeping pill out from his bedside table and pulls the covers over himself, waiting for it to work.

Even when it does, and there's nothing for me to see or hear but a slight rustling of sheets or the noise of a van driving by outside the window, I'm completely stuck within the walls that surround Breckon.

It's eerily intimate, watching someone sleep, especially a guy my age. It's just a dream and I shouldn't care, but I can't shake the feeling that I'm invading his privacy. No one but me knows about that morning sleeping pill or how he cried in the shower until he was shaking and sick yesterday. I feel an unfair responsibility for him tug at my consciousness and it makes me home in on his breathing again—or more accurately, the breathing *beneath* his being.

Asleep, what previously sounded agonizingly similar to lungs filling up with shards of glass currently resembles a more muted noise, perhaps like that of shredding paper with your bare hands. *Perhaps?* The word doesn't sound like me. This is what I mean about beginning to feel more and more like Ashlyn Baptiste—realizing she doesn't use words like *perhaps.*

Even in my amnesia state, I remember more words than I would probably use in conversation. *Hence, doth, perchance,* each of those feels exotic and ancient to me, though less so than they ever were in life, as though I could think in Shakespearean terms if I chose to. "Good night, good night! Parting is such sweet sorrow that I shall say good night till it be morrow." Why is it that I can recall the story of *Romeo and Juliet* but next to nothing about my own tale?

I'm getting lost in my thoughts again, digging for more bits of Ashlyn while keeping my visual focus on Breckon, when I notice his mother ease his bedroom door open. She watches him for several ponderous seconds that set me to thinking . . . how long has he been asleep? It was only the one pill that he swallowed this morning, I'm sure of it.

Granted, you're probably not supposed to swallow them back to back the way he did last night and this morning, but it would take many more than that to overdose, wouldn't it?

My attention shifts to his alarm clock. Twelve minutes to one. No wonder Breckon's mother is checking on him. "Honey?" she ventures. "Breckon?"

He opens his glazed-over eyes and they remind me of frosted glass windows—it's as though you can barely see through them to the actual person they belong to. Breckon stares hazily at his mother and listens to her say, "Your father and I are meeting Barbara and Sean for lunch. Lily was wondering if you'd like to join her, go out somewhere together?"

I have no idea who Barbara and Sean are but Breckon runs one hand down his face. "I'm really wiped," he mumbles after a five-second delay. "I'll warm up something from the freezer later."

"You don't want to get up?" his mom tries again. "Lily has to drop into the health-food store and run some other errands."

"How does that have anything to do with me?" Breckon asks, sounding like your stereotypical moody teenager.

Dawn Cody drops her hands into her cardigan pockets, her eyes weary but concerned. "I thought you might like to go with her. You shouldn't stay in bed all afternoon today, Breckon." I wonder if Mr. Cody told his wife about Jules's sleepover last night and whether this is the point in the conversation where she'll choose to bring it up.

"If Lily really needs me to go, I'll go," Breckon says. "But not if you just want me to get up for no reason."

"For no reason?" his mother repeats. "How about because I'd feel better if you were doing something?"

"Why should I do something?" Breckon fires back. "Why should I do *anything*?"

He glowers at her from the bed and I feel sorry for his mom, even sorrier when she points her chin down towards her chest and says, "Don't fight me, Breckon. I don't have the energy for it."

"I'm not fighting you," he protests. "I'm just really, really tired, Mom. Can't you tell Lily to go without me?"

His glazed-over eyes plead with her, her own expression revealing she's about three seconds away from caving. "Please eat something," she tells him. "Okay?"

"I will." Breckon yawns and dives under his pillow. Outside a delivery truck is backing up and I've just remembered something else about myself—I'm a light sleeper. I'd never be able to drift off to the annoying sound of that beep, beep.

Well, unless maybe I'd taken a sleeping pill. For the second time today I watch Breckon Cody slip back into sleep.

five

ashlyn

I think I'm beginning to understand what it would be like to live inside a straitjacket. Although time seems to speed up when Breckon's asleep, it can't move quickly enough for me. With every hour that goes by I find myself more and more surprised that the depth of my agitation doesn't snap me immediately into full consciousness.

I think . . .

This is going to sound completely freakish but I think I might be able to remember the moment I was born, and if that's true it's something I want to forget fast. The experience smelled like sweat mingled with disinfectant. Overwhelmingly bright and loud and altogether wrong. I screamed at the outrageous wrongness of it, every cell of my tiny being protesting, but I couldn't make it stop—the incomprehensible flurry of images and sounds, cool air brushing against my newly unprotected skin—*no, no, I don't want this!*

And this next thing is even crazier than my false birth memory—because there's no way that can be real, right?

Anyway, this is *lock me up in a rubber room* crazy (which doesn't matter because for all intents and purposes, I'm already there), but the memories rushing to the surface now *predate* me. One moment I'm all but clueless about myself and the next I'm waking up in my dream within a dream and remembering my parents' love story. I guess I must've heard it over the years so it's not weird that I'd *remember* it, but now . . . well, now I can SEE and HEAR those past events in my mind. High-definition images and surround sound. If my parents had met in a foreign country maybe there'd even be subtitles.

Somewhere in the outside world, they're pumping drugs into my system, making me hallucinate fake memories. That has to be what's happening here. Either that or my brain is beginning to shut down and this is what happens when you die, your prehistory flashes before your eyes right along with the rest of your life.

Shut up, you're not dying!

I'm talking to myself in two different personas now. I'm reaching for a full-throttle meltdown and why not? Why stop halfway? Why not just go for it, jump on and ride the wave?

I want to remember, when it comes down to it. Even if it's fake. My own thoughts and memories and this Breckon dream reality are all I have in the world.

I mean, they're my parents. Of course I want to remember. *My parents.* I can't believe I ever forgot them. The second their faces materialize in my brain they set like cement and make my soul sing. They were so young when they met, practically as young as I am now. They shared a first-year philosophy class at the University of Toronto, Cynthia and Curtis, sitting next to each other in the fifth row of a lecture hall, both of them not fans of the professor or the subject. My dad was a babe back then, which is one of those things you never truly want to realize about your father because that's gross. Gross but obvious, like the way you can't miss that it's pouring rain if you happen to be standing around outside without an umbrella. My mom was pretty too, but in an understated way, an amused intelligence in her face that has always made people wonder what she was thinking. She's paler and smaller than me—her ancestry half Chinese and half Scottish. Her keen eyes crinkled as she and my father quietly but mercilessly mocked their philosophy professor under their breath all semester, bonding over the act of eviscerating him.

As I'm remembering that, another memory swims up to meet it, an old white man with piercing green eyes locking a grin on me and saying his head was hurting with trying to figure out where I was from. I don't think he meant it in an unkind way but now that I remember the question I think it's one I heard a lot when I was a kid. People think they can ask you questions they wouldn't ask an older person, as long as they're smiling.

I don't know if I answered him but the short answer is Ontario, Canada, which is the same place we were when he asked me. And the answer he wanted to hear is really the answer to an entirely different question, which is that my mother is from Canada too and her father was born in Jamaica to Chinese Jamaican parents, and her mother emigrated from Scotland. I see my grandparents' faces in my mind, my memories doubling and quadrupling. My grandmother on my dad's side is African American from Chicago, where she was both a teacher and an amateur singer. She moved to Ontario when she married my French Canadian grandfather, and when anyone meets my grandmother one of the very first things they usually find out about her is that she's quite possibly the world's biggest Tina Turner fan, which is apparently the reason that even when I have amnesia I can still remember the Queen of Rock and Roll and the song "River Deep, Mountain High."

I sing the song in my head a little and I can hear the way my grandmother sings it, almost as good as Tina herself. I love that I can remember that. Bit by bit I'm reclaiming my identity.

I see the three of us—my grandmother, me and my big sister Celeste—shimmying and singing along to Tina in my grandmother's kitchen as cinnamon rolls baked in the oven. A big sister too, yes. One who was long and lean like my father. The prettier, smarter one who always knew the right way to speak and do things, even when we were both small.

My voice would pierce the air in uncontrolled bursts, my elbows and feet accidentally knocking delicate treasures off shelves. Fragile birthday gifts would be broken in no time, clothes torn and holes appearing in almost-new shoes. Even my printing was messy and flopped way over to the left side like it'd been subjected to a strong wind. And, ohhh, at night I would lie in bed with the gigantic teddy bear my dad had won at a company raffle, telling Winston (because that's what the tag attached to the back of one of his paws said his name was) about my day and then lending him my voice so Winston could reply.

Countless nights we'd stay up late talking to each other, and the following day I'd act like a brat from exhaustion, even clumsier and louder than usual, until my parents threatened that Winston would have to sleep in another room if I wouldn't go to sleep. Of course I didn't listen. And then I was distraught when my father came in to take the bear away from me, and I cried so long and hard that my mother had to bring him back.

This was such a long, long time ago, yet the images and feelings are as crystal clear in my head as if they had just happened, the sympathy in Mom's eyes as she handed Winston back to me and stroked my hair. "You save the talking to him for morning, okay, love?" she said.

Love. Like her own mother would say.

And my sister . . . before my life collapsed into this surreal dream-world existence I think I used to be a bit jealous of her, but when I remember Celeste now all I feel is grateful for having an older sister—an older sister and a twelve-year-old brother named Garrett, both of them smarter and quieter than I was. I bubble with happiness as I picture the two of them. Garrett as a baby laughing gleefully as he squirts my diaper-changing father in the cheek. Celeste, years ago, reading me an adventure book about an underground city, sounding, to my young ears, almost as grown-up as my mother although she only has three years on me.

My brain swirls with memories, the sights and sounds catapulting me back to the very beginning. I'd be dizzy if I was conscious. Dizzy and overjoyed at the same time.

So what if this *is* a hallucination? I get to watch my parents fall in love. I see them in philosophy class and want to laugh at how immature they seem. Not like people who are anyone's parents. Solely themselves, Curtis and Cynthia.

Though they clearly have a lot of fun talking to each other, their in-class chats don't develop beyond casual friendship. That doesn't surprise me because now I remember how their version of the story goes, and it doesn't really get started until years later, at a city hospital. St. Mike's in Toronto, Curtis visiting my grandmother after her hysterectomy and Cynthia visiting a friend who had just given birth to her first child.

Toronto is full of hospitals—what are the odds my parents would visit the exact same one on the exact same day at the exact same time? And even so, with a huge, majorly busy hospital, the likelihood that you'd run into someone must be slim. But there they were in the St. Mike's gift shop, Curtis in a light leather coat and dress pants that look like they were tailored to fit him and Cynthia in a turtleneck and shapely brown boots. They spotted each other while each of them was examining the bright assortment of floral arrangements in the gift shop flower cooler, and my father did a miniature double take. My mom grinned widely, recognizing him right away too, and exclaimed, "Hey—it's been a long time!"

"It can't have been that long," Curtis said. "You haven't changed at all."

They stood by the flowers talking for so long that it was obvious they should go for coffee and catch up, which they promptly did, my father extracting my mother's number so that they could meet up again soon.

"But not at the hospital," my mom warned. "Hospitals are bad luck."

"I think this hospital brought me good luck today," my dad told her, an earnest smile lighting up his face. "But I'll meet you anywhere you want to go." Kind of a cheesy line but I guess Curtis's babe status glossed over the cheese because they met for coffee twice within the next ten days. On the third date they graduated to dinner and my dad drove over to the apartment my mom was sharing with her sister to pick her up.

This is the part my parents never owned up to—how my mom asked my aunt Sandra to leave them alone so that when my father showed up it was just the two of them. On their first real date that wasn't just coffee Cynthia invited Curtis in and they started locking lips and mauling each other right on my mom's cream-colored couch. I don't know exactly how far things went because that's the point at which I decide to stop watching and close the door on them, so to speak, but my best guess would be that Curtis and Cynthia didn't get around to heading out for dinner that night.

There are certain things about your parents you should just never, ever see—even in dreams or hallucinations. And it's just as well that I've stopped there because Breckon Cody has gotten out of bed and, like he promised his mother, is reheating himself something to eat. I check the kitchen clock and notice that it's nineteen minutes to three and no one else seems to be around. His parents must still be out at lunch, and it looks like Lily went to the health-food store and wherever else on her own.

Breckon's food, which I think is some kind of linguini, spins in the microwave as he leans against the kitchen counter, waiting. He's put on jeans and a wool sweater, and seeing him up walking around and back in day wear gives me the impression that he's feeling a little better. The more I remember about myself and the more I learn about Breckon the weirder I feel about observing him, but I can't shake the feeling that it's what I'm supposed to be doing.

The microwave dings and Breckon takes his pasta out, sets it on the counter and stares at it. He hasn't eaten a thing all day and maybe he won't go through with it now either but he really should. Even if he doesn't feel like it, he really should eat something. I can't help saying it in my head, kind of like when you shout advice at a movie character, although you know they can't hear you.

Go on, I urge silently. *Just a little. It looks good.*

Breckon retrieves a fork from the cutlery drawer and lowers it reluctantly into his noodles. He doesn't bother pulling up a chair; he just leans against the counter and chews mechanically. *Good boy,* I tell him. He manages to finish off about half of the linguini that way, eating joylessly, but at least he's eating.

Then he stops. Drops the container and fork abruptly on the counter and stalks over to the sink with the same look that filled his eyes when he rushed up to the shower yesterday morning. I brace myself for his tears, not sure where to point my gaze.

"Okay," he says aloud. It's the tone of a person trying to convince himself of something and I watch as he switches the tap on, guides it over to hot and then hotter. Steam begins to rise from the water as it cascades from the tap. Breckon peers at it, transfixed. I still don't understand where this is going but I've decided I don't like it.

Without an awareness of my body, dread doesn't feel the way it should. I miss the beat of my heart. It should be racing—galloping—instead I only feel the weight of fears lying heavy on my soul. It's not just Breckon I'm afraid for, it's me. There are reasons for my prebirth memories that I'm not ready to face, the very same reasons that Breckon Cody's life is being revealed to me in such elaborate, painful detail.

My fifteen-year-old brain didn't invent him for its own amusement. What's happening in front of my eyes is much bigger than that.

He's nothing but a dream creation, I insist, battling back against the terrifying revelation rocketing up inside me. *Just a puzzle to solve. Busy work to keep my mind well-oiled.*

You know that's not true, the more knowing side of myself proclaims. *You understand what's going on here, Ashlyn. No one remembers moments from before her birth, not unless . . .*

And when Breckon pushes his left hand under the scalding-hot water and marshals his willpower to keep it there, I howl like the moment I was born.

six

breckon

Instinct kicks in. I should be able to take the pain—worse things happen to people every day—but I can't. I stumble back, losing my footing as my vision starts to close in on me. Then Moose sprints into the room, barking like a maniac. He runs in panicked figure eights as I fall smack down onto the kitchen floor.

"Shut up!" I shout from the tile. "Shut the hell up!"

Moose whimpers, the speed of his figure eights unchanged. My left hand hurts so much that my lungs have forgotten how to suck in oxygen. I fight for air, my head propped against the washing machine and my left ankle shaking like an epileptic's.

Moose barrels out of the kitchen, his high-pitched barking making my heart beat even faster. "Moose!" I roar after him. What the fuck does he think he's doing anyway? And when has rushing around in the shape of a figure eight ever helped anyone?

The pain crowds out everything else. I can hardly think. I breathe in and out but the air doesn't feel like it's catching in my lungs.

The second Moose is sure there's no one to alert he scrambles back into the kitchen with me, panting hard. A steam cloud's wafting up from the sink where the hot water's still flowing and I force myself onto my feet and whack the tap with my right hand, shutting it off.

I flop to the floor again, my head slipping back to its previous position against the washing machine.

"Sit," I command before Moose can start his barking routine again. If I have to watch him careen around in figure eights again I'll end up banging my head against the goddamn tiles.

Moose does what I say, but not in the way I want. He drops down so that his left side snuggles against my thigh. "I'm okay," I tell him. "Relax." As long as he stays quiet, I don't mind him next to me. I'm in too much pain to care.

My ankle's stopped quaking but my left hand feels like it's being eaten away by battery acid. I train my eyes on the furious red skin, and seeing the evidence makes it hurt worse. I've never done anything like this before; never even thought about it. I can't believe I really did it.

The physical pain's so intense that it's taken me over. I'm 17 percent Breckon and 83 percent burnt skin. It's a relief, ten times better than just being me. As much as my hand hurts, part of me wishes it would never stop. It blocks out almost everything else, or at least shoves it to the back of my mind.

God, it burns. I pinch the fingers of my right hand around my trembling left forearm to hold it still. Running my hand under cold water might help but I don't. I decide to let it sear for as long as I can handle. Moose keeps me company. I've thought it a hundred times before but here it is again—if Moose was in the house last Friday night to howl up a storm when it happened, Skylar might be alive now.

I sit there on the floor with the dog, just feeling myself breathe and burn, for what must be something like ten minutes before I think I hear a car pull into the drive. The noise plugs me back into reality and gets me standing. My mom keeps a bottle of Advil on the shelf over the fridge. I reach for it, pour two capsules onto the counter and then toss them into my mouth, chasing them down with a swig of fruit juice from the fridge.

Nobody comes through the front door. The car must've passed.

I set the leftover linguini on the floor for Moose. Way too much garlic and I'm not hungry in the first place. Moose meanders over to smell the pasta. I guess he agrees with me because he looks up at me without taking a bite.

"I know," I tell him. "It sucks."

I lob the linguini into the trash and go upstairs to do something with the burn. The red spans from my wrist down to my knuckles. I should've thought that over beforehand. If you're going to fuck yourself up and want to keep it a secret I guess you better know how to hide it.

I dig out the first-aid kit from under the sink and pull out a gauze pad and antibiotic ointment. Squeezing the ointment onto my skin stings so bad that my molars bite down on my tongue. I lay the gauze pad gently on top of my left hand and that hurts too. Then I wrap a bandage around the pad, finishing it off with a ton of tape to keep the bandage in place.

My shitty bandaging job probably makes the injury look

worse than it is. I'm already beginning to regret what I did to myself. Nothing's changed except now my singed skin won't quit screaming at me and I've turned into one of those screwed-up people who hurt themselves.

Just once, I tell myself. *It could've as easily been an accident. You won't do it again.* And then I realize, for the thousandth time, that my sister's dead and it doesn't matter what I do or don't do because nothing will ever change that.

I hear my cell ringing from my bedroom as I'm putting the first-aid kit back. I don't want to answer it but that's life, doing thing after thing that doesn't matter and won't change anything. My feet start moving in the direction of my room and next thing I know I have the phone in my hand and am answering it.

"Hey, it's Ty," the voice on the other end of the phone says. "Jules said she was over there this morning and that things were pretty quiet. I was wondering if you wanted to get out for a while, or something. . . ." Ty's voice trails off. He sounds kind of like the first time he came to visit me after my bike accident a year and a half ago, as though he's not sure what to say because he doesn't know whether I'm going to be okay.

But that accident was a walk in the park compared to this. A car rear-ended me when I was riding home from Ty's, throwing me off my bike. I never saw who did it—he or she didn't stick around to see if I was breathing. My dad still starts tremoring like a volcano about to blow when the hit-and-run comes up. "What kind of person can knock a kid off his bike and then speed off without calling for help!" he rants. "I can't believe this sicko's still driving around."

It was a fifty-something-year-old woman on a Vespa who found me and called for an ambulance. I'd fractured my C1 vertebra and spent thirteen weeks in a Miami J cervical collar. No more contact sports for me. The doctor even nixed things like snowboarding and mountain biking. The downside was my parents forced me to give up soccer without even getting a second opinion, the upside is that their fear I'd get hit on my bike again convinced them that buying me a car would be worth the dent in their bank account. They gave me a barely used secondhand Hyundai just two days after I got my full license a few months ago.

"You can't put a price on safety," I overheard my father say to my mom one night, but it turns out lightning doesn't strike twice in the same way. I never used to believe in fate but now my head keeps tripping back to the idea that maybe it was supposed to be me instead of Skylar. If it had to be one of us, it should've been me. Skylar was so young. She barely had a chance to get started.

I remember the last time my parents took her and her best friend Kevin to the museum in February. When they got back Skylar was clutching a kids' book on hieroglyphics and couldn't stop talking about mummies. She said when she was older she was going to become an archaeologist and visit the Great Pyramid of Giza in Egypt. Months before that she went around telling as many people as would listen that when she grew up she wanted to go into space and see the earth from so far away that it looked like a marble.

"Wouldn't you be homesick?" I asked her after hearing that

for something like the fourth or fifth time. "With the earth being this tiny little circle so far away?"

Skylar paused and thought about it. "No, because I'd be in radio and video contact with everyone and that would make it seem not so far away."

But what if you never got back? I remember thinking that if it was me I'd be scared something would go wrong and that I'd never set foot on the earth again. I'd *go* because if I had the chance I'd want to have a look at what was out there but I'd worry about it too. I didn't say anything about not getting back to my sister, though, and I guess it didn't occur to her. I wonder if that's because seven isn't old enough to worry about something like never seeing the planet again or whether Skylar herself was just more fearless than I am.

There are so many things . . . so many things she'll never do. And I'll never know what the older Skylar would've been like. How can that be possible?

Pain drags me under again. It stretches out in all directions like the destruction caused by an atom bomb.

"Breckon?" Ty prompts. "What about it?"

I press my thumb against my bandage until I wince at that different kind of hurt. But it works—it brings me back.

"I hurt my hand," I say with a groan. "Fucking scalded it. There must be something wrong with our kitchen tap." Not the tap but the water heater, probably. My grandmother said something about the water temperature to Lily when she was washing dishes yesterday and then they both probably forgot all about it.

I didn't.

Ty and I ruminate on my latest injury for a second. He and our friend Rory (also known as Big Red) still play for the school soccer team. For a long time after the accident I was pissed with my parents for making me stop, but when I got over it I realized that I didn't miss soccer as much as I thought I would. I wondered if maybe I'd never actually liked soccer as much as Ty and Rory. Then I started sketching, which is something I used to do when I was younger, and picked up a guitar. At first my parents paid for the lessons but then Jules and I got to know each other and for a while most of my time went to us—even if I wasn't with her I'd be *thinking* about her. She isn't my first girlfriend but she's the first one I've felt like that about.

When it happened it was like the opposite of discovering I didn't miss soccer. I thought the sex I'd had with my last girlfriend, Nadine, was pretty good at the time, but Jules and the way our bodies were always in sync blew my mind. And it wasn't just the sex that was amazing; it was every single thing you could think of. Jules and I could have a conversation about the simplest thing, like what we had for breakfast, and it felt engrossing or funny or made me happy in a way that it wouldn't if I was talking to someone else. That's how I got sidetracked from guitar—the feeling that Jules was the best thing to do with my time.

The feeling didn't change, but somewhere along the way we both gradually realized that our relationship didn't hinge on spending every second together. You miss too much if you just do one thing all the time, even if it happens to be your favorite thing. So I started playing guitar more often again, teaching myself this time.

Ty, Rory and I still hang out too. Big Red's father is a recovering borderline psycho soccer dad who used to freak out whenever Rory screwed up and didn't play exactly like the next Ronaldo or Messi. Ty's parents are the kind who are happy as long as he's happy, which is pretty close to what my parents were like for the last seven years, until this past Friday.

"You know Mr. Cirelli asked me about you when I saw him in the parking lot this morning," Ty says.

"What did you tell him?" I don't want people asking about me or trying to talk to me about Skylar. It's pointless. None of that is going to bring her back.

My door swings open as Ty starts to answer. If there was a knock, I didn't hear it, and my dad eyeballs me on the phone and points, in surprise, to my hand. "The kitchen tap's busted," I tell him. "The water temperature—boiling-hot water started gushing out of it."

"You okay?" Dad asks with a concerned look.

"Yeah, yeah, it messed up my hand a little but I'm all right." Ty's stopped talking and is waiting for me to finish with Dad. "You should get it checked out before somebody burns their arm off." I say it like I'm annoyed by the ordeal, the way I figure I would feel if I hadn't done this to myself. "Is it okay if I go out with Ty for a while?" I tack on.

I don't want my mom or Lily making a fuss about my hand. Besides, I think I need to get out. I'm almost as pathetic as Moose, wandering aimlessly from room to room.

"Sure," Dad tells me. "Are you positive you're okay?"

"I'm okay." I switch my attention to Ty. "I'm coming to pick you up, all right?"

I move into the hall, staying on the phone with him as protection against my mom and aunt wanting to examine my hand. I don't run into either of them on my way out—maybe Lily's not home yet—and when I hang up and climb into my car reality shifts sideways.

It's like stepping into a cocoon. The outside world disappears. I didn't need to burn my hand to overthrow reality, all I had to do was get into my car.

I know the feeling won't last, that there'll be another BAM right around the corner, but I'll take what I can get. The Advil's dulled the pain in my hand but not killed it. I loosen my left hand's grip on the steering wheel and curse myself for being an idiot. A few scattered raindrops tap my windshield as I drive. One of the neighbors from down the road is out cycling with his son who's a couple years older than Skylar. They're pedaling fast, probably trying to get home before the sky really opens up.

Ty's house is only about a mile away so I'm there in no time and text him from outside. If I go to the door his parents will only crowd around asking how I am in sad voices. While I'm waiting on him, I text Jules too and tell her I'm with Ty. Then I turn off the phone so no one will bother me.

A minute later Ty trudges out the front door with the same expression on his face that he had at Skylar's funeral. It makes me wish I'd driven past his place and kept right on going.

"If you don't quit looking at me like that I'm going home," I tell him as he gets in.

Ty's frown sinks deeper into his skin but he shakes his head to snap out of it. "Sorry, man. I suck at this. But hey, look, don't go home. We'll do something . . . I don't know . . ." He stares out the passenger window and racks his brain. "Maybe . . . drive to that place with the awesome peppercorn burgers we found on the way to the Red Wings game. Remember that?" His eyes shoot over to my bandaged hand. "Can you drive like that?"

"Yeah—with my right hand," I joke. "And a morphine drip for the pain."

I didn't think I was hungry but my stomach grumbles at the memory of that spicy-hot peppercorn burger, hands down the best hamburger I've ever tasted. Over a year ago Ty's dad scored free Red Wings tickets through a friend and we stopped in London halfway to Detroit and discovered this place called QT-Burgoire. The bizarre decorating scheme uses only primary colors—it looks like it was inspired by Play-Doh—but I don't think anyone cares what it looks like once they've tried the burgers.

"So are you up for this thing?" Ty rubs his hands enthusiastically together. "We've been talking about going back for so long that it's in danger of becoming one of *those things* people bring up all the time but never bother their asses trying to make actually happen." Ty's right—every couple months we mention it and then don't do anything about it.

"I hate *those things,*" I tell him and I know we're both faking that the burgers actually matter, but that pretense is better than the look Ty was wearing when he stepped outside his front door.

"Me too." Ty takes another look at my amateur bandaging job. "I can take the wheel if you want, man. It sounds like your hand is *crisp.*"

An hour ago I wanted my hand to hurt and now I just want it to stop. I'm happy to let Ty take the wheel. I change places with him and he drives us all the way from Strathedine to the QT-Burgoire in London two hours away. The city's a snow trap in winter, and being the end of April the place is freshly naked, the recent thaw exposing scabby patches of grass and pieces of garbage—cigarette butts and crushed pop cans that'll be in a Dumpster somewhere in a couple more weeks. I wolf down my QT-Burgoire burger and every last sweet potato fry that comes with it. The whole time we don't say a word about Skylar. Ty fills me in on the highlights of the Toronto FC versus Seattle Sounders game and any school drama I've missed, which isn't something we usually talk about much but I know he's trying to carry the conversation, fill up all the spare air.

Afterwards we walk around downtown until my hand starts to ache worse and we have to find an open Shoppers Drug Mart to buy more Advil. "Why didn't you ask the pharmacist about that Valium drip?" Ty kids once we're back on the street.

"Morphine drip," I correct. But a Valium drip would be better. What I need is a Valium drip permanently attached to my arm.

We both get quiet when we're back in the car and I realize that the closer we get to Strathedine the heavier I feel. If I could get away with never going home again, I think I'd do it. Just keep driving until, for all intents and purposes, I disappear. If I was someplace else—somewhere far away—I could almost pretend to myself that Skylar was back at home in Strathedine, waiting to grow up enough to be an astronaut.

She wasn't worried about not getting back and now she won't. It feels like a sign—a sign that I missed.

When we reach Ty's house maybe he can see the weight back on my shoulders because he says, "So what's up with tomorrow? Are you . . ." He waits for me to jump in.

"Don't know." I shrug. "Maybe if I wake up on time I'll hit class."

Ty nods patiently. "Right." He reaches between us and claps one hand on my shoulder for a second before throwing the door open. I watch him get out of the car, my signal to climb back behind the wheel and drive home.

It's started to rain again and that makes the night look darker than usual, but someone's left the porch light on for me. Between that and the light seeping through the family room curtains, the house looks normal, complete. I dig my thumb into my hand as I walk up the driveway, feeling my world collapse a little with every step. Inside my father, mother and Lily are huddled together in front of the TV the same way they've been off and on for days. My stomach flips over at the sight of them, and my mom, with her bottomless pupils, is the first to look in my direction and mumble hello. Moose bounds across the room and jumps up on me like I'm back from World War II.

"He missed you." Lily smiles. "Your dad said you got a nasty burn from the kitchen tap."

I wave my bandaged hand dismissively. "It'll be fine tomorrow." Before she can pursue it further I yawn and motion to the door. "I'm completely wiped. I'm going to head up—see you in the morning."

I take the stairs two at a time and swallow a sleeping pill from my diminishing stash. It's not the same as really getting away from here but it's what I have and I wonder, as I begin to drift off, what Skylar would think if she'd seen what I did in the kitchen earlier today.

I try to imagine her getting angry with me, yelling at me for even thinking of running away. It would make me feel better if I could picture her mad at me, but even in my head she's not. I see her wide blue eyes pleading with me the way they did the last time I saw her. "But the boxes are so heavy, Breckon. You know I won't be able to lift them."

"I said *later,* Skylar. You don't need to find it right this second. What did I tell you about bugging me when I'm in the middle of something?"

Skylar pouted in defeat; she knew better than to keep asking me. She was too many years younger than me for me to ever think of being downright mean to her but I know I didn't always act like she mattered. *Why didn't you wait for me, Skylar?* Why couldn't you just have fucking waited an hour?

This is one of two questions I'll ask myself for the rest of my life.

And the other is the reason that I need the pills.

seven

ashlyn

I miss the beat of my heart.

I miss the feel of my lungs expanding as they take in oxygen.

I miss being able to swing my hips to the pounding beat of the latest chart-topping dance hit.

I miss hearing someone say my name.

I miss the feel of sunlight, warm on my face. I can see it when I'm outside with Breckon Cody, or watch it stream golden through his window, but I can no longer *feel* it. Three out of five of my senses are dead along with the rest of me.

No one asks if you want to be born and no one tells you when you die either. If I'd wanted to learn the truth, I might have figured it out earlier. Now that I know, the knowledge burns me the same way Breckon's skin began to melt under scalding-hot water.

Everything I knew was wrenched away from me and I don't even remember how. Did it happen in an instant or did I die a long, painful death? Did I fight until the end, clinging to life until I couldn't hold on another moment or did I surrender quickly, seeking to escape the pain of some terrible disease?

Memories are slowly returning to me, but not of that. My early memories—and the ones of my parents that precede my existence—are the ones that seem to be filtering back first.

I was loved, I know my family must be inconsolable, the way Breckon's family is. Why can't I go to them? Why am I tethered here with Breckon instead and where is his sister? Why can't I see her? Where is everyone else? All the other people who have died? There must be billions.

An eternity of this is unthinkable. There has to be something I can do, a larger afterlife to move on to. I try again to break free, struggling in the only way open to me—thought. I meditate on the names of my family, over and over again. Dad. Mom. Celeste. Garrett. The strength of my desire should fly me to them. It would be only fair. *Only fair,* I repeat. *Only fair.*

Dad. Mom. Celeste. Garrett. *I'm here. I haven't left this earth yet.*

But my soul, because I guess that's what this remaining bit of me is, remains fixed firmly in Breckon Cody's orbit. I've watched him lie sleeping next to his girlfriend, watched him hurt himself, watched him try to hide the pain of his awful loss . . . but what about my loss?

And my family can't be far. I spied Strathedine signs when Breckon was out driving with his friend and that made me remember something else—I lived in Strathedine, Ontario, population circa 140,000, before I died. My family lives at number thirty-seven Heathdown Crescent, in the southwest part of town. I chant the address in my head too, but my efforts come to nothing.

Breckon rolls onto his side not seven feet beneath me. I feel sorry for him but I don't understand what I'm doing here. I'm not anyone's idea of a guardian angel. I wasn't even sixteen years old yet when I died, I have no idea how to fix people (I've only just remembered my own address) and, even if I did, I'm powerless. Only an observer.

Breckon opens his eyes and surveys his clock radio. It's ten after eight. His eyelids are heavy and pull themselves abruptly shut, but only for a few seconds. His smoky blue eyes fight their way open again. He coughs as he rises and I try to feel shameless about watching him tug off his T-shirt. If I'm supposed to be here, why shouldn't I see everything I possibly can?

Breckon's chest is slightly paler than his face. He's not super ripped like someone who haunts the gym but not skinny or flabby either, an almost perfect in-between—the kind of hairless lean body that no doubt many girls would want to run up to on the beach and throw their arms skittishly around. It would look better still with a tan but . . .

I glance away as he drops the green boxers he slept in last night. So much for feeling shameless. I can't take advantage of the view this way when I know what Breckon's been going through. *Do you see that?* I ask the universe. *Do you see how I shouldn't be here?*

And then again, would peeking at his penis be more personal than watching him burn himself on purpose? *I shouldn't be here,* I repeat. *I don't know what you want me to do.*

No one answers me.

It's not fair, I say. *Not fair. NOT FAIR.*

My eyes snap back to Breckon, who has put on a fresh pair

of boxer shorts. He digs into his closet and continues getting dressed. Then we—me trailing him by a couple of feet—go down to the kitchen. I cringe as he eyes the tap.

NO! I lecture. YOU ARE NOT DOING THAT AGAIN.

Breckon shakes his head like he's disagreeing with me. He pours himself a glass of orange juice and has just begun putting together a breakfast for himself when his mother wanders into the room in loungewear and fuzzy beige slippers.

Her breath catches at the flash of red she's spotted on the knuckles of his left hand. The bandage shifted a little during the night and the part of the wound she can see is far from the worst of it, but it would shock me too if I were seeing it for the first time.

"Let me see that," she insists, walking swiftly towards him.

"Mom." Breckon hides his hand behind his back. "It's fine. It hurt worse yesterday—it just needs a chance to heal."

"Show it to me," she demands.

Breckon holds out his hand and, with that moody teenager look from yesterday morning, starts unspooling the bandage for his mother.

She stares, horrified, at his lobster claw. *"Breckon,"* she murmurs, her head tilted to one side and her eyes lit up with alarm. "I'm calling Dr. Siddiqui and taking you in to get that looked at."

Breckon rolls his eyes a little but he really can't protest much. There's no denying that his hand looks like it was lowered into a deep-fat fryer.

His mother's already grabbing the cordless and punching in a quick succession of digits. Two minutes later Breckon has a confirmed appointment with his doctor. "They're squeezing you in," she tells him. "We need to get there as soon as possible."

"We?" Breckon's head snaps forward. "Don't you mean me?"

I don't know what Breckon's mother looked like before she lost Skylar but what I've seen in her face during the past few days are layers of grief that flatten her every expression. The final layer—the one she wears closest to the surface—is the one that reminds her she still has to care about something. While the bottom layers are tangled and heavy, rooted to her bones, the top one lies lightly on her form, like a loose strip of gauze apt to blow away in the face of even moderate opposition.

I'm not sure whether this is something I could've seen with my regular old eyes if I'd looked closely enough or whether it's a new talent, like the ability to pick up on the sound of sorrow in Breckon's breath. All I know is that in Mrs. Cody's eyes, I spy a moment where she could give up and back down, simply cease caring and let Breckon have his way—and somehow I sense that Breckon catches sight of the moment too. His entire being pauses, waiting for the outcome of that moment. For several seconds there is only blinking and breathing between them.

Then Mrs. Cody decides to hold fast to that delicate outer layer. Her previously blank expression morphs into irritation. "We," she repeats. "That looks pretty serious, Breckon. I want to hear what Dr. Siddiqui has to say."

"Suit yourself." Breckon shrugs, the challenge gone from his voice. "But I was thinking of going back to school this morning."

"I didn't know that." Mrs. Cody leans back against the kitchen counter. "Are you sure you want to go in today?"

Breckon shrugs again, and as much as I understand that he doesn't want to talk I feel frustrated on his mother's behalf. How can she help him if she doesn't know how he feels? How can anyone? "I don't know . . . ," Breckon says, letting his words hang. "I thought it might be good to try to get back to things."

Mrs. Cody stares down at Breckon's bandaged hand, nodding slowly. "I can drop you off at school after you see the doctor. The plumber's not coming until this afternoon."

For the second time since my dramatic arrival here I'm able to leave the confines of the Cody property. I sit in the backseat of Mrs. Cody's car, an invisible third passenger, and stare out the window for however long the laws governing my current existence allow. Inevitably my eyes drift continually back to Breckon, whether I want them to or not, but in between times I'm able to survey Strathedine as we travel along Highway 11 and turn onto Richmond Road. The journey allows me to pinpoint precisely where the Codys live, which is an area those of us in the Cherrywood part of town usually refer to as New Strathedine.

The Cherrywood subdivision my own family lives in has more tall trees, big lawns with mature gardens and historical homes. My house is only forty years old but starting three blocks away, plaques from the local historical society become plentiful—hanging on several of the doorways, detailing the date the house was built and the occupation of the owner: shipbuilder, saddler, apothecary, millwright, mariner, bricklayer. Twenty-five years before my parents moved there, Cherrywood was its own separate town, but even the newer residents tend to differentiate between Cherrywood (an old port town) and New Strathedine.

Why can I remember so many unimportant details about this place while I still don't know everything about myself? Yet the pointless facts just keep on coming.

The mall, Strathedine Town Center, is literally situated in the middle of town and halfway between our two addresses. The names of the stores that populate it run through my mind as if on a ticker tape: American Eagle Outfitters. The Body Shop. Guess. H&M. Lucky Brand Jeans. Mexx. Nine West. Old Navy. Pink. Sephora. Sony Style. Etc., etc. For the most part they're the same chain stores you'd see anywhere. Not information that could possibly do me any good, but as we approach the Strathedine mall, a more productive idea somersaults into my mind. I find myself trying to sway Mrs. Cody with the power of thought, at first subtly. When subtle doesn't work, I swoop in front of her to stare her in the face from above the steering wheel and *think* my address with such passion that no one would be able to resist the desire to steer in the direction of the Baptiste house.

Thirty-seven Heathdown Crescent, Cherrywood.

What I wouldn't give to see my parents in the flesh. To look them in the eyes even though they wouldn't be able to look back into mine.

Thirty-seven Heathdown Crescent, Cherrywood.

Dad. Mom. Celeste. Garrett. I miss you all so much.

Thirty-seven Heathdown Crescent, Cherrywood, Strathedine.

I think with such keen focus, such dizzying energy, that I could collapse a brain cell or two if I still had any. *Listen to me, Mrs. Cody. Just for a minute, hear me and take us to Heathdown . . .*

But she doesn't listen, doesn't hear. As usual, my mental efforts yield no results. Mrs. Cody makes a left turn away from the mall and pulls into a squat medical building's parking lot. Soon we're squeezing into a tiny elevator that takes us to the third floor. There's a fourth passenger with us, a bald woman about the same age as Mrs. Cody. I see Breckon notice her but pretend that he hasn't. I wonder if he's thinking the same thing I am: she's sick. Will she survive whatever's the matter with her and live to an old age or is she doomed? Was I doomed? Was Skylar?

Do any of us have a choice or are we just playing out destiny?

I stream along behind Breckon and his mother as they exit the elevator and tread along a nondescript hallway and into a medical waiting room. Breckon's mother gives his name to the secretary, who shows them both promptly into the doctor's office and closes the door behind them.

Not five minutes later I'm watching Dr. Siddiqui examine Breckon's hand. The doctor's professional expression makes it impossible to tell what he's thinking, but he says, "It looks sore."

"It is," Breckon admits, glancing from his damaged hand to the doctor.

"He can take some acetaminophen for the pain," the doctor advises, looking from Breckon to his mother. "But there's no infection." He smooths a burn cream carefully onto Breckon's lobster hand, lays a dressing on top of that and rolls a bandage around it with infinitely more expertise than Breckon did himself. In the end only the tips of Breckon's fingers are showing. "The dressing will need to be changed every day, and if it's not beginning to look any better in a week or so—or if there are any signs of oozing or a strange odor—he should come back to the office."

"Thank you," Mrs. Cody says. "I feel better knowing you've looked at it."

Dr. Siddiqui nods. "Always best to get things looked at. I don't have any samples at the moment but . . ." He grabs a pen and his prescription pad. "I'm going to write out the cream he should use. The pain should begin to subside in a couple of days." He tears out the page from his prescription pad and hands it to Breckon along with a sheet of instructions that explain how to change his dressing. "I'm so sorry about Skylar," the doctor adds quietly.

Breckon's shoulders sag as he takes the papers. I notice his cracked bottom lip again as his lips part. "Thank you," his mother repeats before he can get the words out.

"She was a wonderful girl," the doctor says.

Back in the waiting room Breckon hands over the instructions and prescription for his mother to study. She unfolds the instructions and scans through to the bottom of the page. "We can pick the cream up in the pharmacy downstairs," she says as she gives him the sheet back.

"Good idea," Breckon says without missing a beat. He folds the page into his back pocket and then checks his watch. "I think I can make second period if we're quick."

Mrs. Cody hesitates, her face changing as she says, "You probably can."

With the cream and a fresh supply of bandages in our possession the three of us climb back into the car. I grow anxious when I see Breckon's high school loom in the distance and I don't know why. He *wants* to go back to school, so who am I to be anxious for him?

"Thanks, Mom," Breckon says when his mother pulls up to the curb in front of the school. "I'll catch a ride back with Ty or Jules."

Mrs. Cody reaches out to tousle his hair in what I imagine is much the same way she would've done when he was just a young boy. "Okay, hon."

Breckon's eyes break away first. He slips out of the car and I'm swept onto the sidewalk along with him. Breckon doesn't take any notice of the letters over the school's front doors but I do. They read: Stephen Lewis Secondary School. Because we live in different parts of town there's almost no chance we'd attend the same high school, but it does look vaguely familiar—like someplace I would've cruised by in a previous life.

Memories of my own high school, like so many other bits of my life, still elude me but I'm about to become very familiar with Breckon's. I drift along behind his shoulder as he stalks through the hall and then into the main office. The secretary's eyes give everything away—she knows exactly who he is and what happened to Skylar. Sympathy for Breckon oozes from her pores even before he explains about his hand and the doctor's appointment. "It's day three on the schedule today," she says kindly. "If you're not sure what class you have I can pull it up for you."

Breckon's attempt at a smile doesn't quite reach his lips. "That's okay—I know where I'm going."

He nips into the nearest stairwell, his late pass in his hand and a red binder under his arm, and jogs upstairs like he doesn't want to be any later than he already is. At least twenty-five sets of eyes whip towards Breckon as he edges into a classroom and folds his body behind an empty desk near the window. The teacher's words slow as he registers Breckon's presence and then immediately speed up again. Several, but not all, of the students aim their attention back towards their teacher while he continues to drone on about fiscal policy. An Asian girl in the back row fiddles discreetly with her cell phone, and a white boy, with long blond hair that makes him look like he should be surfing the crest of a California wave rather than sitting in a Strathedine classroom, scrawls graffiti lettering in the margins of his textbook. Three or four students are still glancing covertly at Breckon but only one doesn't bother to hide the fact because Jules, as his girlfriend, is allowed to stare. Thick black eyeliner and a spike-tip nose stud make her look more severe than she did the last time I saw her, but she smiles at him and mouths the word "hey" or maybe "hi." I can't tell which.

Breckon mouths the same back and then fixes his eyes on his teacher. From the sound of things this is either a business or economics class and I wish I could sleep through it or fast-forward to next period but I don't want to hang out in the darkness by myself so I stick with the class and listen to the teacher say, "All right, now back into your groups." People begin scraping their chairs across the floor, pulling themselves into groups for some project the teacher probably mentioned while my attention was wandering. "Breckon," the teacher adds, "why don't you just sit in with Jules, Dwayne, Catherine and Renuka."

On their feet, Jules lounges against Breckon's right side for a brief moment before they begin making their way over to the other side of the room to join the rest of their group. "Is it broken?" she whispers, looking down at his left hand. "What happened?"

For the first of many times that day I listen to Breckon lie about his kitchen tap. He sounds so convincing each time that I'm sure nobody doubts him. His friends are happy to see him back at school, but most react to his reappearance with varying degrees of awkwardness. A guy everyone calls Big Red pulls Breckon from one of those macho handshakes into a hug that lasts six seconds too long. Another boy named Cameron tries to act like nothing's happened but his voice is unnaturally high-pitched and he literally won't shut up until Ty tells him to chill. Having gotten this over with yesterday night, Ty does the best job of getting things right.

I see the way he watches Breckon over lunch, simultaneously trying to include him in conversations and give him space. It's a tough balancing act but Ty does fairly well. I can understand why he's Breckon's best friend.

Generally the girls' reactions seem more irritating than the boys' but maybe it just appears that way to me now that I'm sitting with a bunch of guys, forced to see things from their point of view. When the girls glance over at Breckon it's with dewy eyes, like they want to throw their arms around him and cry with him until he feels better. Especially a girl named Nadine who holds tight to his sleeve as she talks to him.

If it was me that might seem easier—dissolving into tears with the girls, embracing a state of collapse rather than pretending I feel better than I do, but maybe Breckon doesn't want to cry for that long. Maybe a person could cry for years if they let themselves and would that really help? In some ways, from my new viewpoint, the crying feels like a trap, like maybe you better not start in case you're never able to stop. I've seen the way Breckon can cry if he lets himself and I'd rather see him like this, even if he still feels that very same broken way inside.

Maybe that means I'm not strong enough. *Do you hear that?* I ask the universe. *I'm not strong enough for this. He needs better than me.*

The universe, like every single atom within it, ignores me. I'm no better than dust really. Even an ant serves more of a function than I do. But before I can truly immerse myself in self-pity, that same teacher from Breckon's economics class this morning stops him in the hall after lunch.

"Mr. Cirelli?" Breckon says, the knuckles of his good hand knocking against his binder.

"I won't slow you down too much," the teacher—Mr. Cirelli—tells him. "I wanted to catch you on your way out of class earlier but I missed the opportunity." Mr. Cirelli looks past Breckon at the hallway crawling with jostling students. "If there's any extra help you need . . ." He folds his arms in front of his white button-down shirt and stares Breckon directly in the eye. "If there's anything I can do at all . . ." Mr. Cirelli straightens his spine, appearing to grow in direct relation to his offer. "Well, that's exactly what we're here for."

Breckon doesn't react to the statement, possibly because he's been hearing variations of it all day. His two front teeth dig into his bottom lip and remain there. Once it's clear Mr. Cirelli has said all he intended to, Breckon clears his throat. "Thanks, Mr. Cirelli." He cocks his head towards the crowd. "I better get going. I forgot my math book in my locker."

Breckon makes his escape down the hallway but doesn't detour to his locker. His math textbook's hiding directly under the binder squeezed against his side but it doesn't occur to Mr. Cirelli that Breckon would lie just to get away from him. He doesn't suspect, just like no one suspects about Breckon's seared hand, and his secrets—no matter what I hear or see—are safe with me.

eight

breckon

I try to do math homework but my brain won't work the way it used to. I can't do my econ, English or humanities homework either but I thought math might be different—there's no bullshit in math; it is what it is. Normally I find the classes with a high bullshit rate easier because half the work is repeating what you've already read or heard and the other half is confidence and style. I don't have the energy for bullshit right now but I don't have the concentration for math either. That leaves me exactly nowhere, but what does it matter? I don't care about any of those things anyway. I'm only trying to fill up hours with something other than remembering Skylar's gone.

It's not like she was everything before but she's everything now. I don't need another two years like this to know that what people say about time healing all wounds is a lie. Skylar's gone. Nothing can ever be as important as that.

Skylar's even the reason my parents are together. They broke up almost eight years ago—my dad moved into a motel near the mall and both of them told me it was for the best, that we'd all be happier. Before my father left they used to yell at each other so loudly that you'd think they'd bring the walls crashing down on us. They hadn't always been like that—something must've happened between them, but in all the shouting I overheard I never found out what it was. The night my dad went to the motel they woke me up in the middle of the night with their screaming and I lay facedown under the covers with my hands clamped over my ears until he stormed out. It was a rough time but I was so young then that if you'd asked me, I would've said I preferred the idea of them together, but yelling, rather than apart.

Skylar changed them for good. She was their second-chance baby. They'd wanted another kid for so long that when they found out my mom was pregnant my dad moved back in and the shouting stopped overnight—at least, that's how it seems looking back. I know they went to therapy together and that my dad was back at the house with us months before Skylar was born. Since then I've barely heard my parents argue, and when they do they don't let loose like they used to, they just argue the way anyone does.

Skylar never knew them other than the way they are now. Their separation isn't a secret—all of our extended family knows—but since Skylar never saw our parents the old way I bet it didn't seem real to her. They were just her parents, together, in love. You wouldn't think two people could change so much, and I know it wasn't really just having Skylar that did it, but I guess it was Skylar that made them realize there was something about them worth saving.

When my mom talks to people about when I was a baby

she likes to say that I hardly ever cried, even when people I didn't really know would hold me. Skylar didn't cry much either, not with us, but she'd get weirded out by other people.

I remember secretly thinking that it was pretty cool that Skylar would let me hold her without crying like she did when she was in other people's arms. She couldn't say my name for a long time and for some reason none of us could figure out she'd call me Todi instead. Even when she was, like, two and a half, we were Mom, Dad and Todi. Sometime last year I asked her if she remembered that and she shook her head and said, "Are you making it up?"

"I'm serious," I told her. "That was your weird little name for me for a long time."

"Todi?" Skylar asked, wrinkling her nose. "How come?"

"I don't know—that's what I'm asking you."

Skylar didn't know—she couldn't remember—but she thought it was so funny that she called me Todi for about a week afterwards. The first couple of times she couldn't say it without giggling but by the end of the week she was just pronouncing it in a singsong voice and then finally, she went back to Breckon.

I really shouldn't have started thinking about all of that. I need something more than sleeping pills, something that would make me numb.

Todi.

Shit.

My hand doesn't hurt much at the moment. Not enough. I've been swallowing over-the-counter pain pills to make it stop and then wishing I hadn't. I can't do something crazy like my hand again but I know I have to do *something.* Something that a doctor wouldn't need to look at. Something I can hide.

The first thing my brain lands on is the grooming kit in the bottom drawer of my bedside table. At Christmas my parents mostly buy us what we want but my mom usually includes something useful that you'd never think of asking for too. This past Christmas she gave me a deluxe grooming kit in a leather case. That kit had everything in it—a razor, nail clippers, toothbrush, nail file, comb, tweezers, scissors, a shoehorn/lint brush and a corkscrew/pocketknife combo. The razor's actually in the bathroom, on the top shelf of the cabinet, but all the other things are still inside the case. My hand reaches for the bedside table, yanks open the bottom drawer and cradles the kit.

I take a jagged breath as I slide the zipper open and study the contents. What's sharper—the knife or the scissors? I've never used either of them so I know they're equally clean. I take out the scissors and press their point against my thumb. They're pretty flimsy scissors but I just want to make a surface cut so they should be able to do the job. I pull up my shirt, separate the blades of the scissors and hold one of the points against my skin—on my left side, a couple of inches above the waist. I drag the scissors quickly against my skin, not hard enough to do anything other than leave a white line. More pressure. I need to do it like I mean it. Slower, harder. Like I'm digging for blood.

Fuck. That does hurt. The cut doesn't start to bleed until a few seconds after the fact and then it stings like a nick you make with a razor, only those nicks aren't usually two inches long. Will it leave a scar? I don't think it's deep enough for that. I let my shirt fall to cover the mess and then head for the bathroom where I press a wad of toilet paper against my side until it quits bleeding.

We have plenty of bandages since the accident with my hand and I stick a fresh dressing on my side and tape it in place the same way a doctor would. It'll be fine, I'm sure. It'll heal no problem. I don't even know why I bothered.

It's a sick thing to do.

The more I think about it the stupider it seems. It's bad enough to do a stupid thing once but this second time is pathetic. Downstairs I can hear the dishwasher running and the TV up loud but I don't want to be around my parents or Lily, especially after the fucked-up thing I just did.

I don't know *what* to do. I can't do my homework. Can't be around my family. Can't stop thinking all the wrong things.

I wish there was a way to just shut down and not feel or think anything. Just stop.

And then I hear my cell ringing across the hall in my bedroom and I know it's Jules. I don't really believe in ESP but sometimes I can tell it's her. I wouldn't pick up for anyone else right now and I don't want to talk but if there was a way to just listen to the sound of her voice . . .

I go back to my room and snap up the phone before it can go to message. It's Jules, all right, and my heart thumps faster as I think about telling her what I just did.

"Hi," I say quietly.

"Hi," Jules says. "Have you seen the weather out there? It's crazy. I just saw a lightning bolt strike the ground in the yard across the street."

I listen for the rain and she's right, it's pouring outside. Thunder rumbles outside my window like the storm's being choreographed for my benefit. "I had my headphones on," I lie. "I didn't even notice."

"Oh!" Jules says, like this is an interesting piece of information. "What are you listening to?"

Before last Friday happened I was in a four-month-old phase where I wouldn't listen to anything recorded after 1979. A while back I figured out that a lot of the stuff I like sounds derivative of older rock, pop and soul anyway and decided to spend some time going straight back to the source.

"Blue Oyster Cult," I lie again. "And then some Smokey Robinson."

"Cool," Jules says.

"Yeah . . . hey . . ." I sit on the bed, flexing the fingers that peek out of my bandage. "Do you think I could get a couple more of your dad's pills tomorrow?" This isn't something I really want to ask Jules but I can't imagine her telling me no. I should've checked my parents' medicine cabinet while they were out the other day and stolen some of whatever they have. Then I wouldn't have to bring this up. But they're home so often lately that I don't know when I'll get another chance.

Jules pauses before replying, "Not too many because I don't want him to notice but, yeah, I guess I can get you a few more."

I don't say anything about the scissors, I listen to Jules tell me about a book her friend Renee lent her. Then she starts reminiscing about when we first got to know each other on the

New York trip. I know all the details and I love Jules and how she can make the smallest thing seem amazing. But anything I feel about her now is through layers of fog. The feelings can't really reach me.

I try to go through the motions at school the next day. None of the teachers care whether I've done my homework or not or call on me to answer questions. They act like I'm made of very thin glass and shouldn't be disturbed.

After classes I head over to Jules's house with her and she gives me another handful of pills. At the end of the weekend Lily goes home to Sunita and although Lily's not a loud person, the house is so much quieter and emptier without her. Before she leaves she says that my grandparents are going to be around a lot and that she's going to call and email and I should come up to see her and Sunita in Ottawa some weekend.

I tell her sure, that I'll do that, and I try to keep doing the school thing, because I know I should keep busy, but by Tuesday—my fourth day back—I'm skipping classes. Tuesday it's just social science, Wednesday's the whole day except homeroom and Thursday it's the afternoon. Mostly I just drive randomly in any direction, pulling on and off the highway until I need to eat. One day I end up at Niagara-on-the-Lake, which is so picturesque that it looks more like a theme park they'd sweep clean and lock the gates on at night than a place anyone could actually live. Another time I try to watch an "us vs. menacing aliens" movie at the multiplex but it's not any easier than doing homework.

Anything other than walking, breathing or driving is

beyond my capability, and while a small piece of me wants to pile on the distractions until I can't see out from under them, the larger part knows that no matter what I'm doing there'll always be too much time without her. It's an endurance test I can't win.

I still think about going away someplace my parents would never find me but I know I won't, that I'll keep doing these empty things over and over again until the end. Trying to hide from something that doesn't have to catch up to me because it's never left behind. I may as well be in the worst place imaginable—the one she's missing from the most—because I can't make her absence hurt any less. It's like there's no other choice but to run towards the pain.

So I do it. I leave the theater in the middle of a battle scene, drive home and tear up to her room, almost like there's been some kind of mistake and she'll be there, just like she would've been that Friday nearly two weeks ago, hours before we got to the part of the night when she walked into my bedroom and asked me to help her scour through dusty boxes in the basement to find what she was looking for.

"Hey, Skylar," I'd say, before she even had the chance to get the question out. "Let's go look through those boxes downstairs."

And I'd never take my eyes off her. I'd go first and make sure she was careful. We'd rip into the cardboard and leave a mess that would make my mom purse her lips when she saw it later but Skylar would have what she needed. She'd be safe. We'd all be happy. Life would continue the way it was meant to only I wouldn't take it for granted this time; I'd know how lucky I was.

I'd make any kind of deal to have a second shot at that.

I'd take six months left to live or a lifetime without legs to have that conversation with my sister again and do it right. I'd take anything.

And that is the way I rewrite history, sitting in Skylar's room like a stone that will never stop falling, never stop sinking.

nine

ashlyn

If I didn't know who Skylar was, her bedroom might make me guess she was a boy. She has the kind of bed you need to climb a ladder up to and a computer desk underneath it, maximizing space. The walls are painted aqua and decorated with two posters—one of the solar system and the other a photo of a polar bear lying down with its front paws folded up underneath itself. The bear's staring straight at the camera as if observing the photographer, taking its own mental photograph. Lower to the ground, the majority of wall space has been dedicated to shelving and storage bins that are filled with action figures, racing cars, dinosaurs and other unidentifiable weird creatures. The pink beanbag chair under the window looks like it was intended for another room. I wonder if it was a gift from someone who didn't know Skylar very well because there's nothing else in the slightest pink about that room. There are some crafty and scientific-looking kits amongst Skylar's things but not one thing that wouldn't fit on either the boy or unisex shelves of a toy store.

As I take stock of Skylar's room, I realize that while my younger self wasn't quite as much of a tomboy as it appears that she was, I wasn't a frilly girl either. While I'm still waiting for the majority of my own memories to fall into place, much of my early childhood has gradually returned to me. A bit more seeps back every day, in a roughly chronological order. I now know that at Skylar's age I liked dinosaurs as well as dolls and that I had an illuminated ant habitat that glowed in the dark. My sister, Celeste, who only likes pretty insects such as butterflies and ladybugs, deemed it "kind of gross" but I bet Skylar would've liked it. I bet she would've wanted me to take it into the bathroom, away from any natural light, close the door and flick the light switch off so we could watch the ants' industrious little tunnels glow green against a black backdrop.

Sometimes I wonder, if I'm here watching Skylar's family, does that mean she's over in Cherrywood, watching mine? Considering that what's left of me revolves around the space Skylar left behind, it doesn't seem right to me that we can't meet. Given our deceased states you'd think that, at least, should be possible.

I conjure the image of Skylar's face from various photos I've seen around the Cody house and whisper her name in my mind, trying to coax her towards me. I've taken to talking to Breckon recently too, or rather, *thinking* to Breckon. He worries me most when he's alone because then I'm not sure what he'll do. At times his eyes fill with desolation, his neck and shoulders become rigid and the sound of his breathing crackles against the air. It seems to me that the atmosphere around us could turn to ice, break into shards and drown him.

Breckon has that very look in his eyes now, in Skylar's room. He's been sitting motionless in the middle of the beige carpet for the last twenty-seven minutes, color draining from his skin until it's a pasty shade of white that makes him look more like a ghost than I do. Moose, who was a step behind Breckon as he flew up the stairs, attempted to climb into his lap but was instantly dislodged. Instead he sits two feet away, as near as Breckon will tolerate.

The dog is company whether Breckon wants it or not. I'm not even a voice, not even a wisp of a thing, but I stay close to him and say, as I've said before lately, "She wouldn't want this." I *think* the message in as reassuring a tone as I can muster and for that, my mother is my example.

When I was small she'd sense, when I was too quiet, that something was wrong and would lay her hand on the top of my head and say, "Why so glum, chum?" I wasn't sad very often back then but there were instances when I measured myself against my sister and knew I fell short. At a friend's sixth birthday party I leaned back in my chair and one of the slats broke as the chair crashed to the floor with me in it. While visiting my grandmother, sometime during that same year, I picked the dead leaves off one of her plants, and with the unhealthiest plucked started in on those next in line until soon the plant was almost bald, only five green leaves clutching sadly to its stem.

At times like those I was harder on myself than my grandmother or my friends' parents were; I knew Celeste would never make such mistakes. But my mom's warm voice, the tickle within it that reached out to cheer me up, would lift my spirits again.

So this is what I do with Breckon. I think of what my mother would tell him if he was me. Often I tell him that Skylar's okay and that he doesn't need to worry about her. I don't know that for certain but considering my own circumstances I'm fairly confident that Skylar's personality still exists—swimming amongst the stars maybe or hovering around someone else's bedroom the way I am now.

I know Breckon doesn't hear me or feel my presence but I can't stop trying. Moose and I have that in common.

Breckon's still in Skylar's room, in almost a trance state, when his father arrives home. He doesn't hear Mr. Cody's approach and it's not until his dad's standing in the open doorway that he takes any notice.

Breckon's father looks much older than he does in the family portrait hanging in the kitchen. He's folded his shirtsleeves up and his tie has been loosened and hangs askew. "Here you are," he says with a twinge in his voice.

At first Breckon remains still. Then he takes another moment to collect himself, stretching out his hand to run it over Moose's fur. "Did school call you?"

"They say you've been missing classes all week," Mr. Cody confirms.

"Not all classes." Breckon's eyes are on Moose rather than his father.

Mr. Cody jangles his keys in his pocket. His eyes skim Skylar's room and hold on the WALL-E robot in the farthest corner.

"We should just . . . leave it," Breckon murmurs, motioning to the room. "Leave everything how it is right now."

Mr. Cody steps inside Skylar's bedroom and picks up the

nearest dinosaur, a poseable protoceratops. He pries open its jaws and then snaps them shut again. "No one's going to change anything," he says. "Not anytime soon."

My mind begins to drift as Breckon and his father speak, my personal history beckoning me. Until this second I didn't remember Farlain Lake, yet I went there with my cousins several years in a row. My dad's friend lent us his cottage for two to three weeks every summer while he wasn't using it. Aunt Sandra, who had fallen in love with my future uncle Ian in Edinburgh while discovering her Scottish roots, would fly back from Scotland with her family to go to Farlain Lake with us.

My cousin Ellie was half a year older than my sister, and from our very first visit there they were inseparable. Ellie and Celeste tried to negotiate a bedroom swap that would result in them sharing a room while I bunked with Ellie's brother, Callum, who, though only fifteen months older than me, seemed to find me babyish.

At least, this is what I had put his reluctance to play with me down to when I was six. As a result, when my parents consulted me about the proposed swap, I told them I didn't want to share a room with a boy. I was so sorry for that the following year that it stuns me to think that I could ever have forgotten about those summers. The next year, when I was seven—while Ellie and Celeste would do fashion shows on the sand, play badminton together and hog the DVD player watching movies starring teenage guys they pretended to drool over more than I imagined they really did—I'd beg my dad or Uncle Ian to take me out in the canoe or plead with Mom or Aunt Sandra to watch me swim. Sometimes all us kids (except my brother,

Garrett, who was too young) would play a four-person version of baseball or, on a rainy day, have a game of hide-and-seek in the cottage, but I would've spent the better part of that second holiday struggling to keep myself busy or hanging out with the adults, if not for the change in Callum.

On the fifth day of that first week I was making a humungous sand pizza on the beach at the foot of the cottage's property. When my dad noticed me struggling to form a perfect circle he'd suggested using the top of a trash can as a mold, which I did, and I was in the process of adding bits of plastic foods (sliced mushrooms, tomatoes and olives) from one of Garrett's play sets when Callum walked down to the sand to see what I was doing.

"I wish we could have real pizza," he declared, looking down at my sand one. "At home we order pizza from Domino's all the time." The way he said that doesn't look anything like you'd read it on a page—his sentences, like Ellie's and my uncle Ian's, were filled with hills and valleys. Their words danced.

That year my mom and aunt happened to be on a joint health-food kick and were determined that we all avoid junk food for the duration of the trip, so I knew how my cousin felt. Back then I believed most green vegetables were inedible and was tired of avoiding all the lettuce, bok choy and peas appearing on my plate at the end of the day. "I wish we could have chocolate," I told him. "Or Cheetos."

"What are Cheetos?" my three-quarters Scottish cousin Callum wanted to know, his green eyes focusing on mine.

"They're sort of like chips, but cheesy," I explained. "When you eat them all the orange stuff comes off on your hands but they're really, really yummy."

"I wish we could have those too then," Callum said.

It's funny, I remember how the sand smelled while we were hanging out at the beach at that moment—and how I had the taste of Cheetos in my mouth from thinking about them. And I remember wondering if Callum would walk away soon, like he usually did, and whether he would stay longer if I was boy, especially a boy older than seven.

"Do you want to play war?" Callum asked me. I temporarily forgot what war was. "I brought cards with me," he added.

"Okay," I told him. I could feel bits of sand between my teeth as I smiled. I always managed to get sand everywhere.

"I'll get them!" he said, smiling back at me. He raced towards the cottage and brought the cards down to the beach with him. We sat on the sand beside my pizza and played war and then quadruple war for hours. The tide came in, the sun hung low on the horizon and Celeste was dispatched with the message that if we wanted to stay outside we'd need to come into the cottage for a minute so our mothers could douse us in mosquito repellent.

"Why don't you bring us the spray?" I asked my sister in a pleading voice.

"Because Mom says you need to come in," she repeated. "You know you *always* have to put on long sleeves and pants if you want to stay out when it's getting dark."

I stared at my father and Uncle Ian in the distance. They were hanging out on the deck, listening to a baseball game on my father's hand-crank radio while they watched over us. I couldn't hear the game from my spot on the beach but they often listened to games in the evenings, and as I gazed over at them and then back at my sister and Callum, I was conscious, with every fiber of my being, that I didn't want the moment to end. I'd forgotten how strongly a seven-year-old could want something, but an echo of the intensity with which I'd clung to that moment charges through me as the details float back.

I really thought it might not ever be the same if I went inside—that I might never be as happy again as I was playing war out on the beach with Callum.

"Pretty soon it'll be too dark for you to even see the cards anyway," my sister said, making me scowl.

"We'll be fast," Callum declared, already on his feet. "Come on, Ashlyn!"

We sprinted for the cottage, changed into long sleeves and pants and allowed ourselves to be coated in bug spray. Then we raced back to the beach together in the fading light and played cards until every bit of sun was gone. Celeste was wrong—if you tried hard enough you could make out the numbers even in the dark. Callum and I kept right on playing by moonlight and my throat got dry, but I didn't dare go into the cottage for lemonade. Our parents let us stay out on the sand for longer than I would've guessed, but in the end my uncle strolled down to the beach and said we could pick up where we'd left off tomorrow.

The next afternoon, eager to cement my friendship with my cousin, I begged my father to drive us into town to pick up Cheetos and pizza. My dad smiled and said I must be suffering a fierce cheese craving if I needed both those things to satisfy it. I told him the Cheetos would be more for me and the pizza more for Callum and my dad nodded and said he was a big fan of both those things himself but that if he took us we should only tell my mom about the pizza and not the Cheetos.

When Celeste and Ellie heard about the pizza, naturally they wanted to come too, and Uncle Ian said he could never resist pizza and to count him in. Only our moms and Garrett stayed behind. My dad let me get Fun Dip and Gobstoppers as well as a jumbo bag of Cheetos to share with my cousin. Callum said he loved the Cheetos and that the pizza was almost as good as Domino's. As he was eating, a pepperoni slid off his slice and onto his T-shirt, leaving a red mark that he kept rubbing, smooshing the sauce into the fabric just like I would've done.

The six of us were sitting outside the pizza place, taking up their only two tables, when a woman in spindly heels walked past us in the direction of the 7-Eleven next door. The woman was holding a small black dog in her arms and Callum pointed to it and said, "Look at its wee paw." I took a second look and noticed that one of the dog's front legs was swathed in a light green sling.

"*Awww,* poor thing," my sister declared, but her reaction didn't sound a fraction as interesting as the way Callum had phrased his. I hero-worshipped him more with each passing day, and at night, as Celeste and I lay in our shared bedroom, I'd repeat stories about the games we'd played and exotic-sounding things Callum had said. "He's Scottish," Celeste said sensibly. "All Scottish people talk like that, Ashlyn." Then, bored of listening to me rave about our cousin, she began to tease me. "I bet you wish you'd let Ellie and me share a room now. You could listen to Callum talk all night."

I stopped jabbering, hearing the change in her tone, and hoped that she'd drop the subject.

"You know you can't fall in love with your cousin," she continued.

"I don't *love* him," I snapped. I hated that she was trying to turn my fondness for Callum into something weird, and I didn't love him anyway, not in the way she meant. "Do you love Ellie?"

"Don't be stupid," Celeste said.

"*You* don't be stupid," I countered, on the verge of tears. "Just because he's a boy doesn't mean I love him."

"Fine, fine," Celeste said indifferently. "You don't love him."

The following day Callum and I went swimming together, as usual, and then tromping through the heavily treed area next to the house, unearthing bugs and pretending we were exploring the Amazon. Callum and I were as close, for the rest of that trip, as Ellie and Celeste had ever been. We played cards for hours and he taught me how to play snap and spit. We buried each other on the beach, constructed cities in the sand and kicked a soccer ball around. He tried to teach me his accent and I tried to teach him mine. We made a video of ourselves talking in the funny fake voices and when we watched it back, the ridiculous sounds coming out of each other's mouths made us laugh until our stomachs hurt.

There are still so many gaps in my memory that I can't say for certain that those three weeks at Farlain Lake were the best of my life, but I don't need perfect recall to realize they were something special.

Shortly after we got back to Strathedine I remember talking to my mother, who I knew wouldn't tease me the way Celeste had, about all the good times I'd had with Callum. "It's nice that you're friends," she said, and I didn't tell her that I thought Callum hadn't spoken to me much the previous year because I was a girl and younger than him. I beamed at her and said, "I hope next year at Farlain Lake is exactly like this one."

Nothing's ever exactly the same way twice. I can't remember the changes yet—my eighth year is still shrouded in mystery, but there's a strange murkiness surrounding it that makes me wonder if I'm better off leaving the future forgotten and hanging on the near perfection that was that second trip to Farlain Lake. Hanging on for as long as I can, just like that night Callum and I played war on the beach in the moonlight.

ten

breckon

My folks say they want me to see a therapist. They tell me they don't think I'm sleeping well and that they know I'm having trouble settling back in to school. *Settling back in.* Like there's any chance of that happening. Like a couple weeks after Skylar died I'm supposed to be able to go on with my life as though nothing happened.

"Are you telling me you're not having any trouble *settling back in*?" I ask defensively. Going through the motions isn't the same thing as settling back in. I hear muffled crying from behind closed doors every day. My parents both went back to work on Monday but their eyes are permanently tired, and when we talk, our words are just noise.

My mom nestles her fist under her chin. "Your dad and I started going to group sessions just today."

"It's a grief group," my father adds. "And we think you might benefit from talking to someone too."

"I'm not going to any group." It was bad enough everyone staring at me at the funeral and then school, my first couple of days back. If I have to sit in a room with fifteen other people who feel like they're being pulled under, I won't make it out of there.

"It doesn't have to be a group like ours," my mother says. "Barbara and Sean know someone, a therapist who saw their daughter for a while when she was having trouble."

Barbara and Sean's daughter was anorexic. I remember Mom going to see her in the hospital two years ago. She got so skinny that she almost died. Imagine starving yourself until you're just skin and bone and your body essentially begins to feed on itself in order to survive. I didn't get it at the time. I don't entirely understand it now but I think I have an idea of how Barbara and Sean's daughter must've felt when she was starving herself. I bet it didn't feel voluntary at all. I bet that it made more sense to her than doing anything else.

"I worry about you," my mom says, her eyes beginning to mist. "I don't want you to think this was your fault, Breckon."

I can't lie about that. *"It was my fault."* She knows it too. We all know it. I'm the one who wasn't there when it counted.

"It was one of those things," my dad says in a brittle voice. "Just one of those things. Nobody can keep their eyes on anyone twenty-four hours a day."

Logically I understand that to be true but I also know that emotionally he's lying. There's no way in hell that my father doesn't blame me. Even if mostly he doesn't let himself, there have to be times when he wishes I did things differently that day. One tiny choice, in a hundred other tiny choices you make a day, and everything would've been different.

We've had this conversation before, the morning before the

funeral, and my dad told me then that if he blamed anyone he blamed himself for not being there when it happened. "You can't always be everywhere we go," I told him.

"No, I can't," my father replied, looking me in the eye. "And neither can you, Breckon. Don't take that burden on yourself—if you do you'll never get out from under it."

He acted as if I had a choice on how to look at this, but I knew better. Nobody can keep their eyes on anyone twenty-four hours a day but if you're the one who wasn't looking when it mattered, it's still your fault. The facts are what they are.

I didn't reply to my father then, and I don't reply now. I can see in my parents' faces that they won't let up. I've let the therapist idea gain traction by skipping classes and haunting Skylar's room earlier. My parents are in orange alert mode.

"Just give her a try," Mom urges.

I don't say yes or no. It doesn't matter what I think. I hunch over, lock my hands around the back of my neck and stare down at the living room carpet. How can I feel so empty and still want to fight them? After all the pain I've caused my parents I should be willing to do this without making them worry and beg.

I can't ditch any more classes either. From now on I need to convince my mother and father that I'm doing as well as can be expected, given the circumstances. I need to say, the next time we have this conversation, that I miss Skylar but that what happened to her wasn't my fault.

I need to lie.

"I'll go meet her," I tell my mom and dad. "But I'm not promising I'll go into therapy."

My mother nods so readily that it makes my throat swell. "We only want you to have the opportunity to talk to someone about your feelings. We're not saying it has to be permanent."

With that settled, Mom confesses that she's already spoken with the therapist, who has a cancellation tomorrow after school and can fit me in. Her name's Eva Kannan and I'm supposed to speak to her for fifty minutes.

I'm sure what Eva Kannan and I have in mind for those fifty minutes are two vastly different things. She'll want to unravel me—break me down into bruised pieces and shove them under a magnifying glass, but I can't let that happen. The most important thing, during those fifty minutes, is that I don't crumble. I'll have to hold it together, no matter what, because every time I break makes it that much harder to keep going.

And this shouldn't even be about me.

None of this should be happening.

I'm so sick of feeling my parents' sad eyes on me, their cheeks carved into expressions of concern, that I stand up and mumble, "I think I'll head over to Jules's place, if that's okay. We have an econ thing we need to work on."

I haven't been to econ in two days and Jules has no clue that I'm on my way over. She's been trying to check in with me at every opportunity but I've been shitty at returning phone calls and text messages over the past few days.

After a moment's pause Dad tells me not to be too late. I say I won't and then jump in the car, thinking about how I've screwed myself over this week and about all the things I won't tell Eva Kannan. When I get to Jules's house I notice her friend Renee's car in the driveway next to her mom's Acura and almost change my mind about stopping by. Maybe I'd have better luck at Ty's or Rory's. There are aspects of me that they don't know as well as Jules does but they expect less. They don't need to feel like they're tapped into my soul to consider us friends.

I used to like that Jules and I could talk about anything. But now I don't know if I want to talk. My brain's so knotted and foggy that I don't know what I want. But this is the first place I thought of when I wanted to get away. That has to mean something.

So I park next to the curb in front of Jules's house and ring the doorbell before I can change my mind. Jules opens the door in the same punk kilt dress she was wearing at school earlier. She had thick black tights on under it then but now her legs are bare, which makes the dress look shorter and sexier and I know if she opened the door looking like that a few weeks ago—and no one was around—that I'd start running my hands over her the second the door was closed behind us.

Jules gets as horny as I used to, maybe more, and the sight of all that skin flashes me back to the first time she asked me to work my fingers inside her. Being naked with Jules, two of my fingers moving slowly inside her, seemed as intimate as sex, but now the memory feels like it must belong to someone else. I can't imagine wanting to touch her like that.

"Hey," Jules says, jumping forward to hug me. "I'm so glad you're here."

"I saw Renee's car," I tell her, giving her a squeeze before I stand back.

"She and Cameron are hanging out." She swivels to look at the staircase, which I guess signals that they're up in her room.

Renee's a senior but she and Jules know each other from doing school plays together. A month ago both Jules and Renee were in *The Importance of Being Earnest.* Because I helped Jules practice her lines for the audition I still have phrases like, "I hope, Cecily, you are not inattentive," swimming around in my head.

"But they won't be here long," Jules adds. "They have to pick their mom up at the hospital." It's not that she's sick—that's just where Renee and Cameron's mother works. Usually brothers and sisters don't hang out together as friends much but Renee and Cameron are step-siblings and so close that some people at school used to make incest jokes about them when they first moved here.

I hardly knew Cameron before I got together with Jules but now I count him as a friend. Sometimes, when he's not with Renee, he hangs out with my other friends, which is one of the reasons the jokes stopped. So many people have his back now that making a shitty joke isn't worth the trouble it could cause.

I go upstairs with Jules and say hi to Cameron and Renee, who are sitting on the floor listening to music that I don't know how to categorize. It's like classical violin, jazz-rock fusion, folk and pop all rolled into one.

"This is pretty cool," I say. "Who is it?"

Cameron hands over a CD. "Doctor Draw. We saw him at a jazz-blues festival the other night, playing electric violin with a backing band. He tore up the crowd. I thought I was going to get trampled in the line to buy his CD afterwards."

Meanwhile Renee's painting her nails orange and she stops and points one of her orange-tipped fingers at me. "We can't wait to see you at Boleyn's. Do you know when you're playing yet?"

Boleyn's is a café in Bourneville, a bigger town bordering Strathedine to the west. They let anyone who puts their name down on the night play music, do spoken word or read regular poetry. I was planning on having a few songs ready by the time school lets out near the end of June. I'm not a natural and wanted to get a lot of practice hours in first—the only people who've even see me play are Jules and Skylar.

I shrug and say I haven't been thinking about it much lately. The truth is, I have no intention of playing at Boleyn's but I don't want to get into that now.

Jules is standing behind me and she grabs my hand and guides me over to the bed to sit down next to her. "Are your folks on their date night?" I ask. I haven't seen or heard any sign of them since I got here and I know Mr. and Mrs. Pacquette try to have a date night once a week. That sounds like something a person like Eva Kannan would suggest if your marriage was in trouble but Mr. and Mrs. Pacquette just do it because they like to hang out together.

"They went to a new Thai restaurant near city hall," Jules tells me. "My dad's been there for a couple work lunches and can't stop talking about their curry duck."

"How can anyone eat duck?" Renee asks, grimacing as she seals up the nail polish. "We *feed* ducks in the park. They're way too cute to eat."

"Once they're cooked they're charred birds just like chickens," Cameron quips, tilting his wrist so he can glance at his watch. "We should go. Mom's shift's going to be over in a couple minutes."

The three of us exchange goodbyes and Jules follows

Cameron and Renee out of the room to walk them down to the front door. The second before they left there wasn't a bad intention in my head but in a flash I realize there's an opportunity at hand and I'm up slinking soundlessly towards the Pacquettes' bedroom and then their en suite bathroom, throwing their medicine cabinet open and scoping out Mr. Pacquette's sleeping pills. He has a practically full bottle—he won't notice a few more missing, and now I won't have to ask Jules or worry about dipping into whatever my parents are taking, which, for all I know, might not do the trick.

My heart pounds as I open the bottle and stuff a fistful of pills down one of my front pockets. I race back into the hallway and have nearly made it to the safety of Jules's room when she appears at the top of the stairs. Her eyes whip over to me and freeze me to the spot underneath my feet. Air sticks in my throat. I can't stop blinking.

"What's going on?" Jules demands.

I shake my head, and during that pause my brain kicks back to life. "I felt dizzy," I murmur. "I was going to the bathroom for water." The second upstairs bathroom is only a few feet away and I motion to it behind me. "But then everything started going black." I slump down on the floor and duck my head like I'm fighting to stay conscious. "So I thought I better lie down and turned around to go back."

Jules's expression morphs from confusion into worry. "Put your head between your knees," she commands, dropping down next to me.

I nod a little, my head still between my knees. I didn't

know I could be such a good liar; I've nearly sold myself on the idea that I was about to pass out.

Jules watches over me for a couple more minutes before slipping into the bathroom for water. She hands me the blue ceramic cup from her bathroom and I drink. "You really had me scared for a minute there," she tells me. "But I think you're beginning to look a little better."

"I don't know what happened. Everything just started to fade." I finish off the rest of the water. "But I'm feeling okay now. I think whatever it was is passing."

"Sit here a bit longer," Jules advises, her hand on my leg. "To be on the safe side." Then she adds, "Are you sleeping lately?"

"Sleeping, eating, all of it. I guess it was just one of those weird things out of nowhere."

Jules stares skeptically into my eyes. "Maybe it's stress."

"You sound like you've been talking to my parents."

Jules's fingers fall into her lap. Sitting down on the floor like we are, her kilt dress is riding up, giving me a peek at her green panties that makes me want to tell her to cover herself.

"They say I should see someone," I continue. "They think I can't handle what happened with Skylar."

"It's not about *handling* it," Jules says quickly. "I mean, if it was me, I think I'd need to talk to someone. Maybe it's not such a bad idea."

"Just because I missed a couple classes doesn't mean I need to see a shrink, Jules." It doesn't feel good to say that from the floor outside the bathroom with a bunch of Mr. Pacquette's pills in my pocket, and I shoot up and stomp towards her room.

Jules follows me in so that we're both sitting on her bed again. She's quiet the way I need her to be and I add, "I just need space. And time. And for everyone to understand that."

"Breckon." Her little finger locks around mine. "I only want whatever will be good for you." Her finger wriggles against mine. The first time we held hands it was actually holding little fingers, just like this, on the ferry from Battery Park to Liberty Island. We'd been hanging out a lot on that trip but I didn't know for sure anything was happening between us until I felt her finger stroke mine.

"I know," I tell her. I wonder if she has any idea how badly I want to let myself fall to pieces when I'm with her. I could crawl under the covers, drag her under with me and stay there forever. But it still wouldn't be enough. Nothing would. I feel like we're thousands of miles apart, even though she's right here next to me, clasping my little finger with hers.

I'm relieved that Eva Kannan's a middle-aged woman with deep crow's-feet and laugh lines. The closer she is to my age, the weirder this would seem. Her office is above a European bakery and I think about Barbara and Sean's anorexic daughter having to walk by there and face the smell of freshly baked cakes, tarts and cookies before each therapy session. From upstairs, I can't smell them anymore but I should've bought something to munch on so I'd have something to do with my hands.

When I first get inside I call the therapist Mrs. Kannan, but she says I can call her Eva instead, if I like. "Okay," I tell her. Once upon a time I might have wanted to make a stupid joke about feeling free to call me Breckon too but now I don't bother.

Eva Kannan's office looks more like a university professor's than a therapist's. All the leather-bound hardcovers I can see are novels instead of psychology books—classic fiction but newer books too. "It's a hobby of mine," Eva says in a clipped accent when she notices me studying her shelves. Eva looks South Asian but she sounds like she grew up in England. "I like to collect books—preferably signed."

"Why signed?" I bet people are always trying to out-shrink the shrink and I remind myself that's a bad strategy. She's the one with the degree—outwitting an amateur would be a cakewalk. I just need to get out of here without revealing too much about myself—give her the impression that I'll keep my head above water without any kind of intervention from her or my parents.

"They're rarer," Eva says thoughtfully. "But I suppose they also seem more personal."

I nod like that makes sense about the signatures and press my thumbs together on my lap. My bandaged left hand seems like a declaration of guilt. A regular person would ask what happened to me and wince when I explained but here I feel like a deep-sea diver being circled by a shark.

"I spoke to your mother on the phone," Eva tells me. "She seems very concerned about you."

"I know." I nod again. The next forty-eight minutes will be lots of nodding and *I knows*. I want to sound reasonable but the room feels so wrong. She's tried to decorate it sort of like a living room but you know that no one ever hangs out here for fun. There's a small wooden desk pushed against one of the walls—an office chair in front of it—but Eva and I are sitting in high-backed leather armchairs with a coffee table separating us. I could've sat on the couch, which looks more comfortable, but that's marginally closer to her and I want to keep my distance. My eyes land on the globe in front of the bookshelves. If it was nearer I could have a look at it without making it seem as if I'm avoiding the subject.

"I'm very sorry to hear about your sister," Eva continues.

"Everyone says that." *Damn.* Two minutes into this and I'm already messing up.

"Would you rather they didn't?" Eva asks.

"It doesn't matter what they say or don't say." Is she going to dissect every sentence that comes out of my mouth and throw it back at me in the form of a question?

Eva gazes at me, expecting me to explain my answer, but I only stare back, focusing on her dangling earrings. "I realize that it wasn't your idea to see me." Eva leans back in her chair. "But this time really is for you. Not for your parents or anyone else. I want you to think of it like that if you can—you can say whatever you want here."

I fold my arms in front of my stomach and grip firmly. "Did my mother tell you what happened?" I ask.

Eva nods, her eyes calm but not unsympathetic. "She told me you were the one to find your sister."

If I hold any tighter I'll crush internal organs. "I was the only one home." The vacant expression on Skylar's face is burned into my brain forever. The moment's never far from my thoughts, but this is worse because we're shining a spotlight on it.

"You were the one who called emergency services," Eva says, and I don't know if it's a question or not.

"It was too late." My eyes burn. Pressure builds in my ears and forehead, making them ache. The tears sting as they well up from that place inside me that never stops screaming Skylar's name.

But when I made the call, the world seemed infinitely quiet. Like time had stopped. The house was soaked in silence. I couldn't turn up my voice. The woman on the other end of the 911 line kept making me repeat myself and saying she was having trouble hearing me. But inside I was wailing.

Even when the ambulance arrived with its siren blaring, I couldn't hear it in the same way that I would've before. It seemed muted the way everything does now—everyone I know and everything I do. And I kept thinking, even as I was screaming inside, even when my parents showed up and an investigator from the medical examiner's office came to look at my sister and said that they'd be taking her to the morgue, that I could somehow change what had happened.

The cops came next. They asked my parents questions, but mostly me. An investigator took pictures of the scene. The police made me describe what I'd witnessed, and the male cop looked away when I lost it and broke down. It didn't take long for the medical examiner to rule accidental death.

Putting the words *accident* and *death* together seems ridiculous. Spilt milk is an accident. Breaking your arm and needing stitches are accidents.

What happened to Skylar is so much more than an accident and I still can't accept that there's nothing I can do to reverse the past few weeks and bring her back. If I told my parents I couldn't watch her that night. BAM. If I changed my mind and went after her when she asked me about the boxes. BAM. If I died that night on my bike a year and a half ago . . .

"I can't do this," I croak, looking away from Eva. *I can't.*

I blink back the tears so that they don't spill over.

She's gone. She's gone.

"Do you want to take a break?" Eva asks. Her voice sounds piercing but I know it's not. It's just that my brain can't cope with the intrusion into my thoughts. A whisper from my own voice would sound like a shriek right now.

I can't. We've only just started and I need more than a break. I need for this to be over. But opening my mouth and forming the words to get that across is more than I can do right now. I nod mutely and Eva uncrosses her legs, gets up and heads for the watercooler in the corner. Several tall clear glasses balance on a tray atop a small circular table next to it and she takes one, fills it and sets it in front of me on the coffee table. Everyone's getting me water lately and all the things I can't say—about the sleeping pills, stealing from Mr. Pacquette, hurting myself—weigh so heavily on me that it's a wonder I can get out of my seat.

But I do. I ignore the offered glass of water, lope over to the globe in front of her bookshelf and spin it, my eyes still on fire. The sphere part has a bronze metallic sheen to it, and beneath it a Greek-style statue of a man on his knees balances the weight of the world between his shoulders. With the way his arm and leg muscles are bulging, the weight appears to be a strain but he's still succeeding, and I wonder if there's some kind of shrink message built into Eva's choice of this particular globe—some *rah, rah you can do it* message.

I suddenly remember the guy's name. *Atlas.* We did Greek mythology in English last year and Zeus punished him for siding with the Titans in their war against the Olympians by making him hold the sky on his shoulders. So not only is the base of this globe not the most fitting message for a shrink's office, it's also incorrect. Atlas should be holding up sky, not the world.

"I always wanted one of those," Eva says from across the room. "It was the first thing I bought for the office when I started decorating years ago."

I swallow to clear my throat. "I had one when I was younger." I stare down at the vastness of Asia on the globe. "Not an antique-style one like this. Just the regular kind you buy a kid to put on their desk."

We talk about kid things for a while—bunk beds, board games, color markers—and when I do sit down again, minutes later, and take a sip of water, we don't discuss Skylar directly—we talk around her, about the concentration problems I'm having at school and about staying in communication with my parents about what I need from them. Eva thinks I should speak to my teachers and that they'd understand and give me more time to work on things—or even extra help when I need it. She says it's natural that I might want to withdraw from people, like my parents, but that I should try to stay connected to them and my friends.

I'm relieved when I notice that the appointment's almost over and that there won't be enough time to get back to Skylar.

At eleven minutes to five Eva, without checking her watch or anything, asks: "Would you like to come back next week?"

I was never going to come back—the near meltdown I had at the beginning of the session just proves that was the right decision. But I pretend to consider her question before replying, "I don't think so."

"I wish you would," Eva says. "But you can think about it and call me. Even months down the road, if you want to. I'll be here." Eva glides over to the desk, picks up one of her cards and hands it to me. "Hold on to it in case you change your mind."

"All right." I slide her card into one of my back pockets. "Thanks."

I'm not going to walk through this door again. I don't need to come here to feel bad about Skylar. That happens everywhere I am anyway. Maybe therapy works for some things, like eating disorders, but how can it be better to scratch at wounds that will never heal?

Eva has done something for me today, though. She's given me a clearer idea of what going through the motions should look like. It's not enough to show up for classes. I need to go to my teachers and ask for extensions on assignments or makeup tests for the ones I'll fail in the near future. Like the math test next Monday, which I'm guaranteed to flunk because the probability that I'll be able to solve problems involving quadratic functions or wrap my head around the sine and cosine laws is less than zero.

When I think of all the energy it will take to *try* like that—or even *look* like I'm trying—a wave of exhaustion slams into me. It was hard enough getting through this week when I was cutting class—sitting through endless hours of math, English, econ and social science while I feel like this is unimaginable. I unlock my car, climb in, push the seat as far back as it will go and shut my eyes. Only for a second because then I realize Eva Kannan might look down from her window, see me napping in the parking lot and call my folks to confirm that Breckon is on his way to cracking up.

Then it comes to me. There's one other thing I can do that doesn't depend on being able to concentrate but that might still show my parents that I'm settling back in and get them off my back. I cradle my cell in my palm, flip up the lid and dial Zavi's.

eleven

ashlyn

When Breckon was at the therapist's office I thought there was a chance he'd tell her the truth. I knew he wouldn't really want to, that he'd try to fight it, but when I saw his eyes fill with tears and say he couldn't do this I thought there'd be an avalanche inside him that he couldn't contain and that it would all come spilling out.

The sleeping pills.

The burn.

The scissors.

Tell her, I urged in the tone I'm still borrowing from my mother when I speak to him. *You can trust her. She won't judge you. She'll listen. She'll help.*

If the fact that I'm not in a hurry to remember certain parts of my life makes me a hypocrite, so be it. Breckon doesn't have to know that. *Skylar would tell you exactly what I'm telling you if she could,* I said too.

If she were with him instead of me I bet he'd be able to hear her. I wonder, because I have all the time in the world to wonder, if his sister was supposed to be the one glued to him in this way and there's been a cosmic mistake.

I wonder so, so many things and if there are answers on the wind I can't hear them, only Breckon's ragged, pained breath. There's life after death but I don't understand it. I don't remember a tunnel or a white light. I don't remember seeing my body and I don't remember being eight years old.

I just watch. And listen. And whisper to somebody who can't hear me.

When Mr. Cody arrives home from work, for instance, I listen to Breckon tell him that the therapist seemed okay and he'll call her if he needs to but for the time being he wants to see how things go. "I'm going back to work tomorrow," Breckon adds. "I called Mr. Baldassarre and he said he didn't want to bother me but that it'd be great if I could make it because they're expecting it to be busy—you know, because of that new time-travel movie opening at the theater next door. They've got it playing nearly every hour."

Mr. Cody appears to accept this, but over dinner Mrs. Cody makes a point of saying, "We can find someone else for you to talk to if you didn't feel comfortable with Eva."

Breckon's in the middle of slicing into his ham and he stops, with his elbows in midair and the sliver of meat under his fork not yet fully severed. "Mom, please," he says in a voice like a rusty nail. "I tried it and I don't want to go back. Let it go."

Mr. Cody reaches for his wife's hand under the table, to stop her from repeating herself more insistently. "He has her number," Mr. Cody says to his wife. "And she's not going anywhere. She's still a future option."

I can see that they're trying to be understanding and do the best thing for him, but that they can't see what that is in the same way that I can. I have the world's best view of Breckon Cody and I know without a shadow of a doubt that his parents should force him to go back to therapy. He hasn't hurt himself lately and I wish I could believe that's over with but his breath sounds the same as ever and now he's lied to Jules by stealing from her parents' medicine cabinet.

Mr. and Mrs. Cody do as Breckon asks and drop the subject, though, at least for the moment. After dinner Jules comes over and she and Breckon watch a horror movie where every last person is viciously slaughtered, even the psycho killer. Some of the scenes are vaguely familiar and I wonder if I saw the movie in my own teenage life. Breckon's parents disappear, giving him and Jules some privacy, and during an axe attack on one of the main characters Jules nudges her face into Breckon's collar to kiss his neck.

He kisses her back a little, but not much, before easing his face away. Jules seems to get the same idea that I do, which is that Breckon isn't interested in getting physical right now, and stops attempting anything beyond cuddling. When she leaves, their good-night kiss at the door is brief but Breckon runs his fingers through her hair and holds her close.

Watching him do it, I get an idea of what they were like together before Skylar died and I can see why Jules fell for him and why he fell for her. I bet they were a couple who made other people want to be part of a couple too. But I shouldn't think that as though it's in the past. People get through hard times by leaning on each other, and Breckon's lucky to have Jules. He should lean more.

I feel instinctively that I never got to have that with a guy, and that makes watching them feel bittersweet. I must have missed out on a lot of things, dying at fifteen, but that's a big one. I would've wanted that kind of love, even if I couldn't remember it.

Once Jules has gone Breckon pops a pill and slips into dreamland, the only part of his life that I can't see. He remains there until early afternoon, almost as though he's relishing his time away from my prying eyes. Just before five he drives over to the Cherrywood Empire outlet mall, which is actually closer to my house than it is to his. There I learn that his work place is called Zavi's Subs & More. Though I remember the basic layout of the outdoor mall I don't specifically remember the submarine shop. It looks like a small business rather than a franchise and it's sandwiched between a tattoo studio and photography store and across from a gym on one side and movie theater on the other.

I peruse the menu as Breckon slips in behind the counter—most of it's composed of various submarine sandwiches but I noticed that there are also an assortment of salads and flat-bread pizzas. I miss the sensation of being hungry, and the act of satisfying it, more than I would've thought possible. Flavor memories—sweet, salty, bitter, spicy—are stored somewhere other than merely your brain cells and mouth. I know that because I can still remember what it's like to taste, although my taste buds must be six feet under.

My focus on Breckon begins to loosen as I slip into a fantasy about devouring a foot-long submarine sandwich piled high with roast beef, bacon, mushrooms and red onions. Drowning in barbecue sauce, it would trickle down the length of the bread and splash to the floor beneath me. I'd make a mess like I used to so often when I was a child and I wouldn't feel embarrassed about it—only revel in the thrill of tasting again. And if, when I was done, that still wasn't enough, I'd order a veggie flat-bread pizza chaser and finish that off good and slow, savoring every bite.

Even to smell again would be ecstasy. Garlic bread baking in the oven. Warm chocolate chip cookies. Ribs sizzling on the barbecue. Corn on the cob directly under my nose as I chomp through a column of kernels like a beaver.

If I had a beating heart I'd be drooling now. Who knew that a type of hunger that has nothing to do with your stomach being full or empty survives the grave? Do sex addicts still crave flesh? Do alcoholics remain thirsty?

Breckon, why couldn't you have worked in a clothing store at the mall? Why did it have to be food?

"Good to have you back, Breckon," an older man with a potbelly and pencil-thin eyebrows says, lumbering over to him. "Zavi sends her thanks too." The man, who I assume to be Mr. Baldassarre, smiles briefly at Breckon. "She's out with her sister tonight instead of here, thanks to you, but she says anything you or your family need, you let us know."

"Thanks." Breckon's eyes shift to the teenage girl standing next to the man. "Hi, Georgia."

"Breckon, I couldn't believe it," the girl replies in a wobbly voice. Her brown hair's barely long enough to pull into a ponytail but she's done it anyway, and having her hair back like that makes her face look chubbier. "Your beautiful little sister," she murmurs. "She was like an angel."

Breckon's head dips in recognition of her remarks. Meanwhile a mother and twin boys, about ten or eleven years old, are sidling up to the counter to ogle the menu. "Can I help you?" Breckon asks, moving quickly towards them.

Georgia's eyes widen, surprised to see him leap into action.

"I know we want one six-inch tuna," the customer says, looking searchingly at her boys. "What else are we going with, guys?"

"I want the meatball sub," one of the boys pipes up.

"That made you burp for an hour last time," his mother reminds him. "Why don't you get something like turkey or tuna?"

"I want meatballs," the boy repeats. "They were good. It doesn't matter if I burp."

His mother rolls her eyes, smiling in resignation as she faces Breckon. "Whatever he wants. He'll be the one burping later, not me." Her other son orders pepperoni flat-bread pizza, and when the order's ready he snatches his pizza out of the bag and has it half-finished before they leave the store.

"Do you hear that, Uncle Dom?" Georgia kids after they've gone. "She said your meatballs made her son burpy."

Mr. Baldassarre swats the air. "Eat too fast and anything will make you burp."

"Anyway, the kid seemed to think it was worth the belching," Breckon says. "That's practically a recommendation. You should put the quote on a sign. You know: 'I want meatballs—it doesn't matter if I burp.' Under that you have printed 'Customer, age ten.' "

"That would be hilarious!" Georgia cries. "We could make up the sickest quotes about this place and hang them on the wall as publicity."

Breckon's eyes glimmer with a playfulness I haven't seen in them before. "The barbecue chicken sub gave me salmonella . . . but if that's what salmonella tastes like, I'm ready to have it again."

"There was half a spider in my Caesar," Georgia begins, "but the salad was so delicious that I didn't stop to look for the other half."

Mr. Baldassarre groans and shakes his head. "If I turned marketing over to you two, I'd lose all my customers by Monday."

"Except the meatball kid," Breckon points out. "He'd still want the meatball sub."

That makes me want to smile, and I say silently to Breckon, *You can be funny when you want to, can't you?* Clearly being here is good for him, like a flashback of his old life.

Over the course of the next few hours a steady trickle of mall shoppers and people leaving the gym drop in to buy meals ably assembled by Breckon, Georgia and Mr. Baldassarre. A third employee, a lanky tall guy named Takuya who can't be older than twenty, shows up just in time for the movie rush Breckon was telling his parents about earlier.

Breckon's the fastest worker of them all. Takuya gets cranky whenever there's a line and Georgia is slow but methodical. Most of the people who stream in after the movie are teenagers. They're loud and excitable and many of them are trashing the movie when they walk in. I hear at least three different guys, at different times, label it "weak-ass shit."

"I don't get why everybody's so surprised that it sucks," Takuya says to Breckon during a lull between customers. "When studios don't screen for the press first, it's a sure sign the movie's a waste of money."

To me it looks as though the teenagers are as happy to complain about the movie as they would be to rave about it if it'd been any good, so maybe it doesn't matter about the money.

"Breckon!" Georgia yells from the cash register. "Your friends are here."

Ty, Big Red (who it took me a while to figure out is really named Rory) and a couple of other guys I recognize from Breckon's school saunter up to the counter. "What time are you on till, dude?" Big Red wants to know.

"Whenever it dies down in here," Breckon says. "So was the movie as shitty as everyone's saying?"

"And then some," Ty says, puffing out his cheeks. "But hey, man, you want to catch up with us after this place closes?"

"I don't know—where are you guys going to be at?"

Big Red shrugs. "Probably over at Denny's getting shakes or hanging out down by the lake."

"Excuse me," the teenage girl next to him interrupts.

Big Red turns to look at her. "Yeah?"

"Where's the Denny's? Is that around here?" The girl has

long blond hair and a perky smile, and Big Red's gaze drops to check out her body.

"It's at Richmond Road and Blakely—you know, that same strip mall that has a Home Depot and a Sport Chek in it?"

The girl, who's traveling in a pack with three similarly attractive friends, listens to a brunette in a purple hoodie say, "That's way too far to walk. My dad will kill us if I call him to pick us up all the way over there."

"We can give you a ride if you want," Ty offers. "Shuttle service. We'd have to make two trips, though. We're driving a Corolla."

The other brunette raises her eyebrows at the suggestion. "That's either nice of you or serial-killer creepy," she comments.

Ty laughs, showing his teeth. "Is that a *no thanks* then?"

Breckon's watching the exchange from across the counter, same as I am, while Georgia and Takuya begin to take the girls' orders.

"We better not," the blonde who originally interrupted Big Red says. "We just thought if it was close . . ."

"Nah, it's definitely not close." Ty's still eyeing the brunette who shot him down with the serial-killer remark, addressing her instead of her friend. "But why don't you give me your number and I'll give you a call sometime—unless that's creepy too?"

The brunette's mouth stretches into a grin for him. "Depends what you plan on saying, I guess. Give me your phone."

Ty reaches into his back pocket for it and hands her his cell. "I'm Ty, by the way."

"Anya," she says as she keys her number into his phone.

"Anya," he repeats, keeping his eyes on hers. "Thanks. I'll call you later."

The second the girls have left with their sub order Ty hurls pissed-off glances at his friends and says, "What happened to you pricks? You just left me hanging in the wind there when I said we could drive them."

Big Red and the other guys don't have much to say in their defense. "I don't think her friends were gonna go for it anyway," Breckon ventures. "But at least you got her number, man."

"Yeah, she was hot," Ty says, and just then another wave of customers hits. Breckon's friends remind him to catch up with them later and take off.

Breckon's spent so much time alone this week that I don't really expect him to hang out with Ty and Big Red after work, but he does. He drives over to Denny's to meet them and orders onion rings and a strawberry milk shake. In the parking lot a guy in a hoodie and a devil mask—but naked from the waist down except for a pair of Nike running shoes and sports socks—jogs slowly alongside a creeping Mazda crammed with howling teenage guys. They're blasting the Pitbull song "I Know You Want Me" from the car, and the noise of that combined with their shouting prompts Denny's employees and customers alike to stare out the window. *"Uno, dos, tres, cuatro. I know you want me . . ."*

A vision of dancing to this song whirls through my mind. My teenage arms, hips, breasts, I see them all shake and swivel in time to the music. *"Uno, dos, tres, cuatro."* Then, just as quickly, the memory evaporates into thin air, leaving me in a restaurant booth with Breckon and his friends. Outside the devil's shielding his penis from public view, both hands clamped over it as he attempts a few simple dance moves himself.

Big Red chokes on his shake and he and Ty laugh so hard that they gasp for breath. Breckon smiles brighter than I've ever seen, drops the onion ring he was holding onto his plate and says, "Looks like he won the bet—I wonder how much it was for."

"Could just be a dare," Big Red guesses, still fighting for control of his lungs. "Or just for the lulz."

The six of us peer out the Denny's window and watch the devil pry his hands away from his penis to reveal—for the briefest second only—that he's wearing a glow-in-the-dark condom. The devil's friends have opened the back door for him and he dives in, a flash of his skinny white ass the last thing there is to see before the car speeds off into the night.

Breckon laughs out loud and Ty, who's never really stopped, declares, "Damn, that's the funniest thing I've seen all week!"

"Dude," Big Red sputters as he holds his sides. "That's going to give me a fucking asthma attack. That guy's my hero."

I wonder, if I was sitting there with Breckon and his friends in the flesh, what I would say. Obviously they find the streaker funnier than I did. It was stupid-funny but not in a way that would make me laugh out loud. Maybe it'd seem funnier if I was with my own friends, or even the girls Ty and Big Red were talking to in Zavi's.

But I'm glad to see and hear Breckon laugh. I zoom in for a close-up on his cheerful eyes and listen to his breathing with my special hearing, but there's nothing remarkable to hear. He's just a boy having a good time with his friends and suddenly

I'm happier in the moment than I've been since I woke up trapped and dead. Tonight I don't need to say anything to him in my mother's voice. Tonight my Breckon worries can simmer on the back burner, and it's not God I have to thank for that, but the devil.

twelve

breckon

I drive Big Red home and Ty takes Brett and Kostas. The devil's inspired Rory and he thinks we should try to top him by doing some group streak, wearing Bart Simpson masks or Beatles wigs. I know he'll never actually do it but I go along with the scenarios for a while instead of bursting his bubble. Rory can be like an Asperger's kid when he gets really excited about something: he'll talk about it until you're bored to tears, but if you call him out on it he reacts like a kid too—all discouraged and moody—and I don't feel like dealing with that. I was feeling good at the restaurant, but as soon as we left the emptiness was back like it'd never left.

When we get close to his house Big Red goes quiet for a bit and then says, "This is off the record, but remember what Ty was saying about leaving him hanging before with those chicks?"

"Yeah." If Rory thinks he can get a bunch of girls to dance naked through a parking lot with us, he's insane.

"So, the thing is," he continues, "I've been hooking up with

Isabel Castillo but she doesn't want anyone to know. You know, her parents are hardcore Catholic and she figures that we should just keep it under wraps."

Isabel Castillo is good friends with my ex, Nadine, so I know her pretty well. Their families have been close since preschool. Isabel's nice but doesn't go to parties or hang out much. You can see her flinch if you swear around her, like someone who's lived a very sheltered life.

I guess the surprise is plastered on my face because Rory says, "Not sex, dude, you know . . . whatever . . ." He points his face out the window.

"So, like, no one knows about you two?" I ask. *"No one?"*

"That's what I'm saying, man. It's off the record."

"So why are you telling me?"

"I don't know." Big Red exhales in the same deliberate way you do if you're smoking a cigarette. "I guess it just didn't seem real if I couldn't tell at least one other person."

I get it. I don't think they can last long as a secret though. Either someone will find out or sneaking around will become too big a pain in the ass to want to bother with.

"The thing is, there's all this temptation walking around out there," Rory notes. "Like that blond chick with the sweet body at Zavi's. It'd be easier if everyone knew about Isabel. Then I wouldn't have to police myself, you know? It'd be a well-known fact that I had a girlfriend."

I shrug. "Things are what they are." I don't know what he expects me to say. This thing he's thinking of as a problem is so microscopic that he should quit worrying and just be grateful for it.

"Yeah, I guess you're right," he says. "I just thought that you'd have some *words of wisdom* or something, seeing how you and Jules have been together for so long."

Advice on how to stop yourself from wanting to fuck somebody else, that's what he wants from me. I shoot him a tired look. "Maybe you should just break it off with Isabel," I offer as we pull up to his house.

Big Red's face jolts like he's just been struck by lightning. "But I don't want to do that. I mean . . . I really like her."

Just get out of the car, man, I think. Not long ago we were killing ourselves laughing and now I feel like I don't want to waste my breath on him. There were a few seconds back at Denny's when Skylar wasn't in my head at all, not even the corner of my mind, lurking. It didn't matter if she'd ever existed or not. The streaker dude caught me off guard and tipped everything out of my head except the stupid glow-in-the-dark condom he was wearing.

"If she's that important you'll figure it out," I mutter.

"Sure." Big Red's foot jerks but the rest of him is still. "Catch you later."

"Later," I tell him.

He opens the passenger door and hops out of the car without looking back. Normally when I'm driving I plug in my iPod and listen to tunes, but I don't bother with that anymore, so it's quiet. I take a left out of Big Red's neighborhood and turn onto Simcoe Street. It's twenty-five minutes to two so there aren't many cars on the road, even though it's Saturday night. There's really nowhere to go in Strathedine this late;

your best bet for entertainment is running into the devil outside Denny's.

Alone in the car with no one else on the road, the urge to keep my foot on the gas until I end up someplace no one will ever find me burrows back into my brain. I could get a job pumping gas in Saskatoon or busing tables in a restaurant in Halifax. I don't need much, just food and a place to sleep at night.

There are people living like that right now. People who are floating free, not attached to anyone.

I follow this pared-down existence through in my head, wondering what Eva would make of my fantasy. I see myself waking up in an apartment with dirty windows and checking which of my clothes are clean enough to put on again because I'm overdue to go to the Laundromat. I see myself eating alone in a cheap diner or cooking spaghetti on a hot plate after working ten hours straight at some sweaty minimum wage job. There would be days and days of this and really nothing else. And if it would bring Skylar back, it'd be the easiest thing in the world to live like that, but deep down I know that I'll feel the same way wherever I go as I do right now, that I'll never be able to fool myself into thinking she's still around, no matter how far I get from Strathedine. I could make it all the way to Papua New Guinea and I'd still know.

If even leaving won't work, I don't know what to do with myself. I don't know how to keep walking, talking and breathing.

I want to hurt myself again. But I know I shouldn't.

More than that, though, I just want to quit. Say fuck this all and walk away.

I loosen my grip on the steering wheel. About six weeks ago when Jules and I were on our way to Bourneville to hang out at Boleyn's, I let her steer from the passenger seat while I chomped on a slice of pizza I'd picked up along the way. It was a clear night, no snow on the ground or in the air, and neither of us really thought of her driving for a couple minutes as dangerous or even gave it a second thought. But Renee and Cameron were in the backseat and Renee freaked out like we were the *Titanic* going down and there weren't enough lifeboats to go around. I had to grab the wheel again and hand my slice back to Jules to stop Renee from screaming into my ear.

Something could have happened to all of us in the car that night and it didn't. So why Skylar and why when she was just a kid in the second grade, not even old enough for long division?

Tonight there's nobody with me to worry about and no one else to steer for me either. I take my hands off the wheel, still holding them out in front of me, grasping air. Then I shut my eyes and envision the world spinning on without me. Nearly seven billion people in the world. What's one less?

Except to my parents. And Jules. And my grandparents and the guys I was hanging out with tonight . . .

I see all their faces from behind my closed eyelids and I lunge forward. My eyes snap open as I seize the wheel. *You're such an asshole,* I tell myself. *What the fuck do you think you're doing? What if you flattened an old man in a wheelchair trying to cross the street? Or a lady with a sleeping kid in a car seat? How many more people do you want to kill?*

My foot eases up on the gas. The car slows until a jogger could pass it with no problem. I drive home, the feeling that I'm going to throw up clawing at my throat and my hands shaking. What did I just do?

Nothing, I tell myself. *Nothing. Nothing. Nothing. Calm yourself the fuck down before you go inside.*

I plug my iPod in after all, my fingers jerking, and listen to Johnny Cash sing "A Boy Named Sue" three times in a row. Tonight is the kind of thing that Eva would want me to call her for, but what can she do? Unless someone can change history for me they're all just varying degrees of useless.

Breathe, I say inside my head and the voice doesn't even really sound like mine, but after a while I'm stable enough to get out of the car and unlock my front door. The TV's still on in the family room and I follow the sound and find my mother curled up in the fetal position on the couch, with her eyes closed and her favorite china teacup (one her grandmother gave her before she died) full to the brim with untouched tea on the coffee table across from her. Moose lies between the couch and the TV, stretched out on his side, and he opens the one eye I can see but doesn't get up.

A black-and-white movie's flickering across the screen and I decide not to turn the TV off, in case the silence wakes my mother. A week before Christmas Skylar got the flu and camped out on the couch for days with a yellow beach pail on the floor next to her in case she had to puke and couldn't make it to the bathroom. On the second day I was watching basketball with the sound down while she slept and she opened her eyes and looked at me but was too miserable to say anything.

"You want me to get you anything?" I asked.

"No," she whispered in a small voice. She pulled the blanket closer around her chin and drifted off to sleep again.

I think if my mother opened her eyes right now she'd give me the same look that was in Skylar's eyes that night.

"Mom?" I say quietly. Usually she's a light sleeper, but not tonight. I should throw a blanket over her and let her sleep.

That moment in the car . . . I meant it. In those seconds I felt ready to leave everything, but in retrospect I'm terrified, my heart feels as though it will race all night, overclock itself and give out like a fried computer.

"Mom," I repeat, raising my voice, "were you waiting up?"

My mother's eyes open slowly. She stares at me, then thrusts herself up on her elbows to squint at her watch.

"Were you waiting up?" I say again, panic galloping inside me. *Breathe, man. Get a grip.*

"Breckon," my mother mumbles. "It's nearly two o'clock." Her bangs fall into her eyes as she shifts into a seated position on the couch.

"I know—sorry. Some of the guys dropped by work and wanted to go to Denny's after. You and Dad are usually asleep by the time I get home when I work late so I didn't think—"

"You should've called." Mom sweeps the hair from her face. She coughs dryly into her palm and takes a sip of what must be cold tea. "How's Ty? Was he there tonight?"

I perch on the couch's arm. "He's okay. There was a streaker outside Denny's. Some guy in a devil mask." What I'm thinking, while I say that, is that what happened in the car tonight can only happen once. I've promised myself that before, about other things, but this has to be different. Skylar's gone but I need to stay. That's what she would want. That's what everyone would want for me.

That's what she would want, a voice inside my head repeats, and once again it doesn't feel like mine. *Hold on,* it begs. *Hold on tight.*

It should freak me out, hearing a voice other than my own inside my mind, but somehow it doesn't. Maybe because although it's not exactly my voice, it doesn't seem like someone else's either. I don't know how to explain it.

"At Denny's?" my mom says, looking disconcerted.

"Outside—in the parking lot. It was pretty funny. He was dancing around and everything with no pants on." I stare at my mother, knowing she's as hollowed out as I am and that it's unlikely that she'll find anything funny. It doesn't feel funny to me anymore either but I'm glad I woke her up. Talking to her makes me feel a little closer to okay than I did just a couple of minutes ago.

"It's a bit cold for that, isn't it?" she says, looping one of her fingers through the teacup handle and twirling it gently on the coffee table.

"I guess."

And without warning my mother's eyes begin to leak. She brushes the fattest tears away but she can't brush fast enough to catch them all. The strays soak her face, turn the corners of her eyes pink until she squeezes them shut, her mouth dropping open.

I slide down beside her and slip an arm wordlessly around her shoulders. It hurts to see her like this but not in the knife-twist-to-the-gut way it did a couple of weeks ago. Maybe I've gotten used to a steady level of pain and only notice it when it spikes, like it did in the car. I feel spent. Empty, inanimate. If I could stay numb forever the way I am right now I might be able to get through this.

But numb might as well be dead, because what's the difference? Just a beating heart, and that, like other people's good intentions, isn't worth shit on its own.

Hold on tight, the voice murmurs to me, soft but sure of itself. *Don't let go. You'll wish you hadn't.*

"She's always with me," my mom says, a sob lodged deep in her throat. "It's as though she's just somewhere I can't find her, but not gone. I feel that if I only look hard enough . . ." She drops one hand into her lap and lets the tears flow uninterrupted. "But I don't know how . . . and those feelings." She shakes her head, spreads her other hand along her forehead and kneads her temples. "They're a lie. A *trick.*"

I know. And I don't know what to say anymore or how this will ever be better than it is right now. There's nothing to grab on to that will make it stop.

Moose doesn't need words. He jumps onto the couch with us and licks my mother's hand in her lap. She forces herself to chuckle through her tears. "That would mean more if it wasn't just about the salt," she says to him.

My mom bends over Moose, hugging him to her, her hair

dropping over him like a curtain, partially obscuring him from view. She plants a kiss on the top of his head, and predictably, he swings around and slurps at her face.

Normally that would make me groan but not tonight. Mom makes fresh tea for herself and we watch the rest of the black-and-white movie that neither of us saw the first half of, Moose's head resting in my mother's lap.

On Sunday my grandparents (Mom's parents) come over for lunch. A set of grandparents either drop by or have us over every couple of days and Lily calls constantly. She emails me too and then complains about my lousy response rate. Last time she wrote, "You're allowed to avoid other people over the age of thirty and roll your eyes about them but I'm supposed to be your cool aunt! Also, I fully intend to continue pestering you until I begin to hear from you on a more regular basis so you might as well start typing now." I sort of smiled at that one but I still haven't emailed her back.

I don't want to go to class any more than I did last week—I feel like I'm in a daze most of the time while I'm at school—but I show up and stay because if I don't my parents will get on my back about Eva again. That's not the only reason I stay; I need to avoid the rock-bottom place I hit on Saturday night. While I don't want to talk to people much lately, their presence is a safety net. I know there's no danger that I'll do anything bad to myself when anyone else is around.

Not that I would anyway but . . . I mean, I *won't.* I know I won't, but it can't hurt to have that extra safety mechanism.

So I go to school and stay there, even though everyone

around me and everything they say and do feels pointless and/or stupid, like it doesn't matter whether they say/do it or not. Whatever *whatever* WHATEVER whatever *whatever* WHATEVER. It's not their fault that they don't matter but that's what it feels like: Whatever *whatever* WHATEVER whatever *whatever* WHATEVER whatever whatever whatever *whatever.*

And then the single thing in my life that feels real continually bursting through the bullshit like an aftershock that will never end: the paramedics checking for a pulse I knew they wouldn't find.

But I keep going because this is what everyone would want, especially Skylar. For me to hold on.

On Monday I stick around after math class to ask Mrs. Reynolds if I can retake the test that I just finished messing up, and she says yes and do I have a date in mind when I think I'd be ready? I have no clue so I just blurt out "maybe sometime next week," and she says that's fine and that if I want we can set up a tutoring session beforehand to make sure I have a good grasp of the material.

Mr. Cirelli is just as helpful about the econ group assignment I've blown. He tells me he'll take the assignment out of consideration for my final grade and balance it with work I've done/will do over the semester.

On Wednesday I put in another shift at Zavi's, just me and Mr. Baldassarre because Wednesdays are usually slow. His wife Zavi drops by partway through the night and hugs me so hard that I practically feel my shoulders crunch. She looks at me with the kind of soppy sympathetic expression I've begun to hate while I pretend that I can't see what's in her eyes. Things are better when she leaves again and Mr. Baldassarre and I can go back to making small talk and throwing together subs. He loves old movies, like the one my mom and I watched the end of the other night where a guy tries to make his wife think she's going insane. *"Gaslight,"* Mr. Baldassarre notes when I start to tell him about it. "With Ingrid Bergman and Charles Boyer."

"Ingrid Bergman—she's the one in *Casablanca* with Humphrey Bogart, right?" I haven't seen it but it's one of those old movies you sort of know about by osmosis.

"That's her," he confirms. "One of the most beautiful, graceful ladies Hollywood's ever seen."

She did have a nice smile. But most of the time she just seemed really frazzled. "I guess I should watch that one too—*Casablanca.*"

Mr. Baldassarre cocks his head. "You mean you've never seen *Casablanca*? What have you been doing with your life, Breckon? This is essential stuff." He's about to say something else when Toby, one of the tattoo artists from next door, saunters in to order the same veggie sub on whole wheat that he always orders and starts telling us about a first-timer who passed out on him, then came to and threw up the pad Thai she'd eaten earlier, mostly on herself and the floor, but he got splashed too.

"Occupational hazard," Toby comments, absently rubbing the mermaid tattoo that runs from just underneath his elbow all the way down to his wrist.

His story about the Thai food reminds me of the time that someone spiked all the sodas at Lorenzo Casaccino's Halloween party and Jules puked up moo shu pork and rice on her white Abba pantsuit costume. She went to rinse out her blond wig in the bathroom and got sick again. I held her real hair back in my fist so it wouldn't get puked on too, while trying not to look at what she was spitting into the toilet.

"If I find out who fucked with the drinks they're getting kneed in the balls," Jules said between heaves.

Because Jules hardly drinks, her alcohol tolerance is negligible and she felt so dizzy that I had to call my dad to pick us up early (this was before I got my license and car). While we were waiting for him to show, this girl Cassandra from my French class told me she saw well-known asshole Jordan Carroll messing with the drinks earlier. I went over to Jordan and asked him straight-out if he did it. "So what if I did?" he asked with a moronic grin.

I told him in that case he owed Jules and a bunch of other people apologies for being a dickhead, and he stopped smiling. "Look who's talking," he said. "You're the biggest dickhead here. It's a party, dude. Drinks get spiked."

I drew my right arm back and punched him in the jaw. It's the only time I've ever thrown the first punch. Normally I'm not a violent person but 1) I'd had three beers and at least as many spiked 7-Ups and wasn't thinking clearly and 2) Jules isn't the type of person who'd want me to fight over her but I hated seeing her look so sick, and when someone crosses the line with her they're guaranteed trouble from me.

Jordan Carroll stumbled as my fist slammed into his jaw. Stupidly, probably because I was just as surprised that I'd punched him as he was, I waited for Jordan to regain his balance, and when he did he charged into me like a bull, hurtling me back across the room. I fell to the floor, instinctively throwing my hands around the back of my head and neck because my parents had drilled into me that I had to be careful since the accident.

Jordan lunged after me, ready to inflict more damage, but in three strides Big Red was on him, hauling Jordan back by his shirt and shoulders, throwing him against the wall and asking, red-faced, "Do we have a problem here?"

"He went for me first, dude," Jordan said, with his hands in the air like he was surrendering to the cops. "I just reacted the same as anyone would."

Later Big Red, Ty and Jules gave me shit for not considering the cost of potential injury to myself before I swung at Jordan. I expected a lecture from Jules but not from my friends. Imagine how pissed off they'd all be if they knew the things I've done lately.

"Since when do you go picking fights?" Jules asked once she was sober.

"He deserved it for screwing with the drinks," I said. "And you said you would kick whoever did its ass, remember?"

"Well, for one thing, I probably just would've dumped a glass of something wet over Jordan's head, and for another, I've never had a serious neck injury and been told to stop playing sports. Seriously, Breckon, if you ever do something like that again I'm going to kick *your* ass."

I got defensive, even though I knew she was right, and we started to argue about it. But the worry in Jules's face stopped me before we got far. She didn't want anything bad to happen to me. How could I fight her on that?

Anyway, the rest of the Zavi's shift goes by fast and then it's back home to swallow a pill and then over to school again the next day. My hand's finally healed and I've peeled off the bandage and left it naked for the first time since scalding it. When Jules notices, she sandwiches it tenderly between her own two hands. Lunch period's almost over and we're standing in front of her locker, talking about her shitty morning. She got a flat tire two blocks from her house when she was driving her mother's car to school this morning and her dad yelled at her for it when he showed up to put on the spare. Then Ms. Gallardo dumped attitude on her in bio worse than ever.

I know I said that everyone I know feels pointless, and sometimes, to a lesser degree, that includes Jules too. It's like she's standing on the other side of a canyon that neither of us can cross. I can see and hear her from my side but from where I'm standing most of the things that seem important to her aren't even on my radar. The conditions on opposite sides of the canyon are too different for us to understand each other like before, so incomparable that she can't even begin to comprehend how different they are, no matter how she tries.

And I know she's trying and that I'm not, which makes me feel bad because I still love her; we're just different now. Mostly different, but with my brand-new hand between hers I could almost believe we're still the same.

"Hey," I whisper, leaning my head down close to hers. "You want to go somewhere nice tonight and try to turn this day around? What about that Italian restaurant in Bourneville we went to with your grandparents on Christmas Eve?"

It's not cheap, but I just put in two shifts at Zavi's and can afford to take Jules. I really want to do something nice for her.

"We could make something ourselves at my house instead if you want," Jules suggests. "Tonight is date night."

In the past Mr. and Mrs. Pacquette's date night usually translated into an evening of extended sex for us (Jules went on the pill last August) but we haven't been together like that since before . . .

I think Jules must be thinking that same thing because then she adds, "We can just cook some pasta or something and then watch a movie or hang out." She shrugs like it's no biggie. "You know, whatever."

"Okay, sure. Meet you there about six?"

"Sounds good," Jules says.

When I get to Jules's place later, her parents are changing out of their work clothes, getting ready to head back out for their weekly date, and Jules and I drive over to the supermarket to buy ingredients for the ravioli recipe she wants to make. We're searching for pine nuts in the baking aisle and she's walking ahead of me, the pair of ultra-skinny red and black striped pants she's wearing hugging her ass in a way that makes my mind flicker. Then suddenly my old feelings for Jules are drifting to the surface, making me forget all about pine nuts.

I used to have dirty thoughts about her almost nonstop and feeling that way again, even just for a few seconds, is so good that I hang back on purpose, enjoying the view.

"Got 'em," Jules says, grabbing a bag of pine nuts from the shelf. "But we still need to pick up some goat cheese."

I don't care about goat cheese or ravioli. My mind's started to race with snapshots of what I want to do to Jules and what I want her to do to me. I want to lose myself in those thoughts like I used to, bury myself so deep inside them that I forget everything else, and I picture Jules blowing me right here in the aisle, my fingers in her hair as she looks me in the eye. It's one of those things we'd never really do, like with Rory and the streaking, but it gets me going so bad that I can't think what to say to her.

I didn't know it could still be like this.

After a moment or two I drive my fingers through my hair, lick my lips and say, "You know, we could buy something to heat up in the deli section—it would taste just as good and cut down on a lot of work."

Jules turns to look at me with a glint in her eyes like she's beginning to wonder if I'm having X-rated thoughts about her in the middle of the supermarket. "We could do that," she says. "It'd be faster."

"Faster is good," I confirm in a husky voice. The way I feel now, I can hardly stand to wait another minute to be alone with her. To be with Jules like I used to. Nothing held back.

Jules smiles at me, reaches out to lay her right hand along my waist, under my shirt. She feels for my belly button and dips her thumb inside. "Sometimes slow is better."

I grin back and tell her that I don't even think I'm hungry anymore.

"I am," she says, slipping her hand out of my shirt. "And you will be later." She locks her fingers around mine and pulls me along to the deli section where we buy premade ravioli and potato scallion bread.

Back at her deserted house, we don't even make it to her bedroom. We dump the ravioli on the kitchen counter and kiss wet and long, our bodies jamming together hard. I yank off her pants and then her yellow bikini underwear, breathing heavy. Jules pushes my jeans down and dips her hands into my boxers to smooth her palms over my ass. I grab hold of her black T-shirt, pull it up over her head and throw it to the floor. We're speeding faster than we've ever done before and it's still not fast enough. I struggle with her black bra and normally I'm good with the hooks but now my hands feel as clumsy as paws. Jules reaches back and unhooks herself and then she's tugging my boxers down, saying how much she wants me.

And it's going to happen right now because I feel exactly the same.

I lift her onto the counter and she slides to the edge, reaches for me and guides me inside her. The ravioli and foreplay can happen later but in the moment there's no such thing as slow. We grind together as though it's the most important thing we'll ever do, my hands clinging to her breasts, thumbs flicking over the nipples and Jules tugging at my hair and clamping her hands to my ass, trying to push me deeper still, bridging the canyon between us.

thirteen

ashlyn

At first I can't take my eyes off them. I watch the urgent way their bodies move together and can almost feel the heat roll off them in waves, warming the air around them. Seeing them like that, oblivious to everything but each other's skin, nearly makes me imagine that I can feel my body, a phantom body the way some people sense an absent limb. A body that longs for another body. I would've wanted to experience what Breckon and Jules are feeling at least once before I died. I envy them so much that it feels like a poison eating away at what's left of me and that's what makes me stop and offer them the privacy they already believe they have.

I retreat into the dark, muffled place where I'm barely aware of Breckon's existence. *This moment is for them,* I tell myself. *Don't peek.*

But they'll never know, another side of myself replies. *This is as close as I'll ever get to life now, witnessing someone else live out his.*

Equally forceful, the two opposing parts of me wage a mental battle that neither can win and neither can lose. I become the kind of person who would watch the scariest moments of a horror movie from behind her hands, periodically parting them to allow the shocking images inside her mind before slamming her hands together again.

I see Breckon and Jules move upstairs to her room after they finish in the kitchen. I see Jules hold him tight and I see Breckon kiss her lips like she's the most precious person in all the world. I hear the joy in their whispers, and a live demonstration of naked skin, shifting positions and relentless craving unfolds while I open and close my eyes, ashamed at myself for looking but unwilling to entirely stop feeding the compulsion.

If I knew Breckon and Jules in the living world and somehow spied them together like this they'd *know* because I wouldn't be able to look at them in the same way again.

I've never seen Breckon more in the moment and I'm happy for him, like when I watched him with his friends at Denny's, but what I feel is more complex than that. Watching Breckon and Jules floods me with a jealousy for what I'll never have. The discovery runs deeper still, triggering an old Ashlyn melancholy, restoring secrets I would rather have left forgotten.

Intimacy. Its boundless potential and its warped, manipulative opposite.

I remember.

I remember what happened after Farlain Lake—all the good and bad things up to and including the day I wanted to subtract from my memory: the surprise birthday party my father threw for my mother and how she was so happy she kissed him on the lips in front of all of us, her palm pressed into his chest; the second-grade teacher, Ms. Peltier, who I worshipped as though she were a deity; the rabbit Celeste and I convinced my mother to buy us—we called him Honeysuckle and he died after just three and a half weeks, leaving us to wonder whether we'd failed him somehow.

But the thing itself, that memory doesn't hurt anymore, not the Ashlyn who I am now. It's the Ashlyn I was then who I wish I could've protected. Was anyone there for me that day like I'm here for Breckon now? Did they watch and try to warn me?

I don't remember sensing anyone else with me. Just a feeling of rising dread, like a bad smell that makes you want to turn your back and walk away but he won't let you. He knows you sense it but he talks smart, smarter than you because you're so young and you suddenly know that although no one's hurt you before, that's now a real possibility. You didn't think about being safe or not safe because you just *were* and now that's over.

It began with Garrett and what seemed like a cold, but then he began having trouble breathing and my mother took him to the hospital, leaving Celeste and me with my dad. My father called around to try to find someone who could watch us for a while so he could be with my mother and Garrett at the hospital. Celeste had a friend named Daisy who lived a few blocks away and her mother said she would be happy to babysit us for a few hours while my father went to see about Garrett.

I'd been to Daisy's house once before. Her mother's name was Bernie and she wanted everyone to call her that instead of Mrs. Hobson. The Hobson house was full of clutter but it was clean clutter and the place smelled like soup mixed with room deodorizer just like it had the last time I'd been there. The

Hobsons had two budgies that lived in a cage in the kitchen and looked the colorful way I imagined all birds looked in fabulous places I'd never been, like South America or Australia. I liked the way the pretty budgies sang and the funny way they'd bob their heads sometimes but mostly it was boring at the Hobsons' house. Celeste had Daisy to play with but I didn't have any of my usual books or toys to keep me occupied, and Daisy's little brother Aidan was teething and kept wobbling over to me to try to bite my leg.

"Bite him back," Bernie said with a big smile. "Then he won't do it again."

But of course I couldn't bite a baby and I think I probably just looked at Bernie like she was a bit crazy, which made her laugh and ask if I wanted to watch *American Idol* with her.

Mr. Hobson was away on a business trip and so it was just the five of us—Bernie, Aidan the baby, me, Celeste and Daisy—and I kept thinking, while I watched people dance and sing, about how Garrett had wailed when a nurse had taken his blood at the doctor's office and that he would probably wail even more at the hospital. After the show my father called and told Bernie that Garrett had suffered an asthma attack but was doing better and that he would come to pick us up in about an hour while my mother stayed with Garrett.

Bernie went to tell Daisy and Celeste that we'd be leaving soon and Daisy said that they hadn't had a chance to play on the trampoline in the backyard yet. "Well, hurry up then," Bernie said. "You have an hour or so before Celeste's dad gets here."

It was a warm Saturday night in May and Bernie took Aidan out into the backyard and played in the sandbox with him while Daisy, Celeste and I jumped on the trampoline. Celeste and Daisy could flip all the way over because they'd had more practice than me, but I was getting better with every minute and I had it in my head—now that I knew Garrett was going to be okay and that I didn't have to worry about him anymore—that I wanted to do a backflip before I left. The thing was that I really had to pee too and maybe I'd be able to concentrate better once I had, so I told Daisy and Celeste that I was going to the bathroom.

I walked through the sliding glass door into the kitchen and then down the hall to the bathroom. It was quiet in the house and the funny smell of it was in my nostrils, reminding me that I was in a strange place, but I went to the bathroom and washed my hands afterwards, careful not to leave the towel crumpled up like my mom sometimes complained I did at home. Back out in the hallway, with my hands clean and bladder empty, a teenage boy I'd never seen before eyed me up. He was wearing a jean jacket and gray track pants and had a pimple on his chin but he wasn't ugly; he just looked ordinary.

"So who are you?" he asked.

"Ashlyn," I said. "Bernie's babysitting us. My brother went to the hospital." I didn't know that Aidan and Daisy had an older brother, but he was white like them, had dirty-blond hair like Daisy and he was in their house, I figured they must have been related.

"What's wrong with him?" the boy who still hadn't given me his name asked.

"He had a cold and then he couldn't breathe," I said because I couldn't remember precisely what Bernie had repeated to me after getting off the phone with my father. "But he's getting better."

The boy nodded. "I'm sure he'll be fine. That's what they do there—fix people." He was standing in the middle of the hallway, not moving, and I didn't move either because there wasn't much room to get by him and anyway, he was still talking. "Hey, is Celeste your sister?"

I nodded. "She's with Daisy on the trampoline."

The boy flicked his messy blond hair off his face and smiled. "You look like her, but prettier."

Celeste was prettier, I knew that and didn't like hearing him say otherwise.

"I'm serious," the guy said. "And I bet you're more fun too. She seems kind of stuck-up."

I didn't know what to say to that. I just wanted him to move so I could go back to the trampoline.

"And I mean, a trampoline, that's such kid stuff," he continued. "I'm surprised she would bother with that." He leaned his arm up against the wall, still blocking the hallway. "Do you think you're too old for the trampoline?" He stared at the front of my pink hoodie, where there was nothing to see, and then my jeans.

"No." I tried to speak loudly but my voice wouldn't project and fell flat. "I'm just a kid. I'm only *eight.*" I said my age clearer than anything else so he wouldn't miss it.

"Some kids are old for their age." He smiled again. "I was always old for my age."

"How old are you?" I asked.

"Fifteen," he said, his smile growing.

"Fifteen is *old,*" I told him, because if he was old for his age and I was only eight, nothing creepy could be happening like I sensed, in the pit of my stomach, that it might be.

"Yeah? So I seem old to you?" He'd stopped smiling and stepped closer. "It's funny because you don't seem that young to me—like, you seem like you would *know* things, if you know what I mean."

I didn't know. But I knew it wasn't good. I shook my head and repeated myself. "I'm only *eight.*"

"You're just fine the way you are," he said, so near to me now that I thought to run. But just as the thought popped into my head it must've popped into his because he wrapped one of his hands around my arm and squeezed, sort of like he was only kidding. "See, look at these muscles. I bet you're really strong for eight. You want to see mine?"

I shook my head again. He was still holding my arm. I thought of Callum and how he would never hold my arm like that. No one had ever held my arm like that. So tight, like he wasn't being careful not to hurt me.

"No?" he said. "How come?"

My voice dried up. His eyes glistened as he looked down at me.

"You're so cute," he continued. "Do you know that? Do guys tell you that?"

His other hand reached down to hold me in place too, his right hand clamped to my left arm and his left hand locked around my right. Nobody's supposed to touch you if you don't want them to. Nobody. He wasn't touching me in a secret place but he still shouldn't touch me, I knew that.

"Leave me alone," I said hoarsely.

"So you think you're too good for me or something?" he said, sarcasm spreading across his face. "Are you a snob like your sister?"

He bent his head and shoulders down so his face was level with mine. "I'm not going to hurt you—I just want a kiss. Look." He pressed his lips quickly to mine like it was nothing. "See? It doesn't hurt. But hey . . ." His voice and face softened. "Just open your mouth for a second and it'll be better, like when older people do it."

My heart was thumping fast and I'd lost my voice again.

"C'mon, c'mon," he whispered, growing impatient. He put his thumb up to my bottom lip and eased it open. I suppose I could've tried to shout then—or at any point so far—but I was so stunned that the things you were supposed to do when someone tried to touch you leaked out of my head.

So I did what he asked, opening my mouth just a little wider, and he kissed me again but not like the first time. His tongue dove into my mouth, pushing at my own tongue, darting wildly around between my teeth like he was looking for something and was in a rush to find it. I didn't kiss him back, but at first I didn't stop him either. I was frozen inside and out. Then his hand reached swiftly up inside my pink hoodie and felt my chest. One hand. That meant he was only holding me with one hand too and I thawed instantly, wrenching myself away from him with every bit of strength I had. Free, I ran.

But he was fifteen and his legs were longer. He caught up to me outside the kitchen, grabbing me around the waist and pulling me back towards him. "It was just a kiss," he said breathlessly. "It wasn't anything bad. You don't have to tell anyone."

I was quiet, my breath paused, the oxygen stagnant in my lungs. I'd seen my father hug my mother like this, his arms wrapped around her from behind. That's the way we were standing then, his left hand snapping on to his right, keeping me enclosed between them.

"I could've done anything to you," he told me. "And I didn't. I could've put my hand over your mouth so you couldn't scream, but I didn't. Your sister would've screamed. You know what that means?" He wasn't really asking and he kept going, answering the question for himself. "You wanted me to kiss you. You're the kind of girl who knows things early."

A lump was working its way up my throat because of the things he was saying about me. The words felt as bad and wrong as the kiss and they made me think of Callum. Had I had a crush on him like my sister said that night at the cottage? Was I wrong to have wanted to be friends with him so badly? Was I the kind of girl who knew *things*?

I screamed long and loud. Mostly because I was scared but in part because I couldn't bear the awfulness of what he was saying. He released me as soon as I opened my mouth and in my mind that made him more right: I could've stopped him earlier, but hadn't.

I stumbled into the kitchen. Celeste reached me first, Daisy four steps behind her and then Bernie holding Aidan. "What happened?" Celeste asked, her eyes filled with fear. "Are you okay?"

I hadn't turned around yet; I didn't want to see him.

"Her brother," I said, pointing at Daisy. I was sobbing as I spoke. "He *grabbed* me."

Daisy looked confused. "Aidan was outside with us."

"No, no, not him." I'm sure the fact that I was crying made it harder to understand me, but Bernie, dazed, handed Aidan to Daisy and rushed off down the hallway. I heard a door bang open as though she was searching for the boy.

While she was gone, Celeste, who hadn't grasped what I meant although Bernie clearly had, repeated, "Are you okay? What do you mean someone grabbed you?"

Soon Bernie returned, but without the boy. Her face was very pale and long and she looked at Daisy and Celeste and said, "I want you two to sit right here with Aidan for me while I talk to Ashlyn in the living room."

"Ashlyn, honey," she said, "come with me."

I don't know why she'd picked up on what I meant right away—maybe it was the stricken look on my face. We sat in the living room together and she asked me, in a voice laced with worry, to explain exactly what had happened.

I told her precisely what I remembered and then I told my parents and a policewoman who came to our house. The boy was Bernie's nephew Dylan. His mother had died two years earlier and he'd been having run-ins with his father and was staying with his aunt and uncle temporarily. He'd fled when I screamed but didn't have anywhere else to stay and had called Bernie early the next morning. During the course of the investigation the police found out that Dylan had grabbed another friend of Daisy's when she'd slept over two weeks earlier, squeezing her butt and swiping one hand across her chest as he'd passed her in the hallway. She'd kept quiet about it at first but I was relieved when I found out I wasn't the only one.

My father took what happened to me the hardest. For months I felt as though he was trying to chase the sadness from his eyes when he looked at me. I think that look—and what Dylan said about me being a girl who knew things—were worse than the kiss and Dylan touching me. My parents sent me to a child therapist, sort of like Eva (who made sure that I understood that Dylan kissing me had nothing to do with anything being wrong with me and everything to do with him and his own problems) and according to my mom, Dylan got sent for treatment too and had to go live with his grandmother two hours away.

For a long time I felt anxious being around most older boys or men and would clam up around them and stand with my arms crossed in front of me, thinking about how I'd get away if I had to. The feeling faded bit by bit but, as far as I can see into my past, left me with a sharpened awareness of possible danger.

Unfortunately, when I saw Callum again at the cottage, only two and a half months after Dylan had stopped me in the hall, the bad feelings were still fresh. I didn't play with him anymore unless we were all playing together; I tagged along with Celeste and Ellie or hovered around my parents. At first Callum didn't understand and then I think he assumed I'd just stopped liking him and didn't bother asking me to play cards or go swimming with him because he'd figured out I'd only make an excuse and say no.

It's funny how one thing—seeing Breckon and Jules together—has unlocked so much inside me. There are still years of my life that I can't remember but I feel the memories surfacing more quickly now, the details of my daily life and the lives of those around me slotting neatly back into place.

I remember hoping, when I began to feel more like my old self during the following winter, that I could make my aloofness up to Callum the next time we were at Farlain Lake. I thought it would take a lot of effort on my part but that it was within the realm of possibility. But the next time didn't come. My dad's friend ran into money trouble and sold the cottage, making that third year at the lake our last. By the time I saw my cousin again we seemed to have evolved into two whole new people who had never sat by a lake together playing cards in the dark.

I'm not mad or afraid of Dylan anymore—from here nothing scares me—but it still bothers me that my younger self didn't get the summer she could've had when she was eight because of him. And I wonder, even now from the afterlife where maybe it shouldn't matter because what's past is past, whether Callum thought about the times we had at our second year at the lake when he heard the news about me.

I hope he did.

I am what people mean when they say "ashes to ashes, dust to dust" and "I'm so very sorry for your loss," and I can't, for one second, stop longing for my body, my life, Mom, Dad, Celeste, Garrett, my grandparents, the taste of orange ice cream on the tip of my tongue and every single person I have ever loved.

fourteen
breckon

Afterwards Jules heats up the pasta and we fill the tub and sit in the bath forking ravioli into our mouths and tearing off pieces of bread. Jules likes the water so steamy hot that I usually end up with sweat on my forehead when we take a bath together. "It's a bath," she always says when I complain. "It's supposed to be hot."

My line: "Not so hot that you need to take a cold shower after it."

Jules (rolling her eyes but smiling): "The way you like it I'm surprised you don't catch a chill. I'd need a *sweater* in water that cold."

Tonight we do our usual routine about the bath temperature and Jules compromises and adds enough cold water to stop me from overheating. While we eat and soak Jules talks about the musical theater program in Toronto she's thinking of doing this summer. When I tell her it sounds like a good idea she asks, "What about you and Boleyn's? I don't hear you mention it anymore."

We used to hang out there every few weeks and I thought I'd be spending lots of time there this summer, both playing music and listening. I never kidded myself that I was a rock star in the making but for a while strumming a guitar made me feel more in touch with something I can't explain—life, the universe, whatever you want to call it.

That's done with and not something I want to talk about but because this is Jules I stroke her leg and say, "I can't get into playing anymore."

"It'll come back to you." Her hands skim the water, creating slow-motion waves around us. Then she lays her wet head against my chest and we're both quiet, Jules closing her eyes as though we could stay in the moment for hours.

We feel as close as two people can be and the pain that's always with me hasn't stopped but it's not in control of me. I wish I didn't have to go back to the real world but we can't be in the bath together when her folks get home. Soon enough we're drying ourselves off, putting ourselves back together and, by the time Jules's parents return at 9:15, we're sitting in front of the TV conscientiously doing econ homework together.

Mr. and Mrs. Pacquette look happy, like they had a nice night out, and Jules is all smiles because of the earlier mattress gymnastics. I think even I look pretty relaxed. I feel better than I have in weeks—not great but better, stronger—and when I get home I decide this is the night to quit the sleeping pills cold turkey.

It's for the best. I only have a couple left and I don't want to ask Jules for more or break into my parents' supply and risk them finding out. Enduring a second appointment with Eva

Kannan and letting her rummage around in my head so she'll write me my own prescription is also out.

So no pills. I need to stop.

At first I toss and turn, working up a full-body sweat and getting tangled up in the sheets. When I do drift off, I wake up only an hour later to the eerie sensation that someone's watching me. If I told my grandmother (Mom's mom) that, she'd insist it was Skylar watching over me. She says she feels Skylar's presence all the time, especially in our house, but in hers too. My grandfather fixes a detached expression onto his face when she talks like that because he doesn't believe in ghosts but doesn't want to argue with her. Sometimes my grandmother argues with him anyway, calling him closed-minded because of that expression.

You imagine things when you're overtired. Everybody does. There's nobody watching me. I don't even let myself turn on the lights to double-check because there's no reason to.

But the feeling makes it hard to get back to sleep. *Ashes to ashes,* I think in that strange murmur I heard in my head on Saturday night. *Dust to dust.* Tonight the voice doesn't sound especially comforting and I kick off the covers and think about the two remaining pills tucked into an envelope in my bedside table.

I'm staring at the table in the dark, telling myself to stay strong, when the other voice interrupts me. I can't even hear it exactly; I *feel* it shift into a positive tone.

It feels like calm ocean waves, a field of willow trees swaying in the wind or a crescent moon on a cloudless night.

Absolute Zen. A billion blades of grass growing towards the sun. Harmony.

I must still be half-asleep. That's the obvious explanation (either that or someone laced the supermarket ravioli with magic mushrooms) and I don't fight it. *Sleep,* the voice advises.

Sleep on the calm waves.

Sleep in the shade of the willow trees.

Sleep under a crescent moon.

Sleep, sleep, sleep.

I can't say where the words themselves end and the feeling surrounding them begins. Maybe the voice never actually says *sleep* but somehow I know that's what it means. The weirdest things happen when you loosen your grip on the waking world. You accept things that would make you do a double take if you were wide awake.

My grandmother's wrong about Skylar's presence, but the voice, whoever it belongs to, feels right. I sprawl out on my chest, bury my head in the pillow and sleep.

On Friday my ex's little sister, Leila, walks nervously over to me in the cafeteria line, dragging a reluctant-looking friend along with her. "Hi, Breckon," she begins. "I didn't know if you were still . . ." She holds up her hand to reveal a key chain attached to the world's smallest pair of tighty whities.

"It's kind of stupid," she continues, "but everybody knows how you collect key chains and Nadine says you like the weirdest ones the most." Leila squeezes the pair of miniature underwear between her fingers and her friend and I both smirk as the tighty whities fart loudly.

"Anyway, we were in Niagara Falls on the weekend and saw them at this novelty store so . . ." She hands me the farting key chain and for a second I just stare at it. People I barely knew used to come up to me with stuff like this nonstop but not since Skylar.

"Thanks," I tell her. "I'm glad it doesn't make a noxious smell too."

"Yeah." She wrinkles her nose. "Maybe they're saving that for version two."

I watch Leila stride off with her friend, both of them holding their shoulders a little higher than they were a minute ago, and wish that people could just be real with me. Yeah, the key chain's lame but so is almost everything else. Sometimes I wonder if everybody can see through my act and know that I don't care about things the way I used to. I can't decide which is worse, the people who tiptoe around me because they think I'm about to splinter into pieces or the ones who act like nothing's changed as though I actually care what happened in last night's soccer game or whose parents are away for the weekend and therefore might throw a party.

After school it's quiet at home the way it always is now. Just me and Moose wandering through the halls, waiting for time to rewind and make life livable again. When it comes down to it I'm not any smarter than he is. We're both waiting for the same thing.

I hang the key chain Leila gave me onto the end of the bottom rod dedicated to the collection in my bedroom, panic gripping my ribs because for thirty seconds I can't remember Skylar's smile. *Think.* One of her bottom teeth was about to fall out. She kept playing with it, pushing at it with her tongue. That detail doesn't help me. The more I try to picture her, the fuzzier my mental picture gets until I have to stalk into my parents' room and pick up a photograph taken of us together late last summer. Skylar's in her baseball uniform, holding her mitt and smiling big for the camera. All her teeth are in place because that was before she started losing them. My right hand's on Skylar's left shoulder and I'm wearing sunglasses, which I remember my mom asking me to take off for the photo. Obviously I didn't listen.

I stare at the picture for so long that my head and ears begin to ache from the pressure building up inside them. How'd I ever forget—even for a second? I set the frame back on my parents' dresser and force myself to leave the room and then the house. I could unravel down to the bone in a microsecond if I let myself but I don't. I sit outside on the front stoop where it's safer because people can see me—I can't do things I shouldn't.

Sitting still's impossible though. I need to keep moving. I shoot back up and head for the garage. Our lawn looks like shit. Some of the flowers my mom planted last year are coming up in the flower bed in front of the porch but I can't remember the last time someone mowed the lawn.

I do it. Our front yard and then the back. Our neighbors are an old couple who never do much with their lawn either and I start in on their front yard. About five minutes in Mr. Pritchard comes outside in a black Windbreaker, smiles at me and waves me over. I cut the motor and say, "I was doing ours and thought

I might as well do yours at the same time. Want me to fix up the back too?"

Mr. Pritchard smiles more, like I'm being generous or something, and says that if I have the time that would be wonderful. I go around to the back gate before he can start talking about Skylar and then I sink the same die-hard effort into mowing the Pritchards' lawn that other people put into taking their SATs. I'm storing the mower back into the garage when my dad pulls into the driveway at five-thirty. An extra wrinkle's been etched between his eyes since losing Skylar and I see that line quiver when he gets out of the car and thanks me for taking care of the lawn.

"It looks great," he adds, but I know he doesn't care about the grass any more than I do.

It's on the tip of my tongue to tell him about forgetting Skylar's smile. Then Moose barks from inside the front door and changes my mind. My parents have been through enough without me bringing up depressing things about Skylar.

Mr. Pritchard, who's noticed that I've finished his lawn, waves at the two of us from his porch. My father waves back. I watch my dad jab his key into the door, step inside and let Moose jump up against his legs. With the smell of fresh-cut grass deep in my nostrils and a dull ache still stretching along my forehead, I follow him into the house.

Saturday I put in another shift at Zavi's. Georgia and I are scheduled to work until closing, and because Mr. Baldassarre's her uncle she's the one who is trusted with a pair of spare keys. The bad thing about working with Georgia solo (Mr. Baldassarre and his wife have gone to the opera) is that she tries to suck you into all her personal drama—the ins and outs of her codependent friendships and stupid details about some guy named Austin who keeps her on the back burner while he messes around with other girls.

Georgia's nice and all but I just don't give a shit that Austin called her up last night and said, "You're so perfect for me. It's, like, I just need the time to realize that in my heart."

In my heart. You'd think that phrase would set off an asshole alarm in your head, but nope, Georgia thinks if she hangs on long enough this guy will have a revelation, fall to his knees and reward her with undying love.

Bullshit. And I've tried to tell Georgia that before but she doesn't want to know. She's clinging to obliviousness like it's a light in the wilderness.

I was out of patience with her weeks ago and now I'm running on fumes. I try to change the subject, and when the new one won't take I trot out the first excuse that springs into my head. "Hey, I need to make a coffee run. You think you can hold down the fort here for a couple minutes?"

"Pick me up a latte?" Georgia asks.

"No problem."

There's a pretty grungy coffee shop along the next row of stores but I don't go there, nobody goes there. The only way they're making anything from it is if the business is a front for a money-laundering scheme. I follow the sidewalk down to the grocery store, taking my time about it, and buy a latte and an Americano at the coffee stand beside the fruit and vegetable department. I'm holding two paper cups of scalding-hot coffee in my hand when I turn and narrowly miss colliding with Skylar's best friend, Kevin Solomon, and his mother.

"Breckon!" Mrs. Solomon exclaims, her fingers reaching for my shoulder.

"Oh, hey," I say. "How are you?" I'm talking to her but I can't stop looking at Kevin. He used to be over at our house a couple of times a week. Skylar and Kevin were two of the three kids on her coed baseball team last year who weren't a disaster. They both got the exact same remote control car for Christmas and had to stick *S* and *K* stickers on the hoods so they could tell them apart. I must've nearly tripped over those cars half a dozen times when they were racing them around the house.

It's bizarre that I'll never see Kevin anymore unless I'm bumping into him in the supermarket. Next to my family he probably knows Skylar better than anyone else does.

"I'm fine," Mrs. Solomon says, her voice dropping an octave. "I've been meaning to call your mother and drop in. Would you mind telling her I'll give her a call?"

"I'll tell her. She'd like that."

Mr. and Mrs. Solomon were both at the funeral but not Kevin. Looking at him's not the same as seeing Skylar's ghost but it's about as close as you can get—like peering into the eyes of a small part of her that's still here. He just keeps staring up at me with his mouth open. I have no idea what to say to him.

Then Mrs. Solomon surprises me by springing forward to clutch my shoulder again. She bows her head, strands of brown hair streaming down over her face as she blinks back tears. "God. *I'm sorry.*"

"It's okay," I mumble. I'm not sure whether she's saying she's sorry about Skylar or apologizing for getting choked up.

Mrs. Solomon nods somberly and puts a braver face on. Kevin looks from me to her and jiggles one of his loose upper teeth the way I know a million kids do every day but it only reminds me of one.

"I have to get back to work," I tell her, holding up the coffees as evidence that someone's waiting for me.

"Say goodbye to Breckon," Mrs. Solomon instructs Kevin.

"Bye," he says dutifully.

"Bye, Kevin," I say.

I go back to Zavi's, drink my coffee and do my job, but memories of Kevin and Skylar edge their way into my head during spare moments, making me wonder if I'll have to take a pill tonight to get any sleep.

Just before nine-thirty Ty and Rory stop by and want me to go to the lake with them after work. I text Jules and ask if she wants to meet up with us there later. All anyone does by the lake at night is hang out on the promenade (some of them drinking or acting up) until the cops show up and tell everyone they're being too loud (even the people who aren't) and should leave the area. Because it's boring and kind of a waste of time none of us go there much. It's a Plan B place and tonight there's no Plan A.

Georgia and I close Zavi's up for the night around ten. Then I sit around with Ty, Rory, Jules, Cameron and Renee at the lake until four assholes on skateboards whiz by breaking bottles on the concrete and the cops make everyone disappear.

In the end I go home to bed and lie there, restless and hot, fighting the instinct to take a sleeping pill. I must win because when I open my eyes it's morning. The sun's storming into my room in the form of a white light that's as blinding as the night is dark. It takes a few seconds for my eyes to focus, and when they do I see Skylar sitting on my bed, cross-legged, with Moose in her lap and her bike helmet on her head.

"Can you take me out on my bike?" she asks as soon as she notices that my eyes are open.

I can't breathe. I'm like a fish flapping around on the floor of a boat, dying. And she's here. Staring right at me and waiting for me to say something.

"This isn't real," I croak.

"What's not real?" she chirps. "Can you *pleeease* get out of bed so I can go out on my bike?"

I sit up and stare at Skylar's hands, then her missing bottom tooth. I point at it and say, accusingly, "Your tooth." It was loose the last time I saw it, not gone.

"I pulled it out." Skylar slips her pinky finger into the space. "I'll put it under my pillow tonight."

"So where is it now?" I can't believe we're having this conversation. I can't believe she's here and God, why is it so bright? "This can't be happening."

"Stop saying that," Skylar lectures. Moose, snuggled in her lap, has his eyes closed, one side of his face pressed against Skylar's pant leg, and I know if there was a scientific way to measure happiness he'd score at the top of the list in this very moment. "Want to see the tooth?" she asks excitedly. "I can get it." She reaches down to move Moose but I get up too. I'm not letting her out of my sight for a second.

I follow Skylar into her room and she plucks the tooth from her dresser and hands it to me. It looks and feels real, just like a seven-year-old's baby tooth, and I can't figure out what's happening. She was gone, wasn't she? My brain's in a fog, cocooned. I can't remember. I just know I need to stick with her.

"Wow," I say as I study the tooth. "That's weird."

Skylar shrugs like I'm acting too impressed. "It's just a tooth."

I look at it in my palm. Skylar's tooth is a little bloody at the bottom where it used to be attached to her jaw. I hand it back to her and she dumps it back onto her dresser.

"So let's go then," I say. I haven't had a bike since mine got busted up in the accident. When I want to take one out, which isn't often now since I mostly drive, I use my dad's.

I don't know what my parents are going to do when Skylar's old enough to go for a ride without them. There are going to be a lot of years between that day and the one when she'll be old enough to get a driver's license. My folks don't even like her cycling now but at least they can keep an eye on her.

I borrow Dad's helmet along with his bike and let Skylar ride ahead so I can keep an eye on her. She comes to a full stop at stop signs and is careful about waiting for cars to pass but I still feel antsy watching her. We ride up the sidewalk until we reach the nearest park—the place she found the frog that day. It's so insanely bright outside that the sun brings tears to my eyes. I can't remember the last time it was this dazzling, and that should probably worry me (what's happened to my memory?) but it doesn't really—my only worry is watching Skylar.

She drops her bike in the sand that cushions the playground area, bending to let the sand sift through her fingers before she runs for the monkey bars. I drop my dad's bike too and say, "The sun's burning my eyes. Do yours hurt? Maybe we should go back and get shades."

"We can't go back yet," Skylar says with absolute certainty. She's funny that way. She'll come out with random stuff with such assurance that you have to wonder if she has some secret source.

"Just for a second—to get the glasses."

Skylar shakes her head, climbs up the ladder and swings onto the first bar. "It's not that bright," she says. "Come on the monkey bars with me."

I'm too tall, my feet drag on the ground. I have to bend my knees and while I'm doing that, from four bars behind her, I realize that I never changed out of my green plaid pajama bottoms. One more thing that I forgot, I guess. There seem to be so many of them now.

I trail Skylar over towards the opposite end of the monkey bars, my hands shifting my weight between the yellow bars, and she pulls her feet and legs up over the final bar, hauling herself skyward so that she can sit on top of them. "Up here," she beckons. She slides along the top of the monkey bars to make room for me.

"Be careful," I instruct, anxious again.

"I won't fall," she promises. Then she knocks one of her hands against her helmet. "And I'm wearing this anyway."

"You could still break your leg," I point out, joining her on top of the bars.

"No, I can't." She laughs at me but it sounds nice, like a tickle.

"So, what, you're like super girl or something?" I kid.

"Super Skylar!" she exclaims. In a flash she's standing, her left foot balanced on one of the yellow bars and her right rooted to the top of the frame.

"Skylar, don't!" I shout, really losing it now. My heart knocks against my ribs as I reach for her. She sits down again—safe, whole—before I can touch her.

"I'm okay," she says calmly. "Don't worry."

"But don't do that again! If anything happened to you—"

"Then it wouldn't be your fault," Skylar says. "It would be just one of those things."

That last part doesn't sound like something Skylar would say and my heart beats faster. I shade my brow with my hand as I gaze at my sister. Something's wrong here and I can't pinpoint what it is.

"But nothing's going to happen," she assures me, beaming a generous smile in my direction. "Don't worry, Breckon. We can get down if you want. We can go on the swings."

The sweat's pouring off me in buckets. I'm baking in the sun like a sweet potato but Skylar looks cool as a cucumber. I don't understand it.

"That's a good idea," I tell her. "Let's swing."

We leave the monkey bars behind and settle ourselves on the swings. We pump our legs through the air, send ourselves soaring towards the blazing sun. "I wish we could do this forever without our legs getting tired," Skylar says.

Me too. I feel like a kid again, nearly as young as she is.

"Higher!" Skylar calls to me. "We can go higher."

Higher, higher. Blue, orange and white swirl by us. I could swear that we're flying free, that we don't even need the swings.

"We don't need them," Skylar agrees in a tone that's pure confidence. "We never did."

I don't know what she means but that's all right, as long as we can keep flying. "Super Skylar!" I holler, making her grin and show off her missing tooth.

And then, without a moment's warning, that perfect morning is torn away from me, the sights and sounds disintegrating into dust and silence. I don't even have the chance to say goodbye. I open my eyes to search for her but she's long gone, weeks gone. Broken. Dead. Buried.

And I can't stand losing her a second time. It's too much to take. It slices me down the middle and spills my insides out. I jerk my head away from the bed and lean over the floor, just in time. The tears scorch my eyes. I gag on air. Shiver like something left for dead in the woods.

This is how life is now. How it will always be.

She's never coming home.

fifteen

ashlyn

I see Breckon hurt himself. He carves into his thigh with a pocketknife he pulled from a grooming kit in his bedside table. There've been times, over the past week or so, that I could've sworn he's heard me, but now my screams come to nothing.

He doesn't stop until he sees blood.

Once he's still I shriek more, admonishing him for what he's done, begging him not to do it again and to call Eva and let her help. Then I rail at whoever or whatever has abandoned me here alone with Breckon.

I think of my time amid the stars. I long for them. I stretch my mind out to reach for them. Back across the universe to the place where my new life began. *Take me back,* I plead with them. *I will float with you forever and never ask another question if you only allow me that peace.*

The stars' silence is deafening. I am alone in the universe. Mute and forgotten.

That's not true. I know my family remembers and that

they'll miss me for as long as they live. But they're as powerless as I am.

"What are we going to do, Breckon?" I ask.

He presses a facecloth to his thigh to soak up the blood and ignores me. I am useless to him and he's a burden to me. We're chained together, both begging, in our own ways, to be freed.

"I'm not giving up on you," I say stubbornly. It feels like a cheesy lie but I don't know what else to say. When I watched Breckon with Jules the other night I was hopeful that he'd turned a corner. Running into that woman and her son, Kevin, in the supermarket bothered him, I could tell, but he seemed all right afterwards. Whatever affected him so deeply must've happened in his sleep.

I revert to my knowing voice and repeat things I've said many times before, that Skylar wants him to be happy and that he still has so much to live for. He lies on top of his bedspread, his hand pressed down on his thigh, applying pressure, and gives no indication that he can sense me.

In the afternoon his folks convince him to go over to his grandparents' house with them. While helping his grandfather bag fallen branches in the backyard he uncovers a mauled bird. "Must be the cat next door that done it," his grandfather remarks. "I see that thing scooting around here all the time."

His grandfather lights himself a cigarette and then offers one to Breckon like I've seen him do once before. "How're things at school?" he asks his grandson. "And how's that girlfriend of yours with the dark hair?"

Breckon takes the offered cigarette and says, "Jules. She's fine. School's all right, I guess. Same as always."

Breckon's grandfather leans forward to light Breckon's cigarette and nods like this is to be expected. "I was never much for school myself but it's good to be busy."

"So I hear." Breckon frowns.

Breckon's grandfather adjusts his newsboy cap, pulling it closer to his eyes. "It's the truth. Once you stop *doing* you begin to wind down like an old clock."

Later, back at Breckon's house, I watch him flip through his homework like he's prepared to give his grandfather's theory some credence. Not ten minutes later he's hurling his math textbook against the wall. It lands, pages splayed, on top of a lone navy sock that has occupied the same position on Breckon's carpet for several days, and keeps it company for the remainder of the night. Meanwhile Breckon watches multiple episodes of *Dexter* on his laptop, writes three lines to Lily in response to a new email from her that appears in his inbox and stands in Skylar's doorway (while his parents are downstairs and won't notice), staring at the remnants of her life.

At bedtime he downs a sleeping pill, drops quickly off to sleep and then heads out to school the next morning with all his homework unfinished. First stop after homeroom is economics and, although I know he slept through the night, Breckon sits at his desk propping his head up with his palm and yawning repeatedly. I'm as bored as he is. I spend most of his time at school staring at the guys and girls in his classes, trying to figure out what their stories are. The boy with the long blond hair looks like a mindless surfer or skateboarder but next to Mr. Cirelli he's the most knowledgeable person in the class. A drop-dead gorgeous South Asian girl named Renuka is the lead singer/bassist in a secret garage band that she and her friends have dubbed Secret Garage Band Girls, and a tall white boy with deep-set brown eyes regularly spends half the class staring at her in fascination, although they never speak. These things I know just from observing and listening.

One girl named Violet can't make it through the period without checking her cell phone at least once and today Mr. Cirelli catches her at it and says, "We've been through this before, Violet. You know your cell phone is off-limits during class."

Violet bites the inside of her cheek, nodding. "Sorry."

"Bring it here." Mr. Cirelli motions with his hand. "You can come back and reclaim it at the end of the day."

"I've turned it off," Violet says with a pleading look.

"Well, that's a start but I want it here."

Violet slinks up to the front of the class and hands Mr. Cirelli her cell.

"Thank you." He grips her phone. "Whatever you were texting can wait. It's not more important than this class."

Breckon snickers, snapping my gaze back to him. He's been holding his cheek up with his left hand for so long that I have to wonder if it's fallen asleep.

"You have some commentary you want to add, Breckon?" Mr. Cirelli asks in an even tone.

Breckon shakes his head without even bothering to lift his head from his palm, and Mr. Cirelli, thinking the matter is done with, opens the top drawer of his cheap-looking beech melamine desk and drops Violet's cell phone inside.

"Actually, yeah," Breckon says suddenly. "I just think it's funny that you believe this class is more important than whatever she's texting. I mean, you have no idea what she's texting, do you? So it's not like you can truthfully judge how important it is." Breckon has shifted his hand away from his cheek so that both arms rest on top of his desk.

A smile flits across Violet's lips but Breckon doesn't notice. A lone anonymous student near the back of the room claps.

Mr. Cirelli's eyes narrow as he concentrates on Breckon. "I'm sure Violet appreciates your concern but this doesn't strike me as an emergency."

"I don't think learning about circular flow in a market economy is exactly crucial for a lot of people here either," Breckon says leadenly. He slips his fingers around his ballpoint pen and idly taps the desk with it. "But maybe you're so wrapped up in it that you don't notice the effect this class has on the rest of us."

Mr. Cirelli's bottom lip twitches. He hesitates briefly before saying, "Breckon, do you want to step outside with me for a moment, please?"

Breckon shrugs but Mr. Cirelli's pointing firmly out towards the hall.

He waits for Breckon to rise from his desk and follows his argumentative student into the hall. They step away from the door and Mr. Cirelli, his face pinched and his head tilting to one side, says, "I know this is a very difficult time for you and I can understand that it's not easy to focus, but what was happening in there wasn't productive."

Breckon's head slopes up towards the ceiling. He swings his hands behind his back, locking them together as he stares silently at Mr. Cirelli.

"Are you okay to go back in?" Mr. Cirelli continues. "Or do you want to take a couple of minutes?"

Breckon shakes his head, his eyes hardening. "I don't need to take a couple of minutes and I don't want to go back in. It's just going to be more of the same bullshit theory—mixed economy, global economy, market economy. Just theory bullshit with nothing real attached to it." He shrugs again—this time like the conversation is an act of futility. "We'd get more out of running our own lemonade stands than we do from this joke of a class."

Mr. Cirelli clicks his back teeth together but otherwise keeps his cool. He steps closer to Breckon and lowers his voice. "You're upset. Why don't you drop in to the guidance office and have a chat with Ms. Harris. I can walk you down."

"No thanks," Breckon retorts. "I have a better idea." He reels past Mr. Cirelli, whips open the door to his economics class and lurches down an aisle without meeting anyone's eyes. He stops at his desk and sweeps his notebook and textbooks into his arms.

"Breckon?" Jules ventures, reaching out to touch his right arm.

Mr. Cirelli, who has followed Breckon back into the room, watches him without making any move to stop him from leaving.

Breckon swings away from Jules and retraces his steps out of the room. "Adios," he says under his breath to no one in particular.

He treks along the school hallway keeping his head down but I, of course, can examine his face regardless. His pupils are dull and his skin is paler than a sliced almond. He looks like someone in danger of fading away and I ask, knowing that there'll be no answer, "Where are you going?"

Near the gym he passes a cabinet overflowing with trophies and then a display of artwork dedicated to the theme of peace. Someone has adopted the blood-donor slogan and captioned their poster: "Peace—it's in you to give." The painting itself is of the traditional white dove symbol soaring against a rainbow background.

But the poster that truly catches my eye is a black-and-white comic-book-style drawing of a long line of people of various ethnicities, genders and ages holding hands and smiling back at whoever stops to look at them. There's a woman in a wheelchair and a man with a prosthetic leg too. Printed across the bottom of the page in itty-bitty text is the word *peace* in what has to be over a hundred different languages.

La paix. Shalom. Damai. Mabuhay. Pingan. Santipap. Rukun. Heiwa. Salam. Amaithi. Der Frieden. Sulh. Ukuthula. There are countless more, but those are the only ones I have time to process as I whiz along with Breckon.

Martin Luther King Jr. said, "True peace is not merely the absence of tension: it is the presence of justice." I know that the same way I know Dalí and Pink Floyd. The world I passed through—and the one that Breckon lives in now—is always at war. That makes me sadder now than when I was alive. People waste their limited time on earth fighting. They squash other people under their heels, make them crawl, make them beg, make them die.

I've left my life behind me and I don't understand the greed and cruelty any better from the other side. *The other side,* what a massive, knee-slapper of a joke on me. All the other side is, it seems, is the flip side of a mirror. I'm Ashlyn Through the Looking Glass without the benefit of the Red Queen or Humpty Dumpty for my amusement. I'm clueless and useless. No one has explained the *through-the-looking-glass* rules to me and I'm floundering. No, not floundering, more like failing . . . I'm failing him.

Jules catches up with Breckon about fifteen feet beyond the peace art. I'm relieved to see her but not surprised.

She must've dyed her hair on Sunday. It has thick purple streaks through it that weren't there when Breckon hung out with her on Saturday night. The nose ring she's wearing today is a tiny cluster of three periwinkle-colored stones. They match the T-shirt Jules is wearing under her black-and-white-striped overalls dress.

"Where are you going?" she asks, her cheeks rosy from rushing after him. "What did Cirelli say to you out in the hall?"

Breckon shakes his head. Their eyes connect for a second before he looks away. "Not much . . . Jules, just go back to class, okay? I don't want you to get in shit for this."

Jules stands her ground. "You didn't say where you were going."

"Because I don't know."

"So . . . we could hang out together and when Cirelli calms down you can probably talk what happened through with him." Jules folds her arms in front of her and leans back against the wall. "You know he can be pretty cool."

Breckon presses his eyelids shut like he's making a statement.

When he opens them again he says, "Look, thanks for the concern but I'll handle it how I want, okay? Just . . ." He waves her away. "I don't need you a step behind me for everything."

"That's not how it is," Jules counters. "I'm just checking on you. It's not like you to pick up and leave in the middle of class. Cirelli was stunned. His face hit the floor."

"Like I care." Breckon's tone sharpens. "Anyway, I'm on my way out. And we're not conjoined twins, you know. I don't have to account for everything to you."

"O-kay." Jules coils a strand of her purple-black hair around her finger and drags it back behind her ear. "I hope you know that you're being an ass right now."

Breckon's face is as emotionless as stone. "You can call it what you want. But leave me alone." He resumes his stride down the hallway and doesn't look back at her, but I do. Jules stands with one shoulder against the wall, watching until he disappears out the doors to the school's west parking lot.

It's a beautiful May day outside and I crane automatically up to feel the warm rays on my skin. *Not for you, Ashlyn,* I remind myself bitterly. *It's not your sun anymore.*

Breckon tosses his books into the backseat of his car and starts the engine. He heads north, towards cottage country, zipping up Highway 400—the very same highway my family motored up on their way to Farlain Lake—and I begin to wonder if we've developed some kind of psychic link and he's reading my mind without knowing it, heading for the place I used to spend the summer years ago.

But then he pulls into a rest stop with a McDonald's in it and orders medium fries and a large Coke. They sit, untouched, on the formica table in front of him as Breckon rests his head in his arms, facedown. I wish I knew where he was going, what the plan was.

"You should turn back," I say gently. And then, for the umpteenth time, "Where are you going, Breckon?"

I cheat and peek at his face from under the table. His eyes are closed and the sound of his breathing is like someone ripping out a set of brand-new stitches.

No, no, no. "Let's go home," I advise. "*Please,* Breckon. Listen to me."

"Fuck you," he whispers in a voice so quiet that probably only dead people and dogs can hear it.

Was that . . . was that meant for me?

Exhilaration surges through me, my worries for him momentarily pushed aside.

A long-haired boy of about five in a Toronto Maple Leafs T-shirt with a squiggly line of ketchup down the front is leaning over the back of the booth that adjoins Breckon's. "Is that man sick?" he squeaks, his eyes shifting to his mother next to him.

"Shush, honey," she commands. "Don't stare. That's rude."

"But maybe he's asleep and we should wake him up," the boy says, loud enough for Breckon and anyone in our section of the restaurant to hear. "Or maybe he needs to go to the hospital."

"Sit down, Jacob." The woman tugs at the boy's hand.

"Owww!" he yelps, although I can tell it didn't hurt a bit.

A couple of minutes later Jacob's plowed through his Happy Meal and his mother's finished her salad. She throws their garbage away and sets the empty tray on top of the receptacle.

I see her glance furtively at Breckon and then, maybe for the sake of her son, scurry over to the table with Jacob in tow.

"Excuse me," she whispers, staring down at Breckon's curly brown hair and the back of his neck. She pokes her tongue against her teeth and hovers by the table, about to attempt contact a second time.

Breckon lifts his head to stare at her. His eyes seem bottomless and she begins to sink into them but pulls herself back just enough to ask, "I just wanted to make sure you were all right. You had your head down for a long time and . . ."

Breckon glances past her at Jacob. "I know. I heard him."

The woman smiles apologetically. "He's at that age where—"

Breckon's cell rings from his pocket. "I should get that," he says, pulling the phone from his pocket and flipping the top up. I very much doubt he would've answered it if he hadn't wanted to escape from the concerned woman next to him, but her presence forces him to mumble a guarded "hello" into the phone.

The woman disappears with her son and I listen to Breckon defend his behavior in Mr. Cirelli's class, framing it as though his main concern was defending Violet from overzealous criticism. "Dad, I'll fix it, okay?" he stammers. "I'll go back and apologize to him tomorrow, but is there any way you can just keep this between us? Otherwise I'm going to have Mom breathing down my neck about the therapist again and, okay, maybe I lost it a little but . . ." He scrambles for the right words. "You know what some teachers can be like, and all I did, in the end, was bust out of class."

Mr. Cody must be leaning towards agreeing because Breckon utters a penitent, "I know, I know. I won't, *I swear.* Stuff was just . . . backing up on me. And then there's my birthday coming up too and I just . . ." He grabs his straw and bends it over, tying it into a knot. "I don't want to do anything for it. I want us to forget about it, okay? Just treat it like any other day."

This is the first I've heard about Breckon's approaching birthday. Maybe I haven't been paying close enough attention. It's impossible to stay focused during every hour of your existence. I don't get physically tired anymore but my mind still wanders.

Whatever Mr. Cody says next is enough to get Breckon back in his car and driving home. The first thing he does when he gets there is scour his parents' bathroom for sleeping pills. Amongst the assorted over-the-counter pain relievers and cold remedies he discovers acid-reflux pills, various outdated antibiotics and a fungal cream. Four remaining tablets rattle around the bottom of the lone trazodone bottle he ferrets out of the medicine cabinet. The length of time Breckon stares at them tells me he suspects they're sleeping pills. But there aren't enough left to help him for long, and certainly not enough to ensure that his mother (it's her name that's printed on the label) wouldn't suspect someone else had been dipping into them.

The next person to arrive back at the house is Mr. Cody. He and Breckon have a powwow in the living room, Breckon sitting on the couch with his hands lost in his hoodie sleeves, nodding at everything his father says, except for the idea of meeting with Eva again. "Are you and Mom going to say I need to get my head shrinked every time I screw up now?" he asks defensively.

"You said things were backing up on you," his father reminds him. "I just want you to know there are people you can talk to." Mr. Cody wearily rubs his forehead. "There's nothing the matter with needing to speak to someone."

"But I don't," Breckon says, eyes blazing. "I tried it. And I'm not going back. You can't haul me out to the car and then carry me up to her office like I'm six. If I don't want to go, I'm not going and *that's it.*"

The strain between Breckon and his father sparked by that conversation hangs in the air for the rest of the night. Most of the infrequent words spoken over dinner are Mrs. Cody's, but it gradually becomes evident that Mr. Cody has kept his word and not told her about Breckon's conflict with Mr. Cirelli.

If Jules tries to call, I'm unaware of it because Breckon switches his phone off and keeps it off. In bed later he stares at the ceiling for hours but doesn't swallow his sole remaining sleeping pill. During this time I test out my inner voice, asking Breckon if he can hear me, just like I've done in quiet points throughout the day.

He has nothing to say in response. If he *can* hear me, could it be that I've been making things worse for him? Maybe he's scared that he's losing his mind and that's partly why he's so adamant about not going back to Eva.

Bright and early the next morning Breckon knocks on the staff room door and apologizes to his teacher. He fixates on the ground, and then his Converse high-tops, and listens to Mr. Cirelli reply, "I spoke with your father yesterday and I think we can put this behind us. I know you haven't been yourself lately."

Breckon bobs his head and quietly thanks Mr. Cirelli but brushes off Jules when she drops by his locker and tries to talk to him. "I'm not in a good head space for any relationship drama," he tells her. "Can we postpone this for a while?"

"What do you mean?" she asks. "Postpone what?"

Breckon curls his fingers around his locker door and sighs. "Talking about what I'm going through and how you think you can help."

Jules stares at him for a long time, waiting for him to face her. If he did maybe things would be different. The way she feels about him shines so strongly in her eyes that it makes me want to cry. Breckon himself doesn't look. He keeps his eyes safely on his locker and, after several seconds, Jules's fingers graze against his on the locker, her black nails a stark contrast to his ashy skin.

"You know I love you," she whispers before doing exactly what he seems to want—lifting her hand off his and falling back into the crowd, away from him.

sixteen

breckon

Mom's parents won't take no for an answer. They say we should at least have some kind of family dinner to celebrate my birthday on Friday, and invite us over to their place. My mother starts to get into a fight with them about it over the phone, repeating that I don't want a birthday dinner. Mom's raised voice is what makes me give in. I don't want her to argue with her parents because of me; I know they've helped her a lot over the past month.

My grandmother makes the blue-cheese hamburgers that were my favorite food as a kid and blueberry cake for dessert. "It's not a birthday cake," she makes a point of saying. "Just a cake." My grandmother told us we could bring Moose, and because he's not used to being here he keeps pacing around their house, looking lost. Watching him skitter around their vintage hand-painted coffee table makes some bizarre kind of statement—like he's a small, hairy substitute for Skylar.

It feels wrong the way everything feels wrong lately. Even the dog seems different. All of us are like those early clones that died too soon because they weren't right inside. We look like identical matches to the original but under the surface we're defective.

I'm seventeen today and I don't know how much longer I'll last.

Jules gave me a birthday hug in the cafeteria earlier, even though we haven't seen each other outside of school since last Saturday and probably won't for a while. I don't want to drag her down and I don't want her knocking herself out trying to cheer me up—she'll just end up hurt and frustrated either way. On Wednesday we stood in the parking lot beside my car and had part two of the conversation that we'd started at my locker the day before. I told her, "Everyone keeps saying that I'm not myself and no one knows that better than you do. Right now I just don't have the energy for anything extra. It's hard enough trying to drag my ass to class—there's nothing left over for you."

Jules bit one of her black nails and said, "It sounds like what you're saying is that you think you need to be at your best for us to be together and that's not true."

"I know it's not like that." Even explaining took too much energy. "But imagine if you were going through something where it was all you could think about. And you needed whatever space and time you could get just to work things out for yourself." My shoe scuffed at the asphalt. "My head isn't in it, Jules. *Us.* When you're talking about summer theater and Boleyn's and all that. I'm just *not there.* I'm so far from that, I can't imagine being there."

"Breckon." She shook her head, her eyes clinging to mine in a way that would normally have made me want to pull her close. I wish it still worked like that. "I want to be with you *wherever* you are. If it's shitty isn't that all the more reason for me to be around?"

There was a time when I would've agreed with her. "I need to be on my own for a while, Jules. Don't make it harder by trying to talk me out of it."

I knew that what I was saying didn't make sense to her. She thinks she can be good for me. Stick by me. What she doesn't understand is that I don't want to swim against the current. I *want* to sink.

Ever since Skylar died but especially since the dream, I can't fight it or pretend to myself that there's some other kind of way through this for me. Jules would want me to try. She'd start off slow, but little by little work on convincing me to do things like start playing guitar again and then follow through with my idea to get up on stage at Boleyn's and make other future plans. And all I want to do is stop breathing.

If I was braver—and if there was a way for me to be done with this without hurting my parents and everyone else—I'd be through with it already.

"I need to step back," I added. From everyone, but from her the most.

Jules's eyes were wet. She said nothing.

Our time at her parents' house last week felt like a dream. I wanted to get in the car and leave her behind but there was still a sliver inside me that her tears reached. It made me say, "I still love you." As much as I could feel anything. "This doesn't have anything to do with that."

And then we were over or on hold or whatever you want to

call it but she still walked up to me today and gave me a hug, forced a closed-mouth smile and said, "You know where to find me if you need me."

"Thanks, Jules." I hugged her back and wondered if I'd been wrong and whether she really could help me. The feeling had dissolved again by the time I let go.

That leaves me right where I am, sitting in my grandparents' light-blue dining room, listening to them coax small talk from me and my parents. My mom and grandmother are discussing natural products that can be used instead of pesticides in the garden when my grandmother turns to look at me, smiles softly and says, "Can you feel her today? She's all around you like a greenish-blue light."

I shake my head. "I can't feel anything." Sometimes I can but I know it's not Skylar and it's not something I want to talk about. My parents would think I was losing it, and in a way I know I am, but whatever the thing around me is it's not Skylar and it's not my imagination. Whatever it is doesn't matter anyway—it's one more thing I don't have the energy for. Something that can't change the past, a gray form drifting in the dark shadows of my mind.

"Can you feel her?" my grandmother asks, shifting her gaze to my mom, who whispers that the feeling my grandmother's talking about is a memory.

"It's more than that," my grandmother insists.

My grandfather stares uneasily at his plate and then I hear my father say, "Sometimes I think I can feel her around me. Certain moments. Sometimes when I'm just drifting off to sleep or . . ." His voice trails off as his eyes land on my mother. Her face projects sadness and skepticism.

My grandmother's slate-gray eyes seek mine out again. "She's with us often, all of us." Inner calm lights her face. "Even if you can't sense that, I want you to know."

I realize my grandmother's intentions are good but her kindness burns. She may be able to convince herself that we're all living a fairy tale but some of us live in the real world. Skylar isn't here and she hasn't been in a month.

My fingers tremble as my fork slices through the blueberry cake. Everyone's watching me, watching the sliver of cake on the end of my fork and how I'm holding it in the air, twitching.

And then my cell rings in my pocket. The timing's so perfect that I couldn't have choreographed it better myself. I'm not supposed to have my cell on at dinner but I excuse myself and answer it as I push my chair out from the table and step into the living room where no one will be able to hear me.

"So what's up?" Ty asks. "You still at your grandparents'?"

I sit on their couch, pointing a cautionary finger at Moose, who wants to jump up and join me but isn't allowed on my grandparents' furniture. "Still here," I tell Ty, aggravation bleeding into my voice. "And it's a nightmare. I don't know why I didn't let my mom turn them down."

"Help is on the way," Ty declares. "I'm in the car with Big Red. Just lay an address on me and we're there."

"You know they live in Middlefield, right? It'll take you at least forty-five minutes to get here." I told Ty days ago, just like I told everyone else, that I wanted to ban any birthday celebrations in my honor, but if having him pick me up means facing down some birthday shit later in the night so be it; it'd have to be an improvement on this.

"Pedal to the metal," Ty assures me. "Shouldn't take more than thirty."

I give him my grandparents' address and hang out in the living room for another seven minutes before slipping back into the dining room and breaking the news. Everyone jumps all over themselves telling me how great and natural it is that I hang out with my friends today. It's another one of those things that make me feel like I don't want to be *anywhere,* but at least I know Ty won't grill me about whether or not I can sense my dead sister.

Ty and Big Red roll up in just over half an hour, like Ty promised, and my grandmother offers them blueberry cake. "I'd love that," Ty says politely, "but we're meeting up with some other friends in Strathedine and I don't want to keep them waiting."

My grandmother chops the remaining cake in two and places the bigger half in a cookie tin with skating penguins on the lid. "So you can eat it wherever you boys end up," she says, handing it to me.

Dad tells me to call him if I need a ride later. "No matter what time it is," he adds pointedly.

Three minutes later we're in the car. Rory has pried the cookie tin open and is scooping his fingers into the cake while Ty warns him not to eat it all because he wants his share. Since Big Red called shotgun first, I'm in the backseat and I notice an orange plastic bag shoved down in front of the seat next to me. A flesh-colored bump of vinyl *something* is sticking out of the top and I reach in and tug at the side of the bag to find out what it is. A grinning full-head Bill Clinton mask, that's what. I set Bill's head on the seat and pull out the masks underneath it: George Bush Junior, Barack Obama and Ronald Reagan.

"What the fuck?" I ask. "I didn't sign up for this."

"Don't worry about it," Ty says, looking over his shoulder at me. "That's not for tonight. You weren't even supposed to see that."

"We just picked it up before we dropped by your grandparents' place," Big Red adds. "We found this cool costume store in Bourneville."

"I wanted to get the Hillary one too but Big Red said it wouldn't go with the presidential theme," Ty tells me.

Rory drives one of his hands through his red hair. "They didn't have any Beatles masks and it's better to have four of the same type. Besides, wouldn't it be a little too freaky to see the Hillary mask on a dude's body?" He shudders at the thought.

I throw all the masks back in the bag, leaving Bill Clinton's for last. Whoever designed it gave him enormous cheeks and a mammoth chin, but the smile sort of looks like his. I've already stopped caring about the masks and the streaking stunt but Ty says, "We're going to pull it off with Brett and Kostas. We didn't want to bother you with it. I know it probably seems . . . I mean, we know you're dealing with more important things and now with Jules—"

Rory faces me in the backseat. "Dude, I can't believe you broke it off with Jules. What happened?"

Ty groans. "Can we maybe not talk about this on his *birthday?*"

"I don't want to talk about my birthday either," I growl. "I just want to get hammered." The path of least resistance. I haven't been plastered since New Year's and never enough to black out. That's going to change.

"Hell yeah!" Ty howls. "I'm down with that plan." He tells me that he and Big Red were on their way to Anya's when they called. I know that he's hooked up with her a couple of times since they met that night at Zavi's but I haven't seen her since. "Her parents are out of town so she's having a few of her girls over," he explains. "They're knocking back vodka coolers as we speak."

Girls. Shit. Just because I want to get loaded doesn't mean I want some random drunk girl trying to ram her tongue down my throat. But I go with the flow and we drive over to Anya's place, which is one of the last houses on a quiet cul-de-sac in Cherrywood.

Her house has a historical society plaque on it that reads: "John Forester, Merchant, 1879." There are only three cars in her driveway and one parked against the curb, and I can't hear any music until we're standing directly outside her front door. Then some shitty generic pop song that makes me frown harder than I already was spits in my ear.

Anya opens the door and throws her arms around Ty, then Rory and then me. "I'm so glad you guys are here!" she cries. Her legs are bare and she's wearing a frilly pink dress that Jules would roll her eyes at. She wraps her right arm around Ty's waist and leads us through the foyer and into the family room where six other girls (some who look familiar from that Saturday night at Zavi's) and three guys are hanging out amongst leather couches, a massive flat-screen TV, plastic cups and bowls of tortilla chips and pretzels. Two of the guys are Wii boxing in the center of the room while four of the girls dance to the bad music and the remaining two huddle on the couch, whispering into each other's ears. The leftover guy's sitting in an armchair, texting with one hand while dropping tortilla chips into his mouth with the other.

Anya turns to explain, "It's just going to be us. This girl I know had a big party three months ago and it spun completely out of control. Her house got trashed beyond recognition and a senior guy ODed and the paramedics had to come so I want to keep this small."

"I think I heard about that party," Ty tells her. "Some people just don't know when to get a grip on themselves. But don't worry, we'll be careful."

"Definitely," I say, scanning the room for whatever alcohol I can get my hands on. "You can't be too careful about who you invite into your house."

"I know, right?" Anya nods. "Some people are total animals."

She must be keeping the booze somewhere else. I hope there's a healthy supply. There's a guy at school whose older brother delivers to underage drinkers for a steep surcharge. I've never been desperate enough to call him before but I'm sure I can find someone who has his number if I have to.

Anya makes Ty hand over his keys and says one of her rules is that nobody gets them back until the personal Breathalyzer her friend brought over gives them a thumbs-up. Ty says that's cool and Anya takes us into the kitchen where a row of large bottles line the counter—brandy, tequila, whiskey, rum, vodka, gin. The smaller vodka-cooler bottles are so colorful that they look like they must be filled with Kool-Aid, and a Rubbermaid cooler stashed with ice squats on the floor in front of the sink. I grab a plastic cup from the stack next to the bottles and start filling up.

Ty and Rory fill up too. Anya and Ty drift back towards the family room, leaving Rory and me to hang out with the bottles. I drink my double vodka down like it really is Kool-Aid. Cherry Kool-Aid on a hot summer's day after playing soccer, my hair sopping and my jersey glued to my back with sweat.

"Are you gonna go in or what?" Big Red asks nervously, his face mimicking his nickname.

I'm not thinking about him; I'm thinking about oblivion—and reaching it as soon as I can. But suddenly I get his subtext anyway; Rory doesn't want to go into the other room because he's afraid he'll hook up with some girl who isn't Isabel Castillo. If he thinks I'll stop him he should think again. I only have one thing on the agenda for tonight.

We go into the family room and take our turn at Wii boxing. I drink more. Rum this time and then two of those vodka coolers, which are so sweet that I have to chase them down with gin. Every time I look at Ty he's got one or both of his hands grafted on to some part of Anya's pink dress. Soon they both disappear, and shortly after that another girl and guy slip away together too.

Big Red and I ignore most of the other action going on in the room and play Wii hockey with the remaining guys for so long that a girl in a black miniskirt and tall boots hops over to one of the guys and plays with his hair until he can't ignore her. He throws her over his shoulder, stomps over to the couch and drops her on her ass, grinning all the while. "Enough with the stupid video games already!" she shouts petulantly, grabbing his arm before he can get away. "I need someone to dance with me."

And so we lose a player, and before long I'm too tanked to see straight anyway. I half-sit, half-lie on the carpet in front of the love seat and watch drunken guys and girls grind against each other to the sound of hip-hop tunes.

It's hard to believe this is the same life where I lost Skylar. I can't get the two separate realities to merge in my head. One of them must be a lie.

A hand falls on my shoulder. I turn to stare at the girl curled up on the love seat behind me. Her name's something like Kathryn, Kirsten or Kaitlin and I thought she was asleep but I guess not. She blinks slowly, like each of her eyelids is as heavy as a freight train, and says, "Hey, I heard it was your birthday."

"Not me," I lie.

"Oh." The girl's blond eyebrows slant in confusion. "Really?"

"No, not really." I'm slurring my words. My teeth taste like sugar and a future atomic hangover. Big Red's swaying to the music while one of Anya's friends does the dancing for both of them. His hands are drifting down towards her ass, which means he could be in trouble here but that's his problem, not mine. I get up and stumble into the kitchen to fix myself a rum and Coke.

There's a hole inside me. It's filled up with alcohol so that I can't feel it at the moment, but I know it's still there. How much do you need to drink to get alcohol poisoning? How much do you have to drink to check out completely and forever?

It's too hot in here. My skin's clammy like I've got a fever. Everything's wrong. The music, the girls. I don't want any of it. I stagger out the front door to get away from it all, my cup still in my hand. Ty forgot to lock the car door and I climb into the backseat and knock back the rest of the rum. My body doesn't want any more but my brain's still in control.

I lie down, close my eyes and wait for sleep to take me.

I don't know how long I'm out for, not long enough. Someone's tapping on the car window, opening the car door and letting fresh air in. I stare out at whoever it is from behind eye slits, my face damp under the vinyl mask I don't remember putting on in the first place but maybe I did. No, wait, I'm missing my shirt and socks too. Did I do all that or was I somebody's easy prank target?

The blond girl from before (Kathryn/Kirsten/Kaitlin) laughs as she leans into the car and stares down at me. My eyes can't focus. Her laughter sounds drunk and I'm not in the mood. "What do you want?" I bark, tearing the mask off and tossing it to the ground.

"I was just getting some air," she sputters, giggling into her arm. "And I saw your foot in the window. Um . . . *Bill.*"

My naked foot. Where the fuck's my sock? I spy the pair of them shoved into the corner of the seat and pull them on. My shirt's down beside me and I start cramming my arms into it.

"What the hell were you doing out here anyway?" she asks with what seems like a permanent grin. "Are you some kind of pervert?"

I don't say anything about passing out or try to explain. I sit up and finish my shirt buttons. They're not easy when you're drunk. I'm a button short.

"You've lined them up wrong," the blond girl says. "Here, I'll do it." She gets into the car with me and begins unbuttoning.

"You're good at that," I mumble. She's not as annoying now that she's helping me. I'm not really into blondes the way some guys are, but her hair's really pretty. Soft too. I let go when I realize I've been touching it. "Sorry."

"It's okay," the girl says. She gets the shirt fixed up right and climbs out of the car. "You coming out to join me or what?"

I want to shut my eyes again and go back to sleep but suddenly I can't stop staring at her hair. I get out, shoeless, and stand with my back against the car so that it's doing most of the work of keeping me upright.

"You're actually pretty cute," she declares, standing so close to me that our knees touch. She's wearing almost the same kind of plaid skirt that Jules would wear, but on her it looks preppy because it's paired with a fitted white top that she probably bought at someplace like Hollister. "But I'm drunk and you're drunker than I am."

"That's true," I say, and it makes her laugh again.

"So you know you're cute, huh?"

"I know I'm drunk." I've started running my fingers through her hair again. This girl doesn't know a thing about me. To her I'm just some wasted guy at a party who stripped off half his clothes in his sleep. I wish I was that guy. Somebody who doesn't have anything on his mind except scoring with a hot blond girl who's decided he's cute.

The girl presses her hands into my shoulders and inches forward. She licks at my lips. I open them and lean forward to catch her mouth, her tongue. The inside of her mouth's warm and tastes exactly like mine, only more potent. I drink her in, pull her closer. I curve my hand around her head, smooth my fingers over her silky hair.

Then her plaid-covered ass is in my hands. My fingers trace her form, creep under the back of her skirt without thinking twice. She's wearing black tights, so that mostly what I'm feeling is a mix of nylon and spandex, but she's under there somewhere, round and soft.

A dog barks from somewhere nearby, breaking my concentration. Three teenage girls, two of them clutching cigarettes, are walking a Doberman pinscher. The trio is approaching the end of Anya's drive and the tallest of the three shouts, "Sorry! We're not looking." She shields her face with her hand to emphasize her disinterest but the two other girls are still rubbernecking.

I've taken my hands off the blond girl and am peering into the distance at the girls with the dog. I could be wrong but I think maybe one of them went to my school in ninth grade.

"I'm going in," the blond girl with the silky hair murmurs, pulling away from me. "I need to pee."

I watch her walk away, still not sure precisely what her name is. All I know for sure is the "K." K turns to see if I'm trailing after her and closes the front door behind her when she sees I'm not. I climb into the backseat of the car again and sleep there, with all my clothes on this time and the doors locked, until Ty and Rory are finished partying and the night of my seventeenth birthday is behind me.

seventeen

ashlyn

My mom was out for the night the first time I got my period. I remember that now too. I remember the more and more infrequent bad dreams about Dylan and how, in later years, it was Celeste's room I crept into in the middle of the night rather than my parents'. She'd wake me up before sunrise, in time to slip back into my own bed without my mother or father noticing.

My parents worried enough as it was. I didn't want to give them reasons to wonder whether I was all right or not because I honestly was. Just, sometimes my subconscious would play tricks and put me back there in the Hobsons' hallway—or other places where I couldn't get away. It's not something that happened a lot but it did happen.

But otherwise I was happy—not the most popular kid in my class but not an outcast either. I'd stopped breaking things and had gained a sense of balance. I could sing a little and dance a little and, for a time, until I got old enough to feel self-conscious about it, my grandmother would show me off to her friends by having me sing "I Say a Little Prayer" or "Reflections."

I wasn't as good as she liked to say I was but I was okay. By the time I was eleven I mostly stuck to singing into my brush while dancing in front of the mirror and pretending I was a diva. You can be a diva and still not be stick-insect skinny. If you're a diva it doesn't even matter what you weigh and yes, I was a little chubby. Enough that kids could've teased me about it but they hardly ever did.

My favorite song to sing back then was Alicia Keys's "No One" and that's what I was singing into the mirror when I noticed that my underwear felt damp. It'd felt like that a lot lately but my sister said it was normal—something that happened when your body was starting to mature enough to have periods. The book my mom had bought me called it "discharge," which made it sound like it had something to do with firearms. But anyway, this time felt wetter than usual, and when I stopped singing to check my underwear I saw that the cotton part that fit between my legs was streaked with brown.

I was eleven years and ten and a half months old and didn't understand that Margaret girl who was desperate for her period in the book I'd read. Periods sounded messy and stupid. Five days of the month that you couldn't go swimming unless you wore a tampon, and I definitely didn't want to do that.

The timing was especially bad because my mom had gone straight from work to spend the evening with an old friend who had just split up with her husband, and my dad was supposed to drop me off at Shenice Campbell's birthday party in thirty minutes.

I knocked on Celeste's door. Half the time she didn't hear

me because she had earbuds in, but she always yelled at me and Garrett if we didn't knock.

"What?" she shouted from inside.

I opened her door and told her I had my first period and that I had to go to a party and what was I supposed to do? Celeste rifled through the linen closet shelf where she and my mom kept their sanitary products. "There's only tampons and panty liners," she complained. "Nothing in between like what you need. I better get Dad to take us to the store."

I frowned like I didn't want to involve him. I wasn't used to grown-up female stuff, let alone having my dad know about it. "It's okay," Celeste teased. "He does realize you're a girl, you know. And we can just get him to sit in the car and wait for us."

My sister went off to discuss my first period with my father while I changed my underwear and stuck on the panty liner my sister had pulled from the box in the linen closet. It didn't matter that I was suddenly a woman, I still had to get in the backseat while Celeste sat up front with my father. My sister and I went into the pharmacy together and she scanned the female-product shelves like an expert. "The ones with wings don't bunch up in the middle as much," she told me, selecting a box from one of the lower shelves and handing it to me.

A man with silver hair and a burgundy walking cane shuffled by us and I felt mortified that he could see me holding the box and guess that I had my period.

I said, "I don't want to go to Shenice's party anymore. What if I . . ." My mouth hesitated, not wanting to say the word *leaked.*

"It starts off slow," Celeste explained. "You'll be okay. Just change the pad when you're home later, okay?" Then she scanned my face with the same evaluating look she'd given the shelves. "Do you have cramps?"

"No." Older girls seemed to complain about cramps all the time. Even some girls in my class. Shenice told me she used it as an excuse to get out of gym.

I didn't like gym. Maybe the period would be good for something after all.

Celeste bought two packages of the pads with wings—one overnight and one regular—with the bills my father had slid out from his wallet. When we got back to the car my father smiled at us and said, "So, all set now?"

"Uh-huh," Celeste said. "All good."

We drove home and I changed into my party clothes, black jeans with sequins down the side and a teal top with sequins on the shoulders. I guess I was big into sequins at the time. The only thing I was missing was a sequined sanitary pad.

Both my parents had gotten better at acting casual about me hanging out at friends' houses, but there were times that I could still spot a difference between their reaction to Celeste socializing and me doing it. "You just give me a call if you want me to pick you up early," my father said once we got to Shenice's. "Otherwise I'll be here at ten." He would've come to the door with me and introduced himself to Shenice's parents except that he'd already met them two weeks earlier, and my mom had called Mrs. Campbell about the party when Shenice had given me the invitation. But none of that's really what I mean when I said my parents were different about Celeste going out, it was just in their faces a little sometimes when I was going to a party or spending time at a new friend's house.

Shenice was a new friend and my dad had that slightly wary look in his eyes as I stepped out of the car. Truthfully, I was surprised that Shenice had invited me to her party because she was one of the most popular girls in the sixth grade and had only really started talking to me about a month before. Someone was crying in one of the stalls in the school bathroom when I walked in during lunch. At first I ignored it, like I figured whoever it was would want me to, but she was still crying when I was washing my hands so I said, "Are you okay?"

"Who is that?" said the girl in the stall in a weepy voice.

"It's Ashlyn," I replied. The girl remained silent and I added, "It's okay, I'm going."

"Ashlyn?" the girl said tentatively.

"Yeah?"

"I've used up all the toilet paper in here—can you check the other stalls for me?" I found her some more toilet paper and passed a wad under the stall. A darker hand than mine took it but I still didn't know who I'd been listening to cry. "Thanks," she said.

"It's okay." I took a step towards the door. "Are *you* going to be okay?"

The girl sniffled from behind the stall. "Yeah, I'll be all right. Thanks."

I didn't know it was Shenice until Ms. Marinangeli paired us up for a geography project two days later. She had to come to my house to work on it and someone called her on her cell phone and she started to cry all over again. When she got off the phone she could see that I'd put two and two together and she told me that her parents had thrown her sister out of the house because she was doing bad things, and now she was going to move to Montreal where she could stay with a friend for free, but Shenice didn't know when she would see her again.

Shenice had three older sisters. One of them had graduated valedictorian of our future high school and was aiming for an MBA, another had a collection of shiny track-and-field medals and was in tenth grade, but the third sister, the eldest, was *trouble.*

Shenice didn't say what kind and I didn't ask. She kept talking to me, even after the project was finished, and she didn't really have to be as nice to me anymore because I was only a regular kid and she was so popular that the popular fourth- and fifth-grade kids tried to look like her by buying the same clothes.

None of my other friends were at Shenice's birthday party, but I knew her popular friends a bit by then. We ate Chinese food and played "I Never" with M&M's, danced and then her dad brought down the iNail machine they'd rented as a surprise and everyone did their nails with funky designs and cartoons. I went to the bathroom to check the progress of my period a zillion times but Celeste was right, it was starting out slow.

Back at home after my dad picked me up I showed him my nails in the kitchen. My mom came home and Dad said I'd had an interesting night and loped off to leave us alone so that I could talk about the thrill (not!) of getting my first period.

I thought, at the time, that although it was a pain to have my period, at least maybe I was getting popular—my star was rising. Sometimes I ate lunch with Shenice and her friends instead of mine and sometimes we danced to music from one of our iPods at recess (while the boys pretended not to watch) or pored over the sexy parts of romance books that Shenice had swiped from her mother. Then a new girl named Bailey joined our sixth-grade class. She had the prettiest blue eyes I'd ever seen but she was fat—much fatter than me. Some of the boys in our class would make oink noises under their breath when she was around, and then Shenice and her friends started making fun of Bailey behind her back too.

The first time I didn't do anything to stop them but on the second I tried to say that she had really nice eyes, and Shenice's friend Vanessa stared at me like I had horns growing out of my head. "Who cares what her eyes look like when she's carrying that much blubber around with her?"

"I mean, she's not just a little chubby like you," Shenice added. "She's *huge.* It's not healthy. You'd have to be stupid to eat that much and let yourself look like that."

Bailey didn't talk to anyone but our teacher, Ms. Marinangeli, and no one talked to Bailey either, unless it was to be mean. Every time I heard someone call her a name or act like she was invisible I winced inside. I told the friends I'd had before Shenice that we had to do something about it. "Why don't you talk to your new friends about that?" my friend Hannah asked. "They're the ones who started it."

I got Shenice alone and told her how I felt about what'd been happening with Bailey. "But we never even say anything to her," Shenice countered. "It's the guys that are calling her all the names."

"But everybody knows that you don't like her and that you say bad things about her."

"What can you expect, Ashlyn?" Shenice sunk her hands into her hips. "She never speaks to anyone. Whenever she has to run in gym class, she stinks. If you want to improve her life, why don't you talk to her about basic hygiene?"

I didn't know what to do. If I took Bailey's side against the boys and everyone else it could make *me* a target. It took me six days to decide that I would risk the consequences and become Bailey's friend. I didn't know the first thing about Bailey, but being her friend, even if that meant turning into a target myself, had to be better than the sadness I felt when people were mean to her. So I sidled up to her during recess and racked my mind for something to say. I had my period again then and had to carry the winged pads to school in my knapsack and make sure I didn't leak. Thinking about it gave me a headache, and I stood next to Bailey and blurted out the first thing that came into my head. "I have killer cramps today. I wonder if Ms. Marinangeli will let me skip gym."

Bailey shrugged and looked the other way.

I tried again. "So where did you go to school before this? Was it nicer?"

Bailey's forehead wrinkled. "It was the same." She bit her lip. Her bright blue eyes stared piercingly into my face. "If you're trying to dig for information for you and your friends to laugh at, you can forget it. I'm not going to tell you anything."

I was shocked. I'd never laughed at her or said anything bad about her.

"I . . . wasn't going to do that," I stammered.

"Right," Bailey said sarcastically. "You're not one of Shenice's followers. I must've mistaken you for someone else."

I started to say that I wasn't a follower, but Bailey scuffled away on me and then Vanessa tromped over, like she must've been listening from around the side of the nearest portable. "You should be careful who you talk to," Vanessa warned, flipping her hair over her shoulder. "You don't want people to think you're the same as her." She poked me in the stomach. "Especially since you already need to go on a diet."

Something sparked inside me when she touched me. I got in her face and shouted at her to keep her hands to herself. Vanessa looked around to see what kind of audience we had and, spotting three boys playing handball not far away, yelled back, "I don't want to touch your blubber, girl! You got more rolls than a bakery."

I lunged forward and pushed her. She fell in a dirty puddle from the morning's rain and her jeans got soaked at the butt. The teacher on recess duty rushed over before Vanessa could get up and smack me back. I got detention and Vanessa, because she was the one with the muddy pants, didn't get punished at all.

If real life was like the movies, Shenice and her friends would've started terrorizing me on a daily basis after that, but that's not how things went. The next morning at school Vanessa sashayed over to my desk and called me a bitch. She shot me dirty looks for the next two weeks. I didn't eat lunch with them anymore and Shenice stopped speaking to me. I didn't become friends with Bailey either but pretty soon most people got sick of picking on her and by June she was hanging out with a girl named Jess who'd cut her hair short and started dressing like a boy.

When Jess changed some kids said mean things to her too, calling her a lesbo and a dyke. One time she punched a boy and made his nose bleed, and maybe that was wrong, but I was glad she'd done it and told her so. After that when I saw kids bugging her I'd shout nasty things back at them. Sometimes they called me fat, ugly and a lesbo too but sometimes more kids would take our side and the other ones would have to stop.

In junior high I began to acquire a reputation as someone who stuck her nose in when someone was being bullied. And not just that but someone who was a good listener and could keep a secret. In eighth grade I met a girl who told me, after we'd been talking on the phone for two and a half hours one night, that the uncle who was staying with her family was sneaking into her bedroom at night after everyone was asleep and touching her. I told her what had happened to me when I was eight and that she needed to tell her mom what was going on, but she was scared and made me swear not to say anything.

I promised but three days later I caved in and told my parents and they called the school and her uncle got arrested. I'd wanted to help that girl so badly but I was in over my head. I needed my mother and father to take charge for me. I have that same feeling now with Breckon. My parents would know what to do to help him but I'm stumped. Sometimes I shout in the darkness in frustration until I can't stand it anymore and want to cry.

Considering how lost I am, adrift in a universe that

recognizes a flea's existence more than it does my own, maybe it's ridiculous to think that something as simple as singing "I Say a Little Prayer" in front of the mirror could make me feel better, but I know it would help some and, as I watch Breckon come apart at the seams, I run through the lyrics in my head in Aretha Franklin's voice until they sound like a prayer themselves.

eighteen

ashlyn

As the sun comes up on Saturday morning Breckon and his friends, still too drunk to pass a Breathalyzer, call a cab to take them to Big Red's house. It's a bloodred sunrise but no one mentions how spectacular the sky is. Breckon, Ty and Big Red look half-dead as they spill out of the taxi and I wonder, did I ever, in the last year or so of my life that I've yet to remember, get wrecked like this with my friends?

I can't really understand why anyone would want to. Dancing, eating, playing video games and making out with someone you're into all seem like things that are just as much fun when you're sober, and as far as I can see being drunk only makes you loud and/or dumb. I don't think Breckon even remembers putting on that Bill Clinton mask and stripping off half his clothes. I guess, for a minute or so before he passed out, that he thought he'd get a jump on his friends' idea and do some streaking himself. Lucky for him he lost consciousness before he could make it out of the car.

Breckon and his friends part ways at Big Red's house. From

there Breckon heads for home, wandering onto a bike path shortcut, and as he nears his house I see him take in the sunrise at last. He stops in his tracks and gazes up at the brilliant deep-orange sky. The sun streams golden from behind a slash of dark red clouds. The neighborhood hasn't sprung to life yet. Newspapers lie untouched on porches. The only noise on the air is of birds singing.

There's a kind of peace in the stillness of the moment that I wonder if Breckon feels.

That's all I do with him, watch and wonder. If I was still alive and knew him, would I be able to do more?

Breckon starts walking again—along the sidewalk, up his driveway, through the front door and up to bed. An hour later Mr. Cody peeks in on him to make sure he's arrived home safely, and when Breckon wakes up at quarter to two in the afternoon the first thing he does is reach for his iPod and listen to Aretha Franklin sing "I Say a Little Prayer."

The moment I wake up . . .

Three times in a row.

Sweet Jesus. He knows I'm here. There's not a shadow of a doubt.

I've been quieter with him than usual over the past few days. Since he seemed to address me at McDonald's I've begun to worry that I could be doing him more harm than good (wouldn't hearing a voice in your head make you wonder if you were crazy?), but I can't stop my private thoughts. I don't know how many of them are sifting through my consciousness to his and how that could affect him. I remain silent as best I can, thinking it all through, but maybe he can hear my silence too?

Breckon says nothing. And I say nothing.

Later he puts in a shift at Zavi's, stays up most of the night watching movies on his laptop and sleeps late. Sunday's a late night too. He thrashes in bed, battling with the covers and his personal demons. I can hear it in his breathing, know what he wants to do and can't keep quiet any longer. *Please don't,* I whisper. *It's not your fault and it won't change anything.*

Breckon gives no indication that he's heard me, and I think, with more vehemence, *What do you think Skylar would say if she could see you? Wouldn't she be horrified? Wouldn't she ask you to stop?*

I watch him cut himself again, a sharp line up the middle of his other thigh. It hurts, I can see that. But not as much as just breathing.

I don't think it's possible to spend over a month watching every hour of someone's waking life and not care about him. Not unless he was bad to the core, and that's not Breckon. I've seen every inch of him now, even the parts I probably shouldn't have. The image of his smoky blue eyes is burnt into my brain. I've spent more time staring into his pupils than anyone else's.

This is not what I thought would become of me. As a child you think you have an entire lifetime ahead of you. You think you'll travel to far-flung places, be recognized for something you're good at, maybe have your own family one day or maybe not, but at least find love. Even if it doesn't last. Even if it breaks your heart.

Deep down I know I've never had that. I can't explain how I sense that when I'm missing a year-plus of experiences, and I hope I'm wrong. But I don't believe so.

I think I've come to love Breckon. Not like a boyfriend and

not like a brother either but in some way I'm not wise enough to put into words.

He needs to be okay. And I can't do that for him but I want to help, if I only knew how.

At school on Monday morning Breckon sits in his car watching the parking lot like he's staking someone out. Then a skinny white guy with a face full of freckles pulls up on a mint-green Vespa. Breckon gets out of his car and intercepts the guy before he reaches the school door.

"Hey, Carl," Breckon says. "You got a minute? I was hoping you could help me with something?"

Carl casts a wary look at Breckon. His spiky hair remains motionless in the face of a wind that sends Breckon's curls billowing out behind him. "I don't know you."

"No, I know. But you've done some business with Cameron Sykes, right? He can vouch for me."

Carl turns and steps away from the door, which is being enveloped by heavy-lidded students trooping towards their lockers and homeroom classes. Breckon follows Carl to a more sparsely populated scrap of lawn near the track field.

Carl skims one of his fingers over his right eyebrow. "If there's anything I can do for you, that has to happen first. So get Cameron to text me and then we can talk, okay?"

Breckon nods quickly. "Sure."

Carl's shoulders swivel like he's about to break away from Breckon. Then he spins back towards him and says, "Want to give me a vague idea of what we're talking about?"

"Sleeping pills," Breckon replies, more mouthing the words than uttering them.

"Okay. We can get more specific later." Carl drops his mask of aloofness for a second. "Sorry, man. It's nothing personal. I just need to take certain precautions."

"No problem, I get it," Breckon says as he begins to stride off.

He sleepwalks through his morning classes. Cameron's in humanities with him in the afternoon and Breckon grabs him on the way out of class and tells him he needs a favor. He fills him in on the details as they inch along the crowded hallway. "I need to keep this quiet," Breckon adds. "I don't want Renee or Jules to hear about it, okay?"

"I hear you. And I'll text Carl." Cameron pushes up his sleeves as they walk. "But you need to be careful. Those things can get you hooked if you don't watch it."

Breckon's eyes scream indifference. "Thanks for the warning."

He has his pills by the end of the night. Forty of them, to be exact.

He swallows one before getting into bed and another the next night. I don't try to discourage him because (a) I don't think I can and (b) the pills work and I know long nights make him feel worse.

On Wednesday Breckon has economics last period and he and Jules arrive at the classroom door at the exact same moment. They were so good together that I can't believe he broke it off, and what's just as surprising is how civil they've been able to remain in the aftermath. If I was in Jules's place I know I wouldn't be handling things as well as she is. Since it happened they haven't been speaking much but they always at least acknowledge each other, and on Monday Jules said she hoped he'd had a good weekend.

Today is different. Today Breckon says, "Hey, Jules. How's it going?"

Jules's black eyeliner can make her almost look mean but when she smiles you immediately know better. But not today. Today she refuses to look him in the eye and retorts, "Fuck you, Breckon" as she slips into class.

Breckon's eyes flick repeatedly over to her as Mr. Cirelli shows a PowerPoint presentation on business and the environmental revolution. When the end-of-period bell sounds, Breckon's up in a shot and out the door where he lies in wait.

Jules's face swells with bitterness as she exits the class, Breckon locked in step with her. "So now it's my turn to say I don't want to have anything to do with you," she says.

"I never said that."

"No, no, you said"—she cups her chin and strikes a mock-contemplative pose—"that you didn't have the *energy* for anything extra." Her long black hair whips through the air as she shakes her head. "And I believed you. Do you have any idea how that makes me feel? You playing me like that when I really thought we had something?"

"Jules," Breckon pleads. "We did, you know we did. I don't understand what you're saying."

Jules stops in the middle of the hallway and burrows her hands into her hoodie pockets. "And the bullshit doesn't stop! You're unbelievable." She glares at him with such contempt that it takes Breckon's breath away. "Lauren Harvey told Renee that she saw you having sex with some girl against a car in her neighborhood on Friday night. Is that specific enough for you?"

Breckon hangs his head. His frame literally seems to shrink under the weight of his navy T-shirt and gray cords.

"I thought so," Jules concludes, swinging away from him.

"No, Jules, wait!" He latches on to her arm as they whisk along the corridor.

"Let the fuck go," she warns in a voice that sounds like a hundred bee stings.

Breckon releases her but keeps pace. "That's not what happened. There was a girl, okay? But we didn't have sex. I was so trashed that I didn't know what I was doing. I don't even know her name."

Jules laughs in a way that says this isn't remotely funny. "So, if you were that trashed maybe you did fuck her. Or would that have required too much *energy*?"

"Jules, c'mon. Please stop." He reaches for her hand and roots himself to the spot. "I know how it sounds."

Jules, who has stopped too, dangles her hand from her arm like it's an inanimate object.

"Did you or did you not have your hands up her skirt?" she asks. "Do you remember that much?"

"I remember," Breckon says. "But can I explain what happened? Ty, Rory and I were at this party Anya was having. You remember me telling you about Anya?" He waits somberly for confirmation that doesn't come and then continues anyway. "I didn't want to be there—I just needed to get away from the dinner at my grandparents' house. And I drank too much, way too much. I think I even blacked out at one p—"

Jules wrenches her fingers from his. "I've heard enough. You're free to do whatever you want. I just wish you'd had the guts to own up to what that was so I wouldn't have been sulking around like a loser, trying to give you space while worrying myself to death about you."

Breckon's eyes drain of emotion. He lets Jules walk away without chasing her. This is what he wanted after all, space.

You should go after her, I tell him. *Apologize. Try to make things right.*

"I'm done," Breckon says aloud to no one but me. "I'm done."

His resigned tone gives me a bad feeling that echoes how I felt when I tried to change Shenice's mind about Bailey and couldn't.

Ty catches up with Breckon at his locker a couple of minutes later and nudges him with his elbow. "Man, I have some bad news. Somehow Renee found out about you hooking up with Kylie at Anya's place."

"Kylie?" Breckon repeats. His eyes are gray-blue marbles. Shiny but lifeless.

Ty smiles. "You didn't know her name?" Breckon shakes his head. "Yeah, man, that was Kylie. The blonde with the super straight hair. She told Anya that you were cute but so wasted that she felt like she was molesting you. Anyway, Cameron said that Jules was really torn up about it when she heard."

Breckon shoves his books into his locker and rubs his eyes. "I just had class with Jules. She hates my fucking guts. At first I didn't know what she was even talking about."

Ty's deflated smile collapses into a full-blown frown. "It's not like you cheated on her. Don't beat yourself up about it. You were completely up front with her, man. And from what I heard, you and Kylie didn't take things very far anyway."

Breckon slams his locker shut. "Lauren Harvey told Renee I fucked Kylie against your car."

"Did you?"

"No, but I think it could've happened that way too," he admits. "I think I'm . . ." His glossy eyes threaten to spill over. He hunches like he's about to break at the waist and crumple into two separate halves. "I don't know what I'm doing."

Ty looks away, scanning the hallway like he's devising a plan of action. "It's okay, it's okay." He claps Breckon on the back. "Walk with me. Let's get out of here."

Breckon follows Ty's lead, trudging out of the school and into the parking lot with his eyes swimming. "Keys," Ty prompts as they near Breckon's car. "I'll drive."

Breckon fishes them out of his pocket and hands them over. "Where?"

"Wherever you want to go," Ty says resolutely as he unlocks the doors and they both climb in. "Think of me as your limo driver."

"I don't know." Breckon stares at the car mat under his feet.

"Okay, so I'll make an executive decision. How about Central America? Costa Rica's, like, number one on the Happy Planet Index. You know, they're the greenest country on the planet." Ty keeps up his commentary on Costa Rica while I listen to the sound of Breckon's breathing and sink lower.

What good am I if I let him bring me down? None. Fight, Ashlyn, I command myself. *Take your cue from Ty and do something constructive.* I let Ty do the talking while I concentrate on trying to generate positive energy. I don't quite know how and have even less clue how to measure whether I'm successful or not, but I think happy, tranquil thoughts. That bloodred sunrise on Saturday morning. Orange ice cream. The lyrics to "All You Need Is Love." Callum and I playing cards on the beach. My father swinging me up into the air in his strong arms when I was small, making me giggle and feel like I could fly. The way he cheered when Barack Obama was elected president of the United States, a light in his eyes that I'll never forget. Mom's nightly soft kisses on my forehead. Puppies. Rainbows. Peace on earth. I try to believe in the possibility, for Breckon.

According to Ty there's a park in Costa Rica, Corcovado National Park, which *National Geographic* called "the most biologically intense place on Earth." Ty explains that he watched a documentary about it the other night and that's how he knows so much about Costa Rica.

After twenty-plus minutes of travelogue Ty admits that when in doubt, his default is to head south and that if Breckon doesn't want to end up at the U.S. border he should suggest another destination. I listen for Breckon's pained breathing. The sound stings but doesn't sear. He's better than he was, for whatever reason.

Ahead, on the right side of the road, there's a baseball diamond where twelve-year-olds in uniforms and ball caps are just beginning an after-school game. An ice-cream truck's stopped as close to the field as it can get and the players' younger siblings are clambering for cones and Popsicles. "Here's as good as anywhere," Breckon says. They pull into the parking lot and take their place amongst parents, teachers and the players' fellow students on the bleachers.

I don't remember going to many of my brother's baseball games, probably wouldn't recognize his team jersey if I stumbled over it, but I'd know my brother. My last memory of Garrett is only a year old and I scan the faces of each of the players as carefully as I can considering the distance we are away from them and my inability to uncouple myself from Breckon.

Garrett's not here.

I've never stopped looking for my family, praying that they'd come into Zavi's or wander by Breckon at the mall. Just because it hasn't happened yet doesn't mean it won't. I have to believe that if I keep my eyes open I'll see my family again someday. As much as I miss them, I need to know that they're okay without me. Breckon thinks his grandmother's silly for believing she can sense his sister, but I believe my family will be able to sense me if I can get close to them.

In the meantime I have to content myself with listening to Breckon ask Ty if he wants ice cream. He strolls over to the truck and buys a chocolate-dip cone for Ty and an orange Creamsicle for himself. *Orange.* In my opinion orange is the freshest flavor in the world. Fresher and lighter than mint. Cold. Juicy. And when it's in cream form, *creamy.* My mind revels in the memory of orange ice cream while Breckon tears into his Creamsicle with his teeth.

Thank you, I tell him, and he nods almost imperceptibly but I'm right there with him; I can't miss it.

nineteen
breckon

Every time I hit rock bottom it's harder to come back. Weeks ago my mother said she felt as though she could find Skylar if she looked hard enough, but that the feeling was a *trick.* A lie. Feeling better, even for a while, is a lie like that. Because I know I'll crash again soon. What's the point in trying to climb back up if it's only a trick anyway?

I've thought about it a lot and the answer doesn't change.

It was better, for a while, at the park with Ty watching kids play ball, that voice in my head acting like a sedative. But I don't want to go to sleep again and see Skylar in my dreams. I don't want that shock of waking up in a world without her.

My sister's favorite color was sky blue. Her favorite cereal was Lucky Charms (Alpha-Bits came second). Her favorite TV shows were *SpongeBob, Wolverine and the X-Men, What's New Scooby-Doo?* and *League of Super Evil,* but she'd also stop whatever she was doing to watch any show with Jamie Oliver in it. She liked to watch him dice, season, stir and talk about cooking, but her favorite food was spaghetti and meatballs out of a can. She'd eat all the meatballs first and then tackle the spaghetti, but whenever my mom made real spaghetti and meatballs she'd only eat half of what was on her plate. Her best friend was Kevin Solomon. She was good at hitting and kicking a ball. She was tough. She learned to ride a two-wheel bike without training wheels when she was four and a half, younger than me. When she fell off a week later and scraped up half her leg, she sniffled and two fat tears streamed down her face but she didn't bawl. Her favorite things to draw were aliens, dinosaurs and mummies. She said that when she grew up she'd be as tall as I was, maybe taller. She had my mom's eyes and my dad's blond hair. She liked Jules a lot, she'd miss her if she was still around but then again, if she was still around I'd still be with Jules too. She loved all animals, not just the cuddly-looking ones. She laughed a lot but she was also a good listener.

A couple of days before Christmas, when Skylar was over the flu and feeling back to normal, she wandered into the kitchen as I was toasting a bagel and asked me if there was really a Santa Claus. Some kids in her class were saying there wasn't, just like there wasn't an Easter Bunny and Tooth Fairy. She said that she knew that the Easter Bunny and Tooth Fairy were made up but was Santa too?

I'd overheard her ask my mother the same question earlier, and my mom had said all the things you'd expect a mother to say in defense of Santa, but Skylar obviously still had her doubts.

"Mom told you Santa Claus was real," I reminded her. "Do you think she'd lie to you?"

"Maybe," Skylar said.

"Why would she lie?"

"To be nice." Skylar's blue eyes pinned me to the kitchen wall. "But I want to know for real. I don't want to believe in him if he's just something made up for kids."

She was so intense about it that I didn't know whether I should keep up the pretense or not.

"You don't think he's real, do you?" she probed. "Or how come you're taking so long to answer?"

"Yeah, of course I believe in him." I tried to outthink my sister, but once somebody has those initial doubts, half the battle's already been lost. "It's just that when people get older they don't think it's cool to *admit* that they believe in Santa. That's why some of the kids you know say they don't—they're trying to be cool and act like they're older. It's like, you don't see adults going to work with SpongeBob briefcases. And lots of people think Santa's for kids like that."

The truth is that none of us—my mom, my dad and I—were ready for Skylar to stop believing, even if she was. Why do the kids who already know have to spoil it for everyone else?

I don't know whether Skylar really believed me about Santa Claus or not, but she decided to go along with it for the holiday. I'm sure next Christmas would've been a different story, but now there isn't any next Christmas.

It's hit me a thousand times in a thousand ways.

It never stops. The loss is what I am now. Loss with just a sprinkling of Breckon.

I've held her hand to cross the street so many times. Carried her in my arms when she was too young to walk, too young to talk. Years later, lifted her on my shoulders because she loved being up high. Played kid stuff with her—from Mega Bloks to Connect Four and Pictionary to making Insta-Snow. Babysat her from the time I was thirteen. Looked out for her even before. At places like the supermarket or the bank when my mom or dad's attention was needed elsewhere. "Stay with her," my mom would instruct before drifting away to inspect apples or carrots. "Can you watch her for a minute?" Dad would ask before lining up for the teller.

I watched her all the time, all the time. I was so much older than her that it felt like second nature. My mother lost her at Toys"R"Us once, while she was trying to pick out a present for Skylar to bring to a birthday party. I was checking out video games when it happened, in a completely different section in the store from the two of them. I didn't even realize Skylar had wandered away on my mother but I found her anyway. This was when my sister still had long hair and my eyes zoomed straight over to her lingering by a display of plush toys.

I was already holding her hand by the time they made an announcement that there was a lost child in the store. Somehow I found her all those years ago, when it probably didn't matter because my mother or an employee would've spotted her in the next minute or so anyway, but when it really mattered I wasn't watching. I let my sister disappear.

April 22 felt like it was just going to be like any other day. At the time it seemed there wasn't a single clue that it would be any different. But when I look back now I can see them all lined up in a neat row.

That Friday morning I woke up a little late and wolfed down leftover cold pizza before jumping in the car. In English

Rob Chen and I presented a media ad we'd made for Emily Dickinson's "Hope is the thing with feathers." At lunch Ty and Rory were still pumped from the soccer team's win over Crestgate High the day before and Mr. Cirelli was back in econ last period after two days off with food poisoning.

It was supposed to rain all day but the downpour had trickled down to nothing by about four-thirty. My parents' friends, Barbara and Sean, were having a twenty-fifth anniversary party and I'd promised my folks I'd babysit Skylar. My mom and dad went early to help Barbara and Sean set up. Normally Jules would come over and hang out with me while I was babysitting but she and Renee had tickets for a play.

I heated up chicken nuggets and broccoli and cauliflower in cheese sauce for her and threw together a stir-fry for myself. All that was fine—Friday, April 22, as it should've been—but after dinner, while Skylar was watching TV, I went up to my bedroom, closed the door and picked up my guitar. "I've Just Seen a Face" was one of the tunes I'd been working on for Boleyn's. Overall it's a pretty easy song but the intro was tough, especially for someone who was still trying to come to grips with some of the basics of guitar playing. Sometimes I spent hours just practicing a good steady strum, trying to lay a solid foundation for myself. Staying in time and developing a sense of rhythm are harder than you might think. Or it was for me, anyway.

There were lots of songs I associated with Jules, but in particular "I've Just Seen a Face" made me think about when I first started getting to know her on the New York trip. Even though I already knew who she was on a superficial level, the real Jules came as an amazing surprise. It's like that line that goes, if it'd been another day, I might've looked the other way. The more time I spent with Jules, the more aware I was that I easily could've missed out on knowing her, and the gladder I was that I hadn't. There's such simple happiness in that song, a sense of wonder that I totally understood.

When I played "I've Just Seen a Face" it was like Jules was in the room with me, like I was reexperiencing all our best moments together. So I wasn't happy when Skylar crept into the room and interrupted me. Sometimes I'd let her watch me play but only when I was ready—mentally prepared—and besides, Skylar didn't want to watch me that night. She was in the middle of her own obsession.

A couple of weeks earlier when we were at my grandparents' (Dad's parents) house for dinner, my grandmother had pulled out a family photo album and Skylar had pored over her baby photos (mine too but hers more). It got late and we had to leave before she'd finished flipping through them all. Then, on April 21, my grandmother dropped in for a visit and brought the album so Skylar could see the rest of the pictures. The one Skylar liked best was from when she was about two years old. She's sitting in her old baby car seat with all her winter clothes on, including a red and gold Winnie-the-Pooh ski hat, and waving through the open car door at my grandfather snapping her photograph.

"Do we still have that hat?" Skylar wanted to know.

"It's probably packed away with the rest of your baby things down in the basement," my mom said.

"Can we find it?" Skylar asked. "I want to see it."

Again, it was too late. "Not tonight," my mom said. "You need to start getting ready for bed."

It was a cute hat and a really cute photo of her. I could understand why she wanted to find it, but when Skylar walked into my room that Friday and made me stop playing guitar to see what she wanted, I was annoyed. "Wait until tomorrow and Mom can help you find it," I told her. "I wouldn't even know where to look."

"All the boxes with baby stuff are probably close together," she said. "If you come down with me I can do most of the looking myself."

"If you can look yourself, why aren't you doing it right now?" I asked, impatient to get back to "I've Just Seen a Face."

I was sitting on the bed, my guitar still in my hands, and Skylar peered insistently down at me. "But the boxes are so heavy, Breckon. You know I won't be able to lift them."

"I said *later,* Skylar. You don't need to find it right this second. What did I tell you about bugging me when I'm in the middle of something?"

Skylar frowned and shuffled over to the door with her shoulders drooping. Then she closed my door hard—not hard enough to be considered a slam exactly, but firmly enough to let me know she was angry.

I didn't think anything of it at the time. I didn't think I was being tough on her and anyway, Skylar wasn't the type to hold a grudge. It really couldn't have mattered less that I didn't drop what I was doing to help her find her old Winnie-the-Pooh hat.

Until about thirty minutes later.

It occurred to me that if Skylar and I were going to take Moose for his nightly walk (which was usually my dad's job) that we better do it before she had to get ready for bed. And then, maybe if there was time, I'd help her look for that hat.

I set down my guitar and went down to the family room to find my sister. *Wolverine and the X-Men* was on TV and she'd left what looked like an unfinished drawing of a spaceship hovering over a bunch of trees laid out on the carpet. Moose barked from outside, not at me but at a squirrel scampering by him in the backyard. I stared at him through the family room sliding door. Skylar must've let him out.

I checked the kitchen next but she wasn't there either. "Skylar?" I shouted, not because I was worried but because it was usually the fastest way to locate her.

Moose barked again from the backyard. Seeing squirrels in his territory always set him off.

I stepped out of the kitchen and back into the hall. I was about to tackle the stairs, figuring she must've been up in her room, when I noticed that the basement door was ajar. I don't know how I missed that before—we usually kept it shut. But obviously Skylar was so excited about the hat that she hadn't waited for me.

"Skylar!" I called again as I pulled the door open wide.

The basement lights were on. We'd never finished the basement, and naked bulbs cast a creepy, stark light into a dungeon-like space.

I thought that somehow the image at the bottom of the

stairs was a trick of that light, like when you think you see something out of the corner of your eye that isn't really there. My brain couldn't register the image at first.

Then my body went cold. My heart punched my rib cage. I ran to my sister.

She was lying on her back with her neck twisted to the right and her eyes shut. Her feet and calves sloped up the bottom two steps of the stairway. One of her arms was down at her side, the other bent up at the elbow and with the wrist swiveled at an awkward angle so that her fingernails pointed to the concrete floor beneath them.

Concrete. Her head smashed on concrete. Her face looked smaller, empty, like the real Skylar had seeped out.

But there wasn't any blood. Nothing to see.

I knew enough not to move her. I watched her chest and it didn't rise. I held my palm less than an inch from her lips to feel the warmth from her breath but there wasn't any.

My heart slammed against my chest. Again and again and again. My lungs evaporated and left me gasping. This wasn't real.

It wasn't like Skylar to fall for no reason.

She shouldn't have gone without me.

Why didn't I help her when she'd asked?

How long can a person survive without oxygen?

How long had she been lying at the bottom of the stairs?

I was wasting seconds Skylar didn't have. I sprang up the stairs, fighting for breath, snatched the cordless phone from the kitchen and dialed 911. Then I sprinted back to the basement with the phone pressed to my ear, nearly tripping myself halfway down the stairs.

I lunged for the handrail and found my footing.

My eyes still couldn't believe what they were seeing. My body was in denial. I couldn't speak loud enough for the 911 operator. I had to say my address four times. "I think she's dead," I kept saying. "I think she's dead."

It wasn't until I saw my mother later that I was lucid enough to consider how terrifying the basement could've seemed to someone like Skylar, who was only seven years old and hadn't stopped thinking about ghosts since that haunted-house documentary. And she'd gone downstairs without me anyway because that's what she was like. She wouldn't have wanted the fear to stop her. In a way that makes me proud of her. She wouldn't give in like I am now. She'd fight.

But I hope she wasn't afraid when she flicked on the light and started down the steps.

It's all bad enough without that thought. It's really all bad enough.

More than I can take. The fact is, I don't have it in me to live with this anymore.

I'm sorry Skylar sorry Mom and Dad sorry Jules and anyone else who'll be sad, but I'm not as strong as you want me to be. I'm really not strong at all.

I'm done.

twenty

ashlyn

Sometimes I try to think back to the moment before the darkness and the stars. Was that previous moment the instance of my death or was there something in between? Instinctively I know I'm almost there now, my memory restored until what must be the precipice of my final days on earth, and I'm wondering—as I wondered about the time beyond my second year at Farlain Lake—if I truly want to know all my own secrets.

What if I can't handle them?

And will the good about being Ashlyn Baptiste outweigh the bad?

Now that I remember being fifteen (and almost sixteen) I know that one of the things that I wanted for my adult future was to have the chance to really help people. I hadn't figured out yet whether that meant being a social worker, a psychologist or even a school guidance counselor. Becoming any of them would have meant that one day I would've been better at helping Breckon Cody than I am now. I wish I could borrow that knowledge from the future I'll never have. *Why not?* I ask the universe. *If it would help him, why not let me?*

The universe never answers. No one does. There are no deals when you're dead. If there were deals to be made I wouldn't be deceased, I'd be walking around in my Ashlyn skin, delighting in things like the feel of raindrops on the back of my neck, dancing with my friends as we sing so hard that my voice gets hoarse, soaking in a hot bath with strawberry-scented bubbles, and staring at Ikenna Shepherd's beautiful face from across our shared history class.

Ikenna . . .

I would have kissed him and more if I'd had the chance. I thought there'd be more time. More time for everything.

I never got to explore most of the exotic places I yearned for. There were two family trips to Florida (mostly just Disney World and SeaWorld), multiple ones to Vancouver to visit Mom's parents, two to Scotland to see Aunt Sandra and one to England. The first time my family went to Edinburgh I was ten and Callum and Ellie were away at summer camp for the entire first week. My aunt and uncle rented a minivan and drove us up to Loch Ness and around the Highlands. The second week, when my cousins were back home, it rained nonstop and I caught a nasty bug and had to be taken to my aunt and uncle's doctor for antibiotics. I spent most of my time in bed in the second guest room, a room that I was initially supposed to share with my sister, but she slept on the family room couch rather than risk getting sick.

Uncle Ian moved the small TV from his and my aunt's

room in with me to keep me from getting bored, and I watched repeats of old American sitcoms, hours and hours of *CSI* and a collection of British shows including *The X Factor,* one show called *Casualty* about a hospital and another called *Waterloo Road* about a school.

The second trip to Scotland when I was fourteen (during ninth grade) was much better. I stayed healthy, for one thing, and though it was Christmastime, the days were mild compared to Canada. We spent three days in London—visited Buckingham Palace, Harrods, the British Museum, the Tower of London and the London Eye—and then caught a train to Edinburgh, where my aunt and uncle met us at the station. One day my aunt took my mom, Celeste, Ellie and me to Glasgow to see the biggest shopping mall in Scotland. The stores were mostly different from the ones at home and my mom let me and my sister each buy some new clothes. Then we stopped in at a restaurant called Wagamama and ate big bowls of ramen noodles and sticky rice.

I didn't think it would feel right being away from home at Christmas but I was wrong, it felt more like Christmas than ever being with my cousins and aunt and uncle for the holidays. The Edinburgh Christmas lights and decorations were beautiful. We stared down on them from the Ferris wheel in the center of town and then went ice-skating at the Winter Wonderland outdoor rink in Princes Street Gardens.

Celeste, Ellie and I became a trio. We shopped together, went to the movies together, baked shortbread cookies together and met Ellie's best friend, Natasha, and her boyfriend, Jack. Callum was out with his own friends a lot, which meant we didn't see much of him, but it'd been so many years since we'd really spent time together that I didn't expect any different. If I hadn't seen him at various points in between I might not even have recognized him as the boy I'd known when I was seven. He was nearly six feet tall, had his hair shaved so short that you could tell his ears stuck out a little, and mostly smelled like a mixture of smoke, citrus body spray and the mint shampoo my aunt stocked the bathroom with. Ellie said her parents were furious that he'd taken up smoking, that it'd been going on for over a year now and that they'd done everything they could think of to make him stop but nothing had worked and now he only lied about it and sprayed himself silly.

On Christmas Eve I couldn't sleep and, after an hour and a half of trying, slunk down to my aunt and uncle's family room to watch TV. Callum was lying in front of the lit gas fire in the dark with his eyes closed but the TV on. All the various smells I associated with him must've worn off earlier in the night because I couldn't smell anything. I scanned the room for the remote so that I could change the channel to something more seasonal than *The Dark Knight.*

In Callum's hand, of course. I slid the remote out from between his fingers and climbed into the armchair closest to the TV.

"Hey," Callum said sleepily as I began flipping channels, "are you not a fan of Batman?"

"He's okay." I flipped back to *The Dark Knight* for Callum's sake. "I was just looking for something more Christmassy. You know, like *The Polar Express* or *A Christmas Story.* Something with snow."

"Go on." Callum yawned. "Watch whatever you like." His cell phone rang and he reached into his pocket for it and then whispered into his phone, facing away from me and into the fire.

I went back to channel surfing and settled on *Die Hard,* which, though it doesn't have any snow because it takes place in L.A., is at least set during Christmas.

After a couple of minutes Callum dropped his cell down on the carpet next to him and eyed the TV. "My girlfriend," he said. "She's still awake too."

I didn't know he had a girlfriend. I only knew the things that his parents and his sister had told me—that he did okay in school although he hardly studied, that he loved scuba diving and fencing, that he and his father fought often, and that he was a volunteer with a government program that helped teach kids sports.

"You found something to watch," Callum observed. "But I don't see any snow."

"It was the best I could do."

We watched *Die Hard* together for a while, Callum from the floor and me curled up in the armchair with my legs draped over one of the arms. Then he sat up, pulled the hood of his sweatshirt up over his head and said, "I'm just nipping outside for a bit."

"For a cigarette?" I asked. I don't know what made me so blunt and nosy; maybe it was just too late at night to sink much effort into censoring myself.

"Aye." He grinned a little. "Filthy habit. Don't start. Everyone will hate you for it."

When he came back in a few minutes later the cold air and smoke smell came with him and Bruce Willis was picking shards of glass from the soles of his feet on the TV.

"So you should tell me your bad habits then," Callum said, taking up his previous spot in front of the gas fire, "and I won't have to feel too bad about mine."

"I think you *should* feel bad about yours," I told him. "Then maybe you'll quit."

"If it was that easy I'd have given up already. The things are bloody addictive."

And maybe it really was because it was the middle of the night that it seemed perfectly natural to talk about things we never would've discussed during the day. He told me that when he'd first tried smoking at fourteen it was one of those stupid things you do just because everyone else is, then he found it stamped out any stress he was carrying around with him and by the time he wanted to stop, it'd already become a habit. His girlfriend, Lucy, was a brand-new one—no one in his family knew about her yet—and I felt happy to have a secret about him.

I would've shared one back if I'd had some kind of equivalent. Because I didn't, and had barely even been kissed, I confessed that I'd never had a boyfriend and that all the guys I knew just seemed to think of me as a friend. Callum looked up at me from the floor and said, "Because you're so easy to talk to, probably." And because I wasn't as skinny as Celeste or Ellie or any of the other girls that had boyfriends. But I didn't want to tell him that and sound like I was feeling sorry for myself. "Blokes are easily confused," he added.

"So I should act bitchy and stuck-up," I kidded.

Callum laughed. He asked me if I still liked Cheetos and said I should've brought some over for him. And suddenly we were those two people who'd played cards together by Lake Farlain in the dark. It happened in the blink of an eye.

Instantly it seemed ridiculous that I'd believed we'd changed too much to be friends. We talked about Callum clashing with his father and how I sometimes still felt overshadowed by Celeste, who'd always been closer to perfect than I was. Then, because it was the holidays and we'd been to church earlier, we talked about God and whether he was really out there, watching, listening and letting bad things happen to people.

Callum said he'd turned into an agnostic and it was another thing that irritated his parents, even though they hardly went to church. I told him that I guessed I was one too—that I wanted to believe more than I actually did—but that if there *was* a God and he was a loving God he probably wouldn't care if we went to church or believed in him so long as we treated everyone with kindness.

Callum agreed but said regardless of whether or not there was a God he was a big fan of Christmas, and with that the topic shifted towards holidays and those magic times at the lake years earlier. "That was one of the most brilliant summers of my life so far," Callum declared.

"Me too!"

Neither of us mentioned the summer before or after. Callum said, "We should play cards before you go—for old times' sake."

We never did get around to cards but that was okay. A couple of days after Christmas we went to an indoor climbing arena with Garrett, and one night the two of us skipped dinner and bought fish and chips from a place a couple of blocks away and sat on the curb eating them, Callum simultaneously smoking a cigarette and being careful to exhale away from me, in the opposite direction. "You don't look right with a cigarette," I told him. "Do you think you'll ever try to give it up?"

Callum sucked in his cheeks. "I'm already trying to cut down. But so far that just makes it worse. I spend all my time figuring out how long until I can light up again."

He smelled like smoke (and citrus and mint) when he hugged me goodbye at the airport. I didn't realize that would be the last time I ever saw him, Ellie and my aunt and uncle. If I'd known I'd have held on to them all longer, but at least Callum and I were able to be friends again. I'm so grateful for that.

After I got home, we stayed in touch online. He and Lucy didn't last. His next girlfriend was Yumi and she did, although she hated his smoking and wanted him to quit just as much as his parents did. I told him a little about Ikenna, downplaying how much I liked him because I didn't want to let myself get too crazy only to be let down later.

Ikenna . . .

Ikenna Shepherd showed up at Hillfield Park Secondary out of the blue in October of tenth grade. By then I'd had a few minor crushes, but the only person I'd ever really kissed was a guy named Anthony. We'd made out a little by a hotel pool during a wedding reception that I'd gone to with my family that past summer, and Anthony kept telling me how pretty my name was but he didn't ignite anything inside me. Looking at Ikenna, on the other hand, made me feel like I'd never been kissed. And being near Ikenna filled me with restlessness and daydreams.

Just when I thought I'd figured out what tenth grade would be like and more or less who everyone in my classes were, there he was sitting in the second row from the window in French, with hazel eyes that made my throat ache and cheekbones so sharp that they could've been lethal weapons. Ikenna's smile looked shy but maybe that was only because he was new. My very best friend since seventh grade (the year after I'd fallen out with Shenice) was Carrie Chappelle and he'd popped up in her English and science classes too. Carrie told me that his mother was from Nigeria and his father was from Calgary and had been transferred here with work. This she learned from listening to Teena Simmons pass on the info to her own best friend, Shenice Campbell (one and the same).

I thought Ikenna would be snapped up by Teena within weeks. It seemed that every time I rounded a corner she was laughing and grabbing his arm or smiling dazzling smiles at him. I kept waiting for the news, bracing myself for the inevitable, and then one cold Wednesday in November I saw Marshall Roy (a power forward from the junior basketball team) and Teena kissing at the top of one of the school stairwells. She didn't bother with Ikenna after that.

Still, I was too self-conscious about my feelings to try to talk to him. The other side of the class may as well have been the other side of the world. The semester went by without either of us saying a word to each other, but I felt like I knew him a little anyway, just from watching him. Ikenna was the type of guy who usually knew the answer when called on during class but looked as if he'd rather not have to give it. When he did speak he was thoughtful about it and I noticed that he wasn't the kind of person who laughed just because everyone else was laughing.

The one thing I didn't like about being in class with him was that he made me want to keep my mouth shut too. When I was around him I felt like I was still the awkward kid I used to be. Knowing he was listening to the sound of my voice made me mangle the French language more than once, and then, when the class ended, I felt even more panicked because that meant no more staring at Ikenna's cheekbones from across the room. I'd had my chance and let it slip through my fingers.

But sometimes there really are second chances in life. Callum and I were proof of that and in January I got *another* second chance—Ikenna and I had history together. When I told Carrie she made me promise to speak to him ASAP. "But about *what*?" I asked. My palms sweated at the thought of it.

"I guess it has to be something about history," Carrie summed up. "Homework or whatever."

I virtually never saw Ikenna in the halls. If I had to go up to him in the cafeteria in front of the guys he'd been hanging out with—Terrence, Lee and Barrett—the odds I'd trip over my words would triple. It was two weeks before I had an opportunity to speak to him alone, and when I did it was rushed because he was hurrying over to one of the portables for class and I was veering away from them, having just finished English in portable 12. By the time I got up the courage to call to him he'd already passed.

"Ikenna?" I said as I turned and caught up to him.

"Hey," he said casually, those hazel eyes of his feeling like the sun as they settled on mine.

"I know this is random," I spit out, "but I spaced in history today—do you know what tonight's homework is?"

Ikenna smiled at me. There's a tiny gap between his top two front teeth that I'd fallen for the first day I'd seen it. Between his eyes and grin I was in danger of burning up. "I wrote it down, but I don't have it on me now."

Except for the fact that he was smiling at me, asking Ikenna about history class already seemed like a dumb idea. If I'd really forgotten to write down my homework, wouldn't I have just checked with my friends from history class?

"Right," I said. "Okay, thanks anyway."

I sped away from him, silently cursing myself for being obvious. But the next morning when I was walking down the hall I heard him say my name from behind me. "Ashlyn?"

"Yeah?" I swung to look at him.

"Did you get that history homework all right yesterday?"

The history homework was a series of questions on Trudeau-mania and naturally I'd known that all along but I said, "Yeah, I did—thanks."

From then on we spoke to each other with gradually increasing frequency until one day in mid-April Ikenna stopped by my locker while I was looking for a hair band that'd fallen out of my knapsack and said he was thinking of calling me over the weekend but realized he didn't have my number.

By then I could look into his eyes without turning stupid and I recited my number and added, "Give me yours too."

We talked for an hour and a half the following Saturday

afternoon. It wasn't difficult speaking to him but I could feel an anticipation-energy between our words that made my heart beat fast the whole time. Before hanging up Ikenna said, "We should hang out sometime—go to a movie or something."

"For sure," I said breezily. My head was whirling like when you're on one of those fairground rides that make you want to throw up and laugh at the same time. I tried to picture myself holding Ikenna's hand at the movie theater, the two of us stealing kisses in the dark. "For sure," I repeated. *For sure, for sure, for sure.* Maybe we could take the bus. Maybe Ikenna had an older brother or sister who could drive us so my father wouldn't have to. Celeste would've done it as a favor but she was away at university in Guelph.

But the details would take care of themselves, I thought. Things with Ikenna were moving in a certain direction—the right direction—and the only thing I needed to do was swim right along with them.

I thought, I *thought* . . . and then everything changed on me in a heartbeat. It happened without warning, and by the time I saw my very best friend again on Monday morning the damage was already done. People stared at me in the hallway, whispering amongst themselves, sniggering and then looking away. Not everyone but lots of people from tenth grade. I glanced down at my jacket and jeans, wondering what they were noticing.

Carrie was waiting for me at my locker, and her eyes were murky. Now that I remember the details from my own life, her apology reminds me of Breckon's to Jules. Saying you're sorry doesn't repair damage. It doesn't take things back.

"Ashlyn, I'm so sorry," she told me. "Please don't hate me."

I didn't even know why she was apologizing. I stared dazedly at Carrie and said, "Why would I hate you?"

Carrie sniffled. She wrapped her hands under the end of her sweater and pulled it taut down across her body. "Because," she rasped. "Because Teena Simmons knows what happened to you and she's twisted it into lies that she's telling everyone."

What happened? My eyes searched Carrie's. I didn't have a clue what she was talking about.

"Dylan," she whispered, focusing on my shoulder. "You have no idea how sorry I am—how much I wish I could take it back."

Dylan. Dylan from when I was eight. The Dylan who'd grabbed me, kissed me and shoved his hand up my hoodie.

My stomach dropped. "What's Teena saying?" I hardly thought about Dylan anymore, hadn't dreamt about him in nearly a year. "I can't believe you told her about that."

"Me neither," Carrie said sadly. "I never thought she'd tell anyone." Carrie explained that she and her older sister had run into Anna Eisler, one of the most popular girls at Hillfield Park, at the movies on Saturday night. Anna invited them to a spontaneous party her boyfriend was throwing and because the only people Carrie knew there aside from her sister were some of the really popular kids from tenth grade, she'd drunk with them for hours.

This was why, when I'd called her on Sunday, Carrie had let her cell go to message all day. When I'd tried the landline, her mom told me she was sick. Although not sick, it turned out, but hungover.

"Teena was really upset," Carrie continued, her hands twisting under her sweater. "Marshall dumped her on Friday night and on top of that her father started going out with a woman twenty years younger than him a couple of weeks ago. The two of us were talking on our own and she kept saying how gross it was, that if he was younger it would be illegal for him to do that, and . . . I was only trying to make her feel better, saying, you know, that it wasn't like what happened to you.

"I was so drunk," she sputtered. "And Teena was talking like she was being real with me. I've never seen her like that—she was almost crying. Not that that's any excuse but . . ." Carrie paused with her mouth open. A fly could've zipped straight down her esophagus if it'd wanted to. "But today I found out she's turned everything I said into lies. She and her friends are saying that, like, you secretly *lost it* to Dylan when you were twelve and that you . . ." Carrie grimaced, her hands popping out from under her sweater as she began to attack her cuticles.

"That I *what?*"

Carrie shook her head like she didn't want to repeat Teena's words.

"I'll find out anyway," I said, already feeling nauseous. I wasn't ashamed of what happened when I was eight. Dylan did what he did and it wasn't my fault, but it wasn't anyone else's business either. No one should've known unless I'd decided to tell them. And now the entire tenth grade would hear about it, but what they would hear would be lies.

"That I *what?*" I repeated.

Carrie looked down at the floor. "Begged him for it." Her eyes snuck up to meet mine as she continued. "And that he should've never gotten into trouble for it because he thought you were older and it was all your idea anyway. She's saying all the guys at school should stay away from you because if anyone gets with you you'll probably say it was rape."

I hung my head and leaned back against my locker. Why would Teena say that about me? I'd never done anything to her.

"Ashlyn, say something," Carrie pleaded. "I swear I didn't know this was spreading until I got here this morning and everyone was acting so weird. I've already started telling people that it's lies."

Some people—my friends—would know Teena was lying right away, but others would inhale the drama like it was oxygen, and I didn't know what to do about it, just that I didn't want to explain the truth about Dylan.

Later that same morning I bumped into a junior guy in the hallway as he was walking with his friends and he pretended to cower and shrink away from me. "Don't call the cops on me—I never touched you," he said with a nasty smirk as his friends laughed. I called him an asshole and shook my head like dealing with them wasn't worth my time, never once looking any of them in the eye.

That entire first day people looked at me differently and talked in hushed voices behind my back. Some of them tried not to look my way and pretended they didn't know my private business, but by the time the end-of-day bell rang I was sure the gossip had filtered down from the most popular kids to the general population, pyramid style. Mostly I tried to act like I didn't care what anyone thought, but inside I felt like an X-ray held up to the light, my secrets exposed for the world to see.

That night the anonymous emails and text messages to my cell phone began. Close to a dozen of them. Cruel stuff that said things like I must have been hotter when I was twelve and asking whether I ever did it for money.

I didn't want to tell my parents and upset them all over again; that bad time was supposed to be behind us. I told myself it would blow over soon and kept the emails and texts to myself—I didn't even tell my friends. At school they stood by me and were fiercely protective, glaring at anyone who gave me a second look and saying that Teena and her friends were lying bitches. But late at night it was just me, reading those awful messages alone, turning them over in my mind. I should've deleted them without looking. I knew that but couldn't help myself.

One of the messages said: "I bet you like it rough. You pretend to be a good girl at school but I always knew looking at you that you were a slut."

That made me feel sick like when it happened, like when Dylan told me I was one of those girls who knew things early, and I wasn't in any frame of mind to talk to Ikenna when I saw him at school but he didn't try anyway. In the middle of the week he started to smile at me from down the hall and then stopped and turned away to say something to his friend Barrett.

I wonder now if he guessed the Dylan rumor was less than truthful and just didn't know what to say to me about it, but I wish one of us had tried before we'd run out of chances.

I don't know how I died but I don't believe I died happy. People say it all the time: life isn't fair. But I wanted a better ending for myself. There's not much left to my life that's yet to be revealed to me, and as I brace for the tail end I feel as though I'm staring, naked and unsheltered, into the face of an approaching hurricane.

twenty-one

ashlyn

Nails on a chalkboard, the squeal of animals as they're slaughtered, a dentist's drill boring deep into a tooth, children screaming in fear—these are the kind of sounds people recoil from, and if you could hear the human heart break like I can, in the measure of someone's shredded but silent breath, you'd know that sound is just as terrible. I can't listen. I've switched the audio off on Breckon's breathing for my own sanity.

It feels like cheating but I can't help him if I can't think. Maybe I can't help him anyway. Maybe no one can.

A few minutes ago Breckon snuck out of his house after pretending to go to bed early. He's driving west as I watch. Heading who knows where and I . . . I can't focus. The past has caught up with me. It burns without heat. Strips away the Ashlyn I've become since my death and reminds me who I was at the very end.

From a distance I've witnessed Jules's calm after Breckon broke up with her and envied it. The calm was of a sort I didn't have. I wanted not to care about what other people thought they knew about me. Even Ikenna.

If he didn't want to talk to me anymore that should've been his problem, not mine. But it still hurt. For all I know the crazy emails and texts (and one printed-off letter that I found slid into my locker) could've all been sent by one person. Would it have helped me if I'd known that for certain? A lone enemy rather than a collection of haters?

I should've changed my email addresses and cell phone number, told my parents and reported what was happening to school. It's easy to see that now, but I didn't feel that way before I died. I felt trapped between wanting to appear strong and feeling vulnerable and afraid, like the child I was when I was eight.

On the first Thursday after the news had spread I walked into the girls' bathroom nearest the front office just before second-last period and found Shenice and Teena both fixing their eyeliner in front of the grimy bathroom mirror. Neither of them had spoken to me since before the Dylan story broke, and Shenice nudged Teena when she saw me.

Teena straightened her skirt like I was invisible. "I should've bought this in black while it was on sale too," she said to Shenice.

"You can borrow mine whenever you want," Shenice offered, her fingers capping her eyeliner and dropping it into her pencil case. "It looks better on you than it does on me anyway."

I stopped directly behind them, staring at the two of them with a fierceness that caught Shenice off guard. She glanced anxiously at Teena before switching her attention to the contents of her pencil case.

"Can we help you?" Teena said in a mean voice, her eyes locking on mine in the mirror.

Shenice reached for her lip gloss, dipping her little finger into the pot to dab cherry red color onto her lips.

"I don't understand why you lied about me," I said, my voice as spiky as Teena's. "I don't get how you can hear a bad thing like Carrie told you—a private thing that wasn't yours to tell—and think it's okay to turn it around and use it against me."

I clamped my mouth shut and waited for Teena to answer.

Then Shenice faced me, giving me enough respect to acknowledge what Teena hadn't. "Look, it's not our fault that Carrie can't keep her mouth shut," she said. "Once these things get loose there's no stopping them. You know how it is, you tell a couple people and then *they* tell a couple people and before you know it, it's everywhere. If you didn't want anyone to know you should've picked your friends more carefully."

"But it's a lie," I said, focusing on Teena's back. "She knows it is. I never . . ." Tears stung my eyes. "I never did anything with Dylan. I was only *eight.*" I thought of the day in sixth grade when I'd pushed Vanessa into a puddle. Some of that old anger rose in me, mixing with fresh ache and brand-new outrage. "Something's really wrong with you if you'd lie about someone who got molested," I rasped.

Shenice's face had fallen, but Teena kept her cool. "I don't know anything about that," she countered. "I only repeated what I heard from your friend. If there's a lie in there, you better talk to her about it."

I couldn't believe Teena was still denying it. Pushing anyone wouldn't help me now. Talking to them wouldn't help either. I spun on my heels and charged out of the bathroom.

Shenice followed me into the hallway, calling after me. I hurried away from her but she caught up to me in the stairwell and asked, "Ashlyn, is that true? Were you really"—she dropped her voice—"molested when you were a kid?"

"Why would I lie?" I felt tears surge to the surface and struggled to hold them back. "Do you think I want to give you more ammunition to use against me?"

Shenice looked as though someone had slapped her. "I didn't know," she said. "I would never have . . ." She shook her head. "*I didn't know.* I'm sorry."

"You didn't have to listen to Teena," I blurted out. "You should've known it wasn't true."

"I honestly am sorry." Shenice's forehead wrinkled as she frowned. "Between Marshall and what's been happening with Teena's dad she's been really messed up lately but I never thought she'd lie about something so—"

"That makes two of us," I interrupted, turning to break away from her.

"Wait, Ashlyn!" Shenice's fingers brushed against my arm as I spun. She sounded concerned and maybe Shenice hadn't meant for the rumors to get out of hand and hurt me the way they had but that didn't mean I trusted her. The only thing I wanted now was to escape.

I jogged away from Shenice until I was outside the school doors, my eyes stinging but dry and my lungs gulping in cold air. In the distance a woman in a Burberry coat and silk scarf pushed her rosy-cheeked toddler in a stroller, along the muddy sidewalk. I wished I were that woman, finished with school and immersed in building my own life. Not with a baby yet, not for a long time, but away from Hillfield Park, where people wouldn't know me.

Away. Allowed to be just Ashlyn without the baggage. No one staring and whispering about Dylan, maybe believing bad things about me or maybe not, but aware of them just the same.

I couldn't handle history and science, but unless I wanted to trudge into the office and fake the flu I couldn't go home either. My father's work hours varied. He could show up at home at any moment.

I went back to my locker for my coat, scanning the inside for a nasty note that wasn't there. So far there'd just been one, but finding it slid into my locker meant whoever had put it there went to my school. Maybe it was Teena herself but it could've been *anyone* and he or she could drop a second, third and fourth letter into my locker at anytime.

Even if the rumor about me had been true, it wouldn't excuse the things said in those texts and emails. There was something wrong with whoever had sent them, like I'd told Teena. Something wrong with *them,* not me. That's what my old therapist would've said to me.

And I knew that for myself but knowing wasn't enough, I needed breathing room. I put on my coat and grabbed my purse from within my knapsack but left the homework and knapsack itself in my locker. They were too heavy to carry around where I was going. If I'd had a car, like Breckon, I would have had more options, but the number seventeen bus route that went by

Hillfield Park ended at two points—the Strathedine Town Center mall and the Cherrywood bus depot.

I caught the bus to the mall. My phone beeped just as I was getting off, signaling that a text message had come in. *Don't look,* I warned. *You know you shouldn't.* For at least an hour and a half, I resisted. I turned off my cell and wandered the hallways, sipping a fruit smoothie. Then I hid out in a corner of the mega bookstore.

Once it was three-thirty it was safe for me to catch the bus home again, and I headed for the exit nearest the bus stop, wishing I could spend every day this way, surrounded by people who wouldn't know anything about me that I hadn't told them. I thought if I could do that it might not even matter so much about the texts and emails. Impulsively, I flipped open my cell and saw there were two messages now. I read the newest first. It was from an unknown number, like all the others, but what it said was very different:

> T tried to hook up with I on Saturday after she left the party but he said he was interested in someone else. Then the rumors about you started. Coincidence??

I wondered if Shenice, feeling guilty for her part in things, was the one who'd sent me the message. I didn't think I could've been any madder at Teena than I already was. So much damage inflicted out of pure spite—apparently just to keep Ikenna away from me—yet knowing where the rumor had sprung from didn't automatically make it easier to stop. Was I supposed to go to war with Teena over this? Drag Ikenna into the mix and start bad-mouthing her back? Or would that only make a bigger mess? I felt overwhelmed thinking about it, like I was floating in a sea of toxic sludge that I'd never be able to wipe off.

But the second message—filled with a nastiness similar to what I'd read so many times before—made me want to crush whoever had sent it underneath my heel. My fingers flew over the keys as I texted back:

> I know what the truth is and so does everyone who really knows me. Maybe you (whoever you are) don't care about the truth. But you should. Karma is a bitch.

My blood was boiling as I pressed send and stalked out the door—rage, sadness and confusion braided so tightly inside me that I couldn't tell one emotion from the other. Hot tears were rising and they wanted out. I blinked them back, rubbed my eyes roughly like they were just itchy, not emotional. My purse rolled off my shoulder as I stepped from tile floor onto pavement, upending and scattering its contents on the sidewalk. My mascara rolled for five feet and then fell off the curb and into the road that edged the parking lot. The lip gloss landed near my wallet and house keys. My cell phone's battery cracked loose and spun away from the rest of the phone.

Spearmint gum. One wrapped panty liner. A gold glitter hair clip. A pink ballpoint pen. Hand sanitizer. Four loose quarters and two dimes. One purple rubber band. A tiny leather notebook that I never wrote anything in but that I'd persuaded my father to buy me at a stationery store two months earlier because I liked the inspirational messages at the top of each page. A small package of salted cashews. All these items sprawled out on the sidewalk around me. My brush was the only remaining thing tucked safely away in my purse.

A tear sprung loose as I dropped to my knees to pick up my purse. A guy bent down next to me and scooped the cashews and notebook into his hands. With his head bent all I could see was curly brown hair. "Here," he said, raising his head to look at me as he dropped the nuts and notebook into my open purse.

Breckon Cody's smoky blue eyes peered into mine. The single fugitive tear continued to snake down my cheek as I peered back at him.

"Are you okay?" he asked, reaching for my change and hair clip.

"Do I look like I'm okay?" I snapped. I'd never seen him before in my life but I'm as certain it was him as I am of my own identity. I've spent what feels like a lifetime watching him since then. His voice alone would be enough to give him away, but in my memory he's a different Breckon—everything about him felt healthy and happy, whole. On April 21 he was the boy he was supposed to be.

Breckon blinked in surprise, probably wondering why I was giving him attitude. He held his palm open so I could pluck the quarters from it. He was wearing a brown down jacket, and now that I remember meeting him face to face in life, I also remember, as I took the change from his hand, feeling envious of this good-looking white boy I didn't know, just like I had of the woman pushing the stroller earlier. It seemed as though his biggest problem would've been a possessive girlfriend or a case of athlete's foot.

"I'm sorry," I told him, suddenly feeling that there was something so mysteriously profound about this boy who was a stranger to me picking up my things from the pavement that for a moment I forgot to breathe. "You're just being nice."

Breckon ambled to the curb and rescued my mascara. "It's okay," he said kindly. "You got everything now?"

I felt light-headed and I don't know . . . strange, like something was wrong with me although I couldn't have explained what, but I scanned the immediate area and, finding nothing remaining on the pavement, zipped my purse shut. "Yeah, thanks."

"No problem."

We walked away from each other, him into the mall and me through the parking lot and towards the bus stop. One moment I was moving forward, my purse looped over my shoulder, and the next I was dropping like deadweight. I didn't feel myself smack the pavement. The end came faster than light.

Somebody, somewhere in the darkness said, "sudden cardiac arrest." Someone said, "stay with us" and then later, "hypertrophic cardiomyopathy," but I'd already disconnected from the husk of my body and didn't know what the words meant or even who I was. No more Ashlyn Baptiste. No tunnel with a white light or visions of my body below me. I had been swallowed whole by death.

And then there really was nothing for a time, the absence of all things.

No in-between period of revelations or reunions with others who had died. Before I fell from the stars there was nothing upon nothing and before that there was Breckon Cody, the last face I looked into before I died. I should've had an opportunity to say goodbye to my family. We all deserve that chance, but it's a longing—a regret—that I can't hold on to any longer. I'll love them for as long as my consciousness persists but I know my story in full now and it's over.

Something happened to Breckon and me that day in April. I sensed it when I stared into his eyes but didn't recognize it for what it was then—a moment out of time, a moment during which my soul recognized that I was leaving before the rest of me caught up to that reality.

I wasn't ready to go. I clung to life—even when it was finished. I clung to *him,* that final face in my mind's eye. Maybe the stars understood both that and Breckon's own need and allowed me to return. I don't know what the stars know—I don't share in their wisdom and can only guess at their intentions. It's taken me this long to gain even a sliver of understanding, but I'm filled with gratitude now for my fall to earth because Breckon still has a chance and I'll fight for him to the death.

The Bourneville Water Bridge arches over the gap separating Bourneville Bay from Lake Ontario. The bridge is about a hundred and twenty feet high and has to be closed in high winds and other bad weather conditions. I remember once, last year near Christmas, that the winds whipping around up there tossed a tractor-trailer onto its side. If it had been in the right lane rather than the middle the tractor-trailer might have been blown right over the edge and crashed into the lake below.

When I see the bridge loom in front of us I know what

Breckon's planning. The ache inside me is deeper than the Nile. I say anything I believe he'd want to hear—I shout, I beg, I try to reason with him. None of that changes his course. He's already pulling over in the right lane, killing the engine. There's no real shoulder, just a couple spare feet of asphalt separating the right lane from the guardrail, but he opens the door and climbs out. He treks decisively alongside the guardrail, towards the highest point of the bridge, his eyes pointed at the pavement. It's four minutes to eleven and the traffic is light. Tonight there's no wind. Anything that happens will be on purpose.

Breckon stands flush against the guardrail and stares down at the lake below. It's calm and dark but it would be deadly from such a height. Massive internal injuries from hitting the water too hard.

I summon serene, healing thoughts as he gazes into the darkness. It worked before but it doesn't work now. His breath sounds like a gasp of defeat.

And what can I do? Without a body, how can I stop him?

All I am is thought. *Shackled.* If I could go for help . . .

It's never worked before. If it did, where would I go?

Breckon's parents. Jules. Ty.

I know where they all live. I can see their streets, houses, rooms inside my mind. *Help him.*

Desperation swells my power. What happens next is so wracked with confusion that I lose myself in the act. A plea for help that I beam out to all of them simultaneously. There is nothing in the universe that can hold me back. I split in four. I spy into their rooms—Breckon's parents sleeping, Jules spooning yogurt into her mouth at her kitchen table and Ty playing a video game in his bedroom. I see my own panic reflected in Jules's and Ty's eyes, and Mr. and Mrs. Cody fight for consciousness as if their sleep was shattered by the noise of a smoke alarm. For a moment I'm such undiluted *message* that my own identity is three-quarters lost, but the final quarter remains with Breckon on the bridge. That anchor summons the other parts of myself like a magnet.

Breckon curls his hands around the top of the guardrail and climbs over to the other side where there's just enough room for him to stand, facing out towards the lake a hundred and twenty feet below, his arms locking around the guardrail behind him. No boundaries keeping him in place now, nothing promising to keep him safe except his own two arms. His phone rings in his pocket. That proof of his connection to the living world makes him tremble but it's not enough. Another minute and he'll be gone.

Cars whir behind us. I would beg him to stay for hours, days, months if that's what it would take to make him listen. If I had a body I'd be on my knees.

But he'll go anyway. I can see it in his face. Hear it in his lungs. He's ready to leave the world behind.

I brace for that moment. I cry without tears.

And then . . . with a chime of music that isn't music at all but the sound of eternal stars, my solitary existence as Breckon's shadow gives way to something more beautiful than I have ever known. I have no body, but I can feel the phantom hand that takes mine in hers. Warmth floods my soul. Fear and uncertainty disappear into the cracks in the pavement. My loneliness retreats into the night, conquered.

I can't see her but I can sense her, and I know without question that she's the girl who would've loved my glow-in-the-dark ant habitat, young Skylar with the white-blond hair. It was her who turned Breckon's phone on the day after her funeral. I sense that too. It was the only sign she could send him from such a distance. She didn't cling to life like I did. She's been somewhere beyond reach, until this moment, when Breckon's need has never been greater.

There's no reason to speak. We understand our purpose perfectly and together we fling our invisible arms around Breckon squeezing love, light, hope and forgiveness into his bones. Tears hurtle down his cheeks as we crush him to us. The heat's so great that we melt into a single burning entity. Life force doesn't die with death. I'm not the only one. We *all* live.

She lives still.

Breckon feels her also; I see it in his eyes. He recognizes her in the swirl of warmth surrounding him, and he scrambles—his face wet—over to the safe side of the guardrail. His phone's still ringing in his pocket as I feel Skylar recede slowly back into a part of the universe I can't touch until all that's left is the memory of her presence and a kind of gold twinkle in the sky. Stardust.

Breckon's trembling worse now, his fingers shaking so hard that he struggles to answer his phone. On the bridge a black minivan slows and pulls over to us. The driver, a guy in his thirties with a shaved head, rolls the passenger window down and leans towards it to shout to Breckon: "You okay out there? You need a boost or something?" The man cocks his head in the direction he came from. "That your car down there?"

"I'm . . ." Breckon's voice splinters as he pulls his cell away from his face. "It's okay . . . It needs more than a boost. I'm . . . getting a tow."

"You sure, buddy?" the guy repeats. "You positive you're all right?"

Breckon nods, his red-rimmed eyes countering his words. "I'm fine. Thanks."

"Okay," the guy says doubtfully. He closes his window and drives away into the night.

Breckon presses his phone close to his ear again, silent but nodding at the voice at the other end of the line. Still with me and still with the living. Safe on the Bourneville Water Bridge on a night with stardust but no wind.

twenty-two
breckon

"Breckon," Jules repeats as I lurch back towards my car. "Hello? Are you there?"

But I can't answer her yet. My voice is in pieces.

I don't know what I felt out on the other side of the bridge. My mother would say it was a memory and my grandmother would swear it was Skylar herself, in the form of a greenish-blue light. I didn't see any light but whatever it was, I know I can't follow through with ending things. However much I want to escape, I need to stay. Not just because it's what Skylar would want, although it feels that way right now, but because someday, eventually, it's possible that it could be what I want too.

I don't know, but I hope so. There's always a chance I could change my mind again tomorrow or the day after that; realize I'd been tricked by misfiring brain cells faking some kind of ethereal experience that never really happened.

But for tonight what I know is that it would cost too much to give up. I can't stand the pain but I don't want to die.

"Yeah," I whisper to Jules. "I'm here." I still sound like shit. I can't hide it and I wonder why I ever tried.

"Where are you?" she asks urgently. "Who was that asking if you need a boost?"

"Just a guy," I rasp. A bead of sweat rolls down my forehead and mixes with tears. I'm still warm from whatever happened out there. "Jules . . . I'm out on the Bourneville Water Bridge."

My call waiting beeps and I let it. A BMW honks at me as I near my car.

Jules says, "What are you doing on the bridge? Did your car break down?"

I shiver. I'm hotter than hell and I can't stop shaking.

I open the car door and climb in. I can't drive like this. I can't do anything but *stay.* All my energy's clinging to that one thing, that and the shock that I almost didn't make it. My heart's beating as fast as a hummingbird's. I'm running circles around my own mind. Tripping, falling. Alive.

"Jules, I almost jumped." I slouch in my seat, my eyes closing in relief because I've confessed. I'm done pretending. "I couldn't do it."

"You . . ." Jules's voice breaks. She tries again. "I'm coming to you." I can hear that she's scared but I hear her strength too. "Don't do anything. *Don't do anything.* Promise me!"

"I promise."

"Okay, look, I'm getting in the car right now but I'm staying on the phone with you."

I don't argue. She could get pulled over by the cops for that but I want her with me. I pushed her away before and now I can't stand to be apart from her voice for fifteen minutes. "That's . . . good," I stammer, "but I don't think I can drive, Jules. I'm too . . ."

I don't have to explain, Jules gets it. "Okay," she says slowly. "What about if I pick up Ty to come drive your car home? He'll . . . you know . . . he'll understand."

I know he will. It's fine, let him come.

"But the only thing is, I'll need to get off the phone with you for just a second to call him," Jules continues.

"It's okay," I tell her. "Call him. I'll wait."

She's gone for less than a minute before my phone rings again. This time it's Ty and he says, "We're on our way, man. You sitting tight there?" The way his voice bends lets me know I've scared him shitless and I can't believe it's come to this. I still can't believe Skylar's dead and gone and that my life will never be the same. The shocks explode in my head in quick succession. Gone, gone, gone.

But I'm still holding on. I'm going to fight after all. Skylar would approve.

Jules and Ty pull up behind my car on the bridge soon enough. I open the door and get out. Jules runs into my arms, crying, which makes me cry again too. Ty, who before April had never seen me cry at all, watches us shuffle towards him. When we get close he grabs me and hugs me until it feels like my bones will snap. "You know, I tried to call you just before Jules called me," he says. "I don't why. It was like . . . just a feeling, a hunch."

Somehow I'm not surprised. It has something to do with that voice inside my head and maybe Skylar too. I can't explain it in any way that won't sound delusional. I don't know that I'll ever be able to fully figure it out, but two people called me at the moment when I was ready to dive off a bridge tonight. That can't be coincidence.

"I'll be right behind you guys on the way back," Ty adds. "We'll talk more after."

And so I get into Mrs. Pacquette's car with Jules. After everything we've been through she's still here, and when things get better I need to make it up to her. "I'm sorry about everything," I tell her. "What happened at the party . . ."

Jules shakes her head. "That doesn't even matter, Breckon, you know? That's for some other time."

I know. When we get to my house I'll tell my parents everything. I won't argue about Eva Kannan, I'll volunteer to see her. Let's face it, I need help—maybe even more than once a week, maybe pills that I won't have to buy illegally, whatever I can get that will stop me from crawling out onto bridges.

I will never stop missing Skylar. That's a fact. But I need to learn to live with it. Even as I think that to myself I feel like I should apologize to her, as though dealing with something is the same thing as forgetting.

It's not. She'd know that and think I was being stupid, apologizing for the wrong thing when what I should've been sorry about was trying to kill myself.

Jules keeps eyeing me from the driver's seat, like I'm going to spontaneously combust. I can't really blame her. In fact, I'm as glad to be with her as I could possibly be about anything at this moment and I have one more thing to ask her. "Do you think . . . do you think you and Ty could come in with me when I talk to my parents?"

My phone rings before Jules can reply. It's my home phone number, my parents calling. Three calls in the last few minutes—what are the odds? I don't pick up. We'll be home soon and then I'll explain everything. My parents have enough problems without this, but I need them to know the truth.

Jules is tearing up again. She reaches out with her right hand, her fingernails digging into my shoulder, and whispers, "Yeah, of course."

"Thanks." My voice is small. I owe my friends so much—and that extra voice inside my head, whoever it belongs to. I clear my throat and repeat myself, louder, *"Thank you,"* so that it will know it hasn't gone unnoticed and that I'm grateful. I should have said something before now.

Inside my head Aretha Franklin sings "I Say a Little Prayer." Gold stardust sprinkles behind my eyes as I remember the serenity and love that I felt out on the bridge. And I'm not sure what I believe or how exactly I'll get through this but I'll welcome a little prayer in my favor any day. *Thank you.*

twenty-three
ashlyn

Breckon Cody walks to his front door with his friends close by his side. His father opens the door before Breckon can reach for his house key. Mr. Cody surveys the trio, his eyes steeped in a relief that mutates swiftly into unease, the wrinkle between his eyes deepening. I watch Breckon step inside the front door, Jules's fingers intertwined tightly with his, and I know he's in good hands. He can manage without me for a while.

So now it's my turn. I broke free from the chains binding me to Breckon out on the bridge when I sped to the people who currently surround him. I no longer have to shadow his every move.

Where I go now is up to me. All it takes is one thought. *Home.* And I'm through the front door, no need to wipe my feet on the taupe area rug my mom bought on sale at Home Depot last summer. The house is dark but I can feel how it's changed in the air. Because of me, my death. I've left a hole and I need to tell them—Dad, Mom, Celeste and Garrett—that they don't have to worry about me. My heart stopped beating but I haven't ceased.

But even now something tells me I won't be able to stay, not with my family and not with Breckon either. This is an in-between time. My journey's not finished and leads elsewhere, maybe the place where Skylar lives now. The universe has begun to peel back its secrets. Light streams in where previously there was only darkness. In the distance unseen voices murmur. Others like me. Within reach.

Soon I will go to them. Soon I will know whatever there is to be known, but I'm not finished here quite yet.

Up the stairs I fly, into my parents' bedroom where Curtis and Cythnia sleep, my mother curved onto her side and my father stretched out on his back, one of his feet poking out of the covers. Like the house itself, my parents look the same as before I left them but feel different. Grief is in the slope of my mother's shoulders, the slackness of my father's jaw.

This is not what I want for them but I understand loss, from my time with Breckon, in a way I couldn't before. It doesn't stand still. This is only a moment, like a single link in an endless chain. In time my mother and father will move forward, not away from me but towards life. That is my biggest hope.

I hover over their bed, marveling at the sight of my parents and bursting with love for them—every last thing they are and every piece of themselves they gave me. Hands for me to hold. Praise and encouragement sung loud. The timbre of my father's voice when he called me "baby girl." My mother, stroking my hair when I felt sick or had a childhood nightmare, her hand rubbing tender circles into my back. The knowledge, right at the core of me since before I could speak, that there was nothing they wouldn't do for me. Their love will never end.

I'm more myself than I have ever been, and from here, Curtis and Cynthia feel almost like children. My wishes for them are those a parent has for their kids—that they be safe and happy and that their future be filled with peace. I kiss their fretful foreheads with my phantom lips and pray that they can feel it in their sleep. *I'm free,* Mom and Dad. *Don't be sad for me.*

Live.

Next I go to Garrett, my beautiful baby brother, just twelve years old, who will have to do the rest of his growing up without me. Baseball trophies, plaques and ribbons line the shelf next to his bed. He was always so proud of them. So smart too, and infinite pride for him wells up inside me as I slip further into his room. My brother will be whatever he wants in life, I know he will. There's no limit to what he can do. He rolls over as I approach, burying his face in his pillow so that all I can see is a fraction of his cheek and chin until he flips onto his back again. Then I kiss him too. *I've missed you, Garrett.*

Of all my family, only Celeste is awake, home from university for the summer, her face drawn and her body thinner than I remember. I watch her sitting hunched over in the same bed she's had since she was thirteen, scribbling in a tiny leather notebook—the one that I kept in my purse but had never written in. I glance at the page beneath her pen, only for a few moments because it's my sister's face that I really want to see. It doesn't take long to realize every word on the page is meant for me, a letter intended to reach across the divide. She wants me to know that I'll never be forgotten, that she is always thinking of me, carrying me with her.

My sister. She's the first person I wanted to be like, the first and best friend I ever had.

I remember every minute of those days at Grandma's, Celeste. Dancing with the smell of fresh baking all around us. I remember the bedtime stories you read me, sitting next to me with your legs stretched out on top of the blankets. And years later, the way you let me creep into your bed when I'd had bad dreams about Dylan.

You never stopped watching out for me. I haven't forgotten. I remember *everything.* And I want everything for you that you would've wanted for yourself before I left. You can want those things and still remember. I hope you know that.

I wrap my arms around Celeste's shoulders, kiss her temple and radiate warmth. *Feel this,* I tell her. *I'm here and I love you.* Celeste puts down her pen and leans back against me. We sit on her bed together until she drifts off to sleep. I sing into her ear, wish I could stay with her and Garrett and my parents forever, wish I could have turned sixteen.

But there are the secrets and the others and I long for them too.

I reach towards the light and tug back the curtain, still singing to myself, still Ashlyn Baptiste. And this time I do not have to fall. I soar.

acknowledgments

Special thanks to my husband, Paddy, for reading, believing and always being there. How did I get this lucky?

Many thanks to writers Courtney Summers and Kathleen Jeffrie Johnson for listening, understanding and offering sage advice. I appreciate it more than you know.

Thank you, Shana Corey, for being the kind of editor I always dreamed of having.

My gratitude goes out to all the Random House folks involved with this book and the ones that preceded it. In particular I want to thank editor Amy Black for her faith in this novel, Nicole de las Heras for her stunning cover designs, and Emily Pourciau for being such a pleasure to work with.

Thanks to my brother, Casey, for reading my first draft of this book and for sharing his thoughts.

Finally, thanks to my agent, Stephanie Thwaites, for accompanying me down this path and for her guidance over the years.

about the author

C. K. Kelly Martin is the critically acclaimed author of *I Know It's Over, One Lonely Degree,* and *The Lighter Side of Life and Death.* She began writing her first novel in Dublin and currently lives in greater Toronto with her husband. She's perpetually working on new novels and redesigning her website and blog. Visit them both at ckkellymartin.com.